PERFECTLY CRIMINAL

with contributions from

CATHERINE AIRD
KATE CHARLES
MAT COWARD
LINDSEY DAVIS
EILEEN DEWHURST
MARTIN EDWARDS
GÖSTA GILLBERG
LESLEY GRANT–ADAMSON
REGINALD HILL
H. R. F. KEATING
PETER LEWIS
PETER LOVESEY
JOHN MALCOLM
VAL MCDERMID
SUSAN MOODY
IAN RANKIN
ANDREW TAYLOR
TONY WILMOT
KEITH WRIGHT

PERFECTLY CRIMINAL

edited by Martin Edwards

with contributions from

CATHERINE AIRD
KATE CHARLES
MAT COWARD
LINDSEY DAVIS
EILEEN DEWHURST
MARTIN EDWARDS
GÖSTA GILLBERG
LESLEY GRANT–ADAMSON
REGINALD HILL
H. R. F. KEATING
PETER LEWIS
PETER LOVESEY
JOHN MALCOLM
VAL MCDERMID
SUSAN MOODY
IAN RANKIN
ANDREW TAYLOR
TONY WILMOT
KEITH WRIGHT

This first world edition published in Great Britain 1996 by
SEVERN HOUSE PUBLISHERS LTD of
9–15 High Street, Sutton, Surrey SM1 1DF.
First published in the USA 1997 by
SEVERN HOUSE PUBLISHERS INC. of
595 Madison Avenue, New York, NY 10022.

British Library Cataloguing in Publication Data

Edwards, Martin
   Perfectly criminal
   1. Detective and mystery stories, English
   I. Keating, H.R.F.
   823'.0872'08 [FS]

   ISBN 0-7278-5132-2

Typeset by Palimpsest Book Production Limited,
Polmont, Stirlingshire, Scotland.
Printed and bound in Great Britain by
Creative Print and Design, Ebbw Vale, Wales.

LIST OF CONTENTS

FOREWORD

It is my privilege and pleasure, as Chairman of the Crime Writers' Association, to welcome readers to this anthology. Forty years ago the first anthology of the CWA, *Butcher's Dozen*, was published, followed by a series of collections issued by various publishers and with a number of distinguished editors. Now, after a one-year hiatus, we have an exciting new beginning under the editorship of Martin Edwards.

This seems a fitting time to launch a new sampling of the talents of the CWA. Interest in good crime writing has never been higher. In our increasingly fragmented society, marred by unspeakable real-life crimes (James Bulger, Fred West, Dunblane), more and more readers are turning to crime fiction. Some are looking for escape: for the tidy make-believe world of the "Golden Age", where all loose ends are neatly tied up at the end and ugly reality never intrudes. Others want a more "realistic" reflection of today's world. Both approaches are valid, and there is no reason why we can't have it both ways. Why must we all leave the village rose garden to be dragged down the "mean streets", as some would suggest? There is room in the genre for all tastes, and the more choices we give our readers, the more the genre will flourish.

One thing is unquestioned: the quality is better than ever, as this anthology demonstrates. In spite of the prevailing snobbery of the literary establishment, some of the best writing being produced in the U.K. today is coming from the pens (or more likely computers!) of crime writers. It is time to stop being apologetic for our status as "genre" writers, and declare proudly that we are *writers*, practising our craft within an area which

Kate Charles

still demands that we tell a good story and tell it well. *Perfectly Criminal* does just that, to the credit of its contributors and the CWA.

Kate Charles
Chairman, Crime Writers' Association

INTRODUCTION

Welcome to the first in a new series of annual anthologies from members of the Crime Writers' Association. *Perfectly Criminal* is distinct from its predecessors, not simply because it has a different editor and publisher, but also because all the stories have been freshly written and are linked by a common theme – that of the perfect crime.

My aims in putting this collection together have been to showcase the depth of talent in the CWA and the diversity of stories that its members write. One of the genre's enduring strengths is the breadth of work that it encompasses. The contributions in *Perfectly Criminal* illustrate how variously contemporary crime writers may tackle a theme which has intrigued mystery enthusiasts ever since Edgar Allan Poe wrote "The Murders In The Rue Morgue". The concept of the perfect crime, moreover, pre-dates the emergence of crime fiction. As Hercule Poirot pointed out in *Curtain*, for example Iago was the perfect criminal: "The deaths of Desdemona, of Cassio – indeed of Othello himself – are all Iago's crimes, planned by him, carried out by him and *he* remains outside the circle, untouched by suspicion – or could have done so." The stories in this collection show that the elusive perfect crime continues to fire writers' imaginations.

The first CWA anthology, *Butcher's Dozen*, appeared exactly 40 years ago and my predecessors in the editorial chair include such luminaries as Julian Symons, Michael Gilbert, Elizabeth Ferrars, Harry Keating, Michael Z. Lewin and Liza Cody. I take particular pleasure in following them, since my first introduction to the CWA came at the age of 13 when I asked for – and received – the 1969 anthology as a Christmas present. For many years, CWA anthologies have brought marvellous crime stories of all types to a wider public, but these are difficult days for short story collections. In 1995, for the first time in three decades, no national CWA anthology appeared, although members of two regional chapters of the CWA produced local collections. Testing market conditions are nothing new, though; the introduction to *Butcher's Dozen* expressed the fear that the outlook for the crime short story was "bleak". So I am especially glad that, 40 years later, *Perfectly Criminal* is seeing the light of day and confounding all prophecies of doom.

The broad unifying concept of the book has, I believe, brought out the best in the contributors. They have to their credit a cabinet-full of awards, including two CWA Diamond Daggers for outstanding achievement in the field and four CWA Gold Daggers for the year's best crime novel. The line-up includes several of the great names from the past 30 years – Harry Keating, Reg Hill and Peter Lovesey – as well as writers of the new generation. I have also been keen to include work by authors who, although not widely known, are talented entertainers. Three familiar series characters, William Dougal, C. D. Sloan and Kate Brannigan, appear; as well as private eye and police stories, *Perfectly Criminal* offers a history-mystery founded in fact, a good deal of rich comedy and twists-a-plenty.

The idea for this collection has been around for quite a while, even though in the end the book has been produced under considerable pressure at times. But although three of the stories have appeared in magazines a little in advance of publication, this is to all intents and purposes a collection of original work, (and to tease Reg Hill's future bibliographers, I have included his first-written version of "The Perfect Murder Club", which has a different ending from that published elsewhere).

My editorial task would have been impossible without a great deal of support and goodwill. I am grateful to Kate Charles for contributing a foreword at a time when she was recovering from a major operation, and her predecessor as Chairman of the CWA, Peter N. Walker, for his constant encouragement as the project took shape. Eileen Dewhurst's work on the proof-reading at short notice has been invaluable and a number of literary agents have

Introduction

provided ideas and assistance of varying kinds: my thanks go to Mandy Little, Teresa Chris, Jane Gregory and Lisanne Radice. Edwin Buckhalter of Severn House, himself a CWA member, deserves much credit for helping to turn the idea of a themed series of anthologies into reality and I have had a good deal of editorial assistance from his colleague Humphrey Price. Finally, I must express my appreciation of all those CWA members who submitted contributions to the book, not just for their enthusiasm (and patience) but also for the quality of their work. I hope readers will agree that *Perfectly Criminal* shows that, 40 years on, the crime short story continues to flourish in the hands of members of the Crime Writers' Association.

Martin Edwards

GRAVE IMPORT

Catherine Aird

Reports of the death of the classic detective story have been exaggerated. The tradition of Christie, Sayers, Marsh and company lives on in the hands of expert contemporary practitioners such as Catherine Aird. Her stories set in the county of Calleshire featuring Detective Inspector Sloan and his team have earned much praise for their combination of intricate plotting and gentle wit. She once even wrote a novel in which "the butler did it". This, the latest Sloan story, was inspired by a real life case concerning an apparently inexplicable death and provides a good example of the way in which her amiable style conceals considerable art. Note in particular how a vital clue is inconspicuously planted early in the story. Aird plays fair by her readers, but my guess is that very few of them will beat "seedy Sloan" to the solution.

"I still don't see what it's got to do with us," said Superintendent Leeyes testily.

"No, sir," said Detective Inspector Sloan. "It's the Coroner who . . ."

"Ah!" exclaimed Leeyes. Not even an optimist would have described the tension which existed between H. M. Coroner for the County of Calleshire and the Superintendent as being a creative one.

Sloan started again. "It's actually Mr Locombe-Stableford who . . ."

"After all," continued Leeyes in aggrieved tones, "I understand it all happened on some odd little island . . ."

"Mecredos," supplied Sloan from his notebook.

". . . in the Mediterranean." The Superintendent was always prepared to take a keen interest in anything against the law that went on in his own manor of Berebury, (otherwise known as 'F' Division of the County of Calleshire Constabulary), but not, if he could possibly help it, beyond its boundaries.

"Actually, sir," Sloan coughed, "I believe Mecredos is in the Aegean Sea."

Leeyes shrugged his shoulders and said, "Comes to the same thing, doesn't it?"

"Yes, sir."

"And after all, Sloan," he said ineluctably, "wherever it happens to be, it's not as if we had any say in what goes on there, is it?"

"No, sir." Detective Inspector Sloan did his best to sound sympathetic. The state of mind identified by the biologists – or was it the anthropologists? – as the Territorial Imperative was stronger in Superintendent Leeyes than in anyone else he knew. "No, we don't."

"And would it be Greek or Turkish, then, this little island in the Aegean?"

Detective Inspector Sloan consulted his notebook again. "As it happens, sir, it's neither."

The Superintendent glared at him. "You're not going to tell me they've had another volcano that's gone and turned itself into a new island like that other place with the name like a tonic?"

"Santorini," said Sloan, who had had to turn to an atlas himself. And a gazetteer. "No, sir, Mecredos is a real island all right but it's independent of both Greece and Turkey."

Leeyes grunted.

"After the Chanek Crisis of 1919," Sloan quoted from his notebook, "Mecredos decided to – er – go it alone."

2

"Don't blame them," said Leeyes, not really interested. It was only in Berebury that events were ever described by him as reaching crisis proportions. If catastrophes happened anywhere else the Superintendent was inclined to dismiss them out of hand as "little local difficulties". "She died out there, I take it, this woman you're telling me about and they want the insurance money?"

"Angela Worrow, yes," supplied Sloan. "She was a nurse and she and her husband – he's a clinical psychologist, by the way, sir . . ."

"And what might that be, pray?" Leeyes was always at his most Churchillian when he didn't know something.

Sloan wrinkled his brow. "A sort of psychiatrist, I think."

"I can do without any sort of psychiatrist, Sloan, thank you."

Although this was a matter of opinion down at the Police Station, Sloan forged on. "One who deals with states of mind not necessarily due to disease . . . phobias, alcoholism, criminality, post-traumatic stress syndrome . . ."

Leeyes sniffed. "In my young day we called that shell-shock."

". . . sexual deviancy, fetishism, behaviour modification . . ." The Superintendent, thought Sloan privately, would be a real challenge to anyone trading in behaviour modification.

"How?"

Sloan cast his mind back to the medical dictionary he had just been consulting. "Desensitisation, relaxation and hypnosis – oh, and something called aversion therapy."

"Don't like the sound of that, Sloan."

"No, sir. Anyway this couple went to Mecredos on holiday and the wife died there two days later."

"Not used to the heat?"

"Wasn't out in the sun long enough to get heat stroke . . ."

"These old people with bad hearts will go abroad and overdo things, though . . ."

"She was twenty-four," said Sloan.

"And eat and drink more than they're accustomed to," said Leeyes, not listening, "or is good for them."

"She hadn't had anything to drink," said Sloan. "Nothing alcoholic, anyway."

3

"I should get that in writing . . ."

". . . because she was pregnant."

"Food poisoning?" The Superintendent, who had never willingly stepped out of Great Britain, wrinkled his nose. "Some of the seafood out there's pretty dangerous from all accounts."

"No, sir," said Sloan. "She died in the bath."

"Ha!" exclaimed Leeyes upon the instant. "There's plenty of precedents for that . . ."

"The husband seems to think it might have been the geyser."

"And them, too," said Leeyes sagely.

"Yes, sir."

"Not so much a case, then, of travel broadening the mind," pronounced Leeyes morosely, "as extinguishing the body."

"But," continued Sloan valiantly, "she lived here in Berebury and her husband wanted her buried back here in Berebury."

"Very right and proper," said Leeyes, who had never ever considered some corner of a foreign field a suitable resting place for anyone English, adding, since he had been a policeman all his life, "He wants the insurance money, too, I suppose."

"And the Coroner won't issue a burial order until there's been a post-mortem," said Sloan, making his point at last. The welfare of insurance companies was not his concern. They could – and did – look after themselves.

"I should hope not," said Leeyes piously. "She could have died from anything in a place like . . . what did you say it was called?"

"Mecredos. It's a very small island." Even to Sloan's own ears, that sounded lame. Like the housemaid's baby, the size of the island was immaterial. "I was proposing to see the husband next and take a statement."

"And you can take Detective Constable Crosby, too," said the Superintendent smartly. "That's him out of my way . . ."

"Yes, sir."

"And I daresay," continued Leeyes heavily, "that you'd rather I'd've said 'Take a pair of sparkling eyes' instead . . ."

Time was when the Superintendent had attended an evening class devoted to the works of Gilbert and Sullivan, feeling a total affinity with those authors in their sentiments about punishment fitting the crime. Unfortunately the lecturer had not been prepared to use that famous line from the *Mikado* "Society offenders who might well be underground" as the topic for discussion every single week.

Detective Inspector Sloan and Detective Constable Crosby – he who was *de trop* at the police station – found Nigel Worrow in a sizeable detached house on the outskirts of Berebury. He admitted them at once, ushering them into a sitting-room where he immediately sank back into his own chair in a state of inanition.

He answered their questions like an automaton, admitting to being the husband of the late Angela Worrow. He was, he said, thirty-eight years old and the visit had been an early summer holiday on Mecredos. His wife, he told them, was perfectly healthy and had been expecting a baby.

"A girl," he said listlessly.

"I'm sorry, sir," said Sloan formally.

"The doctor said it would be all right. To go there, I mean. I wanted her fit and well, you see, for . . ." He broke off, sinking his head into his hands.

"Quite so," said Sloan.

Detective Constable Crosby said nothing but appeared to be studying the mantelpiece.

"It was the old geyser," remarked Nigel Worrow in detached tones. "I'm sure it was the geyser. It can't have been anything else."

"What sort of a building were you in?" enquired the detective inspector.

"Self-catering holiday accommodation – we thought we'd better stay somewhere where we could do our own cooking because Angela was still getting those funny food fads that expectant mothers do . . ." He looked at the two policemen and said rather loftily "With the Duchess of Malfi, you know, it was a predilection for apricots . . ."

Sloan said no, he didn't know.

Crosby, who had never heard of the strange cravings of pregnancy, remarked to no-one in particular that "A little bit of what you fancy does you good."

"Actually the building was an old cottage that had been converted for holiday letting," said Worrow. "Mecredos doesn't get as many tourists as most islands."

Detective Constable Crosby said he wasn't surprised.

"Was it your first visit to Mecredos?" asked Sloan hastily.

"It was," said Worrow, aroused to something like animation for the first time. "And I can assure you it's my last."

"And was it the first occasion either of you'd used the geyser, sir?" asked Sloan. That was something the Coroner would be sure to want to know. Especially if he was only holding a "paper" inquest without the formality of a hearing and witnesses.

Worrow nodded. "We didn't attempt to have baths the first night. Too tired after the flight from England." He shifted a little in his chair. "Besides we'd both been in and out of the swimming pool." There was a catch in his voice as he added, "Angela'd been toying with the idea of having the baby under water."

"I've read about that," said Sloan non-committally.

"Sounds daft to me," said Detective Constable Crosby.

"And?" said Sloan, his eye on Worrow.

"The next night Angela went to have her bath first," resumed the husband. "When she didn't come out of the bathroom after quite a while, I went to see why not – she hadn't locked the door – and there she was lying in the bath dead."

"What did you do then?" said Sloan quickly before Crosby could say anything. He was glad to hear that Angela Worrow hadn't locked the door. Superintendent Leeyes didn't like locked room mysteries.

"I pulled the plug out and tried the Kiss of Life."

Sloan wrote down 'Artificial Respiration attempted' in his notebook. The Coroner favoured impersonal reportage.

"And then," said Worrow, "I tried to get hold of a doctor." He stared at the two policemen. "Have you ever tried to raise a doctor late at night in a foreign country when you don't speak the language?"

"No," said Sloan.

"Well, you can take it from me it's not easy." He shuddered. "The doctor was much too late, of course, and he didn't have any oxygen with him anyway."

"Quite so," said Sloan temperately.

"And he sent for the police." He paused at the memory. "I can tell you one thing, Inspector . . ."

"Sir?"

"The police on Mecredos aren't wonderful."

"No, sir?"

He shuddered again. "Talk about the Spanish Inquisition . . ."

"But you weren't there," said Crosby.

"Where?" Worrow sounded bewildered.

"Spain."

"No. We were . . . I was on Mecredos. And when the police found out what had happened they didn't want to know. Nor did the doctors. None of them. They just wanted my poor Angela buried and me off their precious island pronto."

Sloan coughed. "I fear that other – er – regimes don't always share our feelings about justice for the dead, sir."

"Or the living," chimed in Crosby.

"You can say that again." Worrow gave a short humourless laugh.

Detective Inspector Sloan leaned forward, notebook at the ready. "Just for the record, sir, would you tell us how you and your wife had spent the evening before?" That was something else Mr Locombe-Stableford would be sure to want to know.

"At the *orta oyunu*."

"And what might that be, sir?"

"When it's at home," added Constable Crosby gratuitously.

"It was at home," said Nigel Worrow coldly. "It's a form of travelling Turkish folk drama."

"I see, sir," said Sloan. *Orta oyunu* hadn't been a substantial national dish liable to bring about faintness in the bath, but a play.

"Kavuklu – he's always the one in the red coat – gets knocked about by Pisekar," explained Worrow. He hunched his shoulders. "I suppose you could say that an all-male Punch and Judy is the best description of the show . . ."

Sloan made another note, although he didn't think the Coroner would be really interested.

Nigel Worrow stirred in his chair and said languidly, "Better

7

still, you could call it an Eastern Mediterranean variety of *Commedia dell' arte*."

"I'll make a note of it," promised Sloan. Punch knocking Judy about might have given any husband ideas. He couldn't for the moment recall what it was that Judy had done to Punch to provoke him. Something to do with a baby, he thought . . . He coughed and said "This geyser, sir, that you thought might be the cause of the – er – trouble. Tell me about it."

"There's not a lot to tell. I couldn't get the police even to examine it." He looked sadly from Sloan to Crosby and back again. "Believe you me, gentlemen, finding a fault of any sort out there on their God-forsaken island was the last thing they wanted."

"The geyser was still alight when you went into the bathroom and – er – found your wife, was it, sir?" It wouldn't do, of course, to underestimate the importance of their tourist trade to a small island like Mecredos.

"Yes . . ." He frowned. "Yes, Inspector, I'm sure it was. That's right because I remember going back in to turn it off . . . afterwards . . . and being a bit surprised to find it still on. I thought it might have blown out without Angela noticing."

"And the water?" enquired Sloan.

"The water?"

"Was her head above it?" amplified Detective Constable Crosby helpfully.

"Oh, yes," the husband said. "She hadn't drowned if that's what you mean."

"What I meant," said Sloan patiently, "was whether the water was still hot or not."

"Oh, I see. Tepid." He sunk his head down between his hands again. "Angela didn't like hot baths. Besides with the baby on the way she was being very careful."

"What about windows?" asked Sloan.

"There was one little one overlooking the harbour."

"I meant," Sloan did his own amplification this time, "was the window open or shut?"

"Shut. I opened it straightaway, of course."

"And was it windy?"

Worrow looked at him. "No, it was a very still evening, Inspector. Why?"

"There have been cases, sir, where when the wind was very strong, geyser exhaust gases haven't been able to get out of their vents."

He shook his head. "It was a beautiful evening . . . one I shall always remember."

"This cottage," said Sloan tenaciously, "how many storeys did it have?"

"Just the one."

"And do you know if the police looked at the outlet spoilers in the chimney flue?"

"No, but you bet I did," he said warmly. "I shinned up on the roof as soon as I could."

"And?" In England gas poisoning – before North Sea gas came in – used to be known as the October Flush. That was because birds built their nests in chimneys without cowls in the summer when the fires below weren't being used. That blocked the escape of the exhaust gases.

"All I can say," affirmed Worrow, "is that I couldn't see any obstruction in the flue myself but . . ."

Then, remembered Sloan, come October, when gas fires came to be lit again in the colder autumn the fumes couldn't escape. The October Flush was the pink deceptively healthy-looking colour of the deceased that came from coal gas poisoning.

". . . before I could do anything else," continued Worrow, "the friendly Mecredos police came along and hauled me down off the roof."

"I see, sir." Sloan brought his mind back to the present. "And after that?"

"I had a row with them. They'd come to offer me a plot in their cemetery. But I wouldn't take it."

"Why not?" asked Crosby with every sign of real interest.

"I didn't fancy leaving Angela there all alone."

Detective Inspector Sloan's mother – or, rather, the rubric of the Church – would have held that the late Angela Worrow would have been accomplished among the elect wherever she was buried but all Sloan said was "That means they gave you a death certificate, then, sir?"

Worrow gave a hollow laugh. "They gave me something I couldn't read which I was told certified that Angela had died from natural causes."

"Natural gas, more likely," contributed Detective Constable Crosby insouciantly.

"I shall want that certificate, sir, for the Coroner," said Sloan.

"They gave me a certificate of freedom from infection for the airline, too." He stared at them dully. "That was after she'd been embalmed so that I could bring her home."

"A sort of fitness to travel certificate that would be, wouldn't it?" murmured Crosby – fortunately under his breath.

"We're on our way to the post-mortem now," said Detective Inspector Sloan, rising to his feet and hoping Worrow hadn't heard the constable. Crosby got more and more impossible every day.

"Yes, of course." Nigel Worrow sank back into his chair like a rag doll, all animation gone now. "I understand."

"We'll be in touch with you again presently, sir . . . Come along, Crosby."

Dr Dabbe, Consultant Pathologist to the Berebury Hospital Trust, listened to Sloan's account of how and why the body of Angela Worrow came to be awaiting post-mortem. "And you, Sloan, I suppose want to know if it's another case of Johnny being so long at the Fair?"

"Beg pardon, doctor?" The detective inspector was accustomed to levity from the pathologist but not irrelevance.

"Visiting foreigners can sometimes upset local plans," said Dabbe obscurely.

"I don't think, doctor, that the deceased . . ."

"Johnny had been so long at the Fair," remarked the pathologist, "because he'd died."

"Angela Worrow died, too," chipped in Crosby.

"And they pretended poor Johnny had never been there at all," said Dr Dabbe, reaching for a green operating gown.

"Who did?" asked Sloan.

"The City Fathers."

"As far as I am aware," advanced Sloan cautiously, "there isn't any doubt that this woman had been to the island of Mecredos."

"Oh, Johnny had been there all right," said Dr Dabbe, looking round for his rubber gloves.

"Then . . ."

"It's just that the City Fathers didn't want it to get about that he'd died there."

"'Oh, dear'," carolled Detective Constable Crosby, suddenly bursting into song, "'what can the matter be . . .'."

"Crosby!" exclaimed Sloan sharply, "what on earth do you think you're . . ."

". . . 'Johnny's so long at the Fair'," Dr Dabbe completed the couplet. "Exactly."

"Then," said Sloan austerely, "there may be some parallels after all."

"Johnny," said Dr Dabbe, advancing on the post-mortem table body and commencing his external examination of it, "had died of cholera."

"I don't think, doctor, that that's the case . . ."

"And if word had got out," continued Dr Dabbe, "it would have ruined their Great Exhibition."

"Death from carbon monoxide poisoning wouldn't have gone down well with the Mecredos Tourist Board, I agree," conceded Sloan, explaining Nigel Worrow's conviction that it had been fumes from the bathroom geyser that had killed his wife.

The pathologist listened carefully and nodded. "That would certainly account for the colour of the body, Sloan."

"Cherry red," said Crosby, who didn't like attending autopsies.

"Ah, that's the carboxyhaemoglobin," said the pathologist. "Absolutely typical post-mortem sign of carbon monoxide poisoning."

Sloan let his pencil hover above his notebook while he took a policy decision about waiting to see the doctor's report before he tried to write the scientific word down.

"Haemoglobin, you see, has a far greater affinity for carbon monoxide than it has for oxygen," explained Dabbe happily, "and binds with it to get this compound we call carboxyhaemoglobin."

The word didn't sound any easier to spell the second time Sloan heard it.

"And the compound can't carry oxygen so you get your tissue anoxia," finished Dabbe, "and death."

"So what would have happened, doctor?" asked Sloan. The Coroner's questions were always unpredictable and it was as well to be prepared.

"First, Sloan, your Bride in the Bath would have felt nauseated and tired . . ."

"Too tired to get out of the bath?"

"That would depend on the concentration of carbon monoxide." Dabbe frowned. "Not at first, I should say." A little chill came over the room as he added ominously, "There should have been time, I would have thought."

"Then why," began Sloan, adding with a real detective's caveat, "even if she had been locked in . . ."

"Which her husband says she wasn't . . ." said Detective Constable Crosby.

". . . didn't she just get out of the bath and turn the geyser off?" said Sloan.

"Or open the window?" put in Crosby.

Dr Dabbe waved an arm around the post-mortem theatre. "I'm only a pathologist, gentlemen, not a clairvoyant."

"Sorry, doctor." Sloan grinned.

"Don't forget she was pregnant, too." The doctor said, "That doesn't make for ease of movement in the later stages."

"No, but it's odd all the same," said Sloan thoughtfully. "Then what?"

"Then she'd have had a headache . . ."

"Would she? She'd have been aware of that then . . ."

"And gradually gone into a coma with respiratory depression and death," said Dr Dabbe. "How rapidly the symptoms came on would be in direct relation to the dose of gas she was getting."

"With the other Brides in the Bath," remarked Crosby conversationally, "the husband grabbed them by the ankles and held them under water until they drowned."

"Angela Worrow didn't drown," said Dabbe.

"And anyway," said Sloan dismissively, "if the husband had been in the bathroom with her he'd have inhaled as much gas as she did."

"He could have locked her in," persisted Crosby.

"That wouldn't have stopped her getting out of the bath and turning off the geyser," said Dr Dabbe, "and opening the window."

"He said it was shut . . ." began Sloan and stopped. "Funny, that, now I come to think of it. You'd have thought she'd have opened the window on a hot night with a strange geyser. After all, she was a nurse . . ."

"If you ask me it's the husband who's the strange geyser," contributed Crosby.

"He could have said it was shut to make us think that carbon monoxide poisoning was more likely," said Sloan, pursuing quite a new train of thought.

"Carbon monoxide poisoning was what she died from," said the pathologist flatly.

"So," said Sloan, "what we are looking for is something which kept her immobile in the bath while she was overcome by the fumes . . ."

"There was nothing in my superficial examination to show that there had been anything," said Dabbe. He was using the word superficial in its purely technical sense; there had been nothing casual about it. "She might have been drugged, of course . . ."

"But that would show up at post-mortem," said Sloan. "Worrow's a clever chap – after all he's a clinical psychologist, isn't he? If he had thought we'd find anything he could have left her in Mecredos and no one would have been any the wiser." He paused and then said slowly "If he's killed her and brought her body home it's because he wanted to have his insurance cake and to eat it too, and," added Sloan, his professional instincts stirred, "because he was sure we wouldn't find anything."

"He could have shinned up on the roof and put something over the chimney easily enough," said Crosby. "And taken it off again."

Catherine Aird

"He told us – and the Mecredos police – he'd been up there," agreed Sloan. "And if he could get up there once he could get up there twice."

Dr Dabbe looked alertly from one policeman to the other. "The murder of apregnant wife by her husband is usually for one reason and one reason only . . ."

Detective Inspector Sloan gave the pathologist a long hard look. "If this was a question of paternity . . . and there's quite an age gap between the two . . ."

"Then there is one test that could be performed very easily," said Dr Dabbe, adding "With the – er – putative father's consent, of course . . ."

"He could hardly refuse, could he?" said Crosby, "not without incriminating himself."

"It doesn't . . . wouldn't . . . explain how he ensured his wife stayed sitting in the bath long enough to inhale a fatal dose of carbon monoxide, though, would it?" said Sloan. The Superintendent didn't like unlocked room mysteries either.

"No," said Dr Dabbe. "Well, gentlemen, you can take it from me he didn't tie her hands together or put a heavy weight on her trunk . . ."

"If the baby isn't his . . ." began Sloan slowly. Punch and Judy had differed over the baby, hadn't they?

"Which is something that could be demonstrated if it is so," said Dr Dabbe putting in his pennyworth. "The discovery of DNA was a great day for forensic science."

"And he set out to kill her . . ."

"Something killed her," remarked Crosby insouciantly.

". . . in such a way as for him to be confident enough that we shouldn't find out how he engineered it . . ."

"So that he could collect the insurance money as well," said Crosby.

"Then he's a better man than I am, Gunga . . ." Sloan stopped suddenly. "Of course he's a better man than I am."

Crosby looked up, puzzled. "Sir?"

"He's a clinical psychologist, Crosby, isn't he? Scientific, trained . . ."

"Well?"

14

"One of the things he does in the course of treating people," declared Sloan, "is to hypnotise them." He struck the palm of his left hand with the fist of his right. "And I should have thought of that before . . ."

SHEEP'S CLOTHING

(with apologies to Celia Dale . . .)

Kate Charles

*As anyone who has tried their hand at it will confirm,
the short-short story is a tricky form to master. There
is no scope for leisurely plotting or character development and if the central idea is in any way inadequate,
the result will be a let-down. Here Kate Charles shows
how it should be done, skilfully building the suspense
before providing a suitably neat twist at the end.*

A wolf in sheep's clothing – I suppose that's a fair description,
though I don't really like to think of myself in those terms. One
of my friends – one of the few people who know the truth about
me – called me that once, and although it rankled, I have to
acknowledge the accuracy of it. I may be a lot of other things,
but at least I try to be honest with myself.

Yes, it's true. I do pretend to be something other than what I
am, and then I take advantage of people's innocent trust. To be
fair, though, I'm not the only one doing it, but most people aren't
honest enough to admit it. It's easy enough when you know how,
and when you have good protective covering.

One of my biggest advantages is my appearance. I blend in
well with my surroundings, if you know what I mean – just like
the wolf I mentioned. I've reached the sort of age when women

Sheep's Clothing

don't go around broadcasting how old they are – I think it's called 'no longer young' by those inclined to euphemism. And I look ordinary, like anyone you'd pass in the street without a second thought. My clothes aren't showy or expensive – I buy them at the chain stores like everyone else. Good old Marks & Spencers: where would I be without them? I'm afraid that I've put on rather a bit of weight in the last few years, but that all adds to the reassuringly ordinary appearance that I cultivate.

I meet most of my victims in church. Unsporting of me, perhaps, but I find that churchgoers are perhaps a bit more trusting than the average man or woman in the street. They take you at face value, most of the time. And, as I said, with my protective covering, I fit in well in those surroundings – just another dumpy middle-aged woman amongst scores of dumpy middle-aged women. Does preying on church people (no pun intended!) make me more culpable somehow? That's another question, one I don't want to think about now.

You'll understand better if I give you an example of what I do. This is a true story – my latest caper, if you'll allow me to call it that.

As usual, I met her in church. I'll call her Dorothy, for the sake of this story, though that's not her real name. She looked to be in her sixties, though she'd dyed her hair an unlikely colour, so it was hard to tell. The man she was with looked considerably older, small and wizened but well dressed. I was impressed by the way that she treated him, guiding him with gentle firmness to a table in the church hall. It was a Tuesday, the day that this particular church – I'll call it St Mark's – serves reasonably-priced homemade lunches to mostly middle-aged and older parishioners, as well as any outsiders who happen to know about it. I've made it my business to know about this sort of thing, at St Mark's and at other churches in town; it often provides my most fertile trawling-ground for victims.

It was the easiest thing in the world to take a seat next to Dorothy at one of the long trestle tables in the church hall, and it was only natural that we should strike up a conversation. We talked about the food – how good it was, and what excellent value. It was shepherd's pie: I took that as a good omen. "Do you come here often?" I asked innocently.

"We haven't been before, but we'll certainly come again," she told me. "It's wonderful to eat a nice hot meal that I haven't cooked myself, and it does Father a world of good to get out of the house. And me too, of course."

So he was her father – that sounded promising. "How old is your father?" I asked.

"He's ninety-two," she said, pride mingled with weariness in her voice. "He's very good for his age, I think."

I agreed. "Splendid, I should say."

"Though I'm afraid his hearing isn't so good." She raised her voice. "Is it, Dad?"

The old man, who had been intent on shovelling shepherd's pie into his mouth as fast as his creaky jaws would work, turned to his daughter. "What's that?"

"I said that your hearing wasn't good!"

"No," he grunted, returning to his food. Better and better, I thought: all the more opportunity for getting to know the daughter without any interference from the old man. My antennae were twitching; Dorothy looked like she was going to be the ideal victim. She was a talker, and she didn't ask awkward questions. I couldn't have asked for more.

I didn't rush it, of course. That's where a lot of people in my line of work make their biggest mistake. By the end of that lunch I knew that I had hit pay-dirt, but I was willing to take as much time as it needed to mine the ore from the seam.

That first day she told me a little bit about her circumstances: about how her mother had died, a few years ago, and about how she had moved back home to look after her father. "It's not that I mind looking after him," she confided. "After all, it's a matter of duty, isn't it? But I used to have a *life*, a life of my own. Now I'm just an unpaid nurse and servant."

"Your father has a large house, then?" I probed discreetly.

"Yes, quite large, but it's not *my* house, if you understand what I mean. Mother had some beautiful things, and I don't feel that it's my place to change anything."

I left it at that; there would be time to learn more as time went on.

Sheep's Clothing

The following Tuesday Dorothy seemed to be watching for me. She beckoned me to her table eagerly, and resumed where she'd left off the week before. Believe me, I did nothing to discourage her confidences. "I love my father," she said, almost as if she were trying to convince herself. "Of course I do. But it's so difficult. Sometimes I feel so trapped." She looked off into the distance and added wistfully, "Sometimes I wish that a knight on a white charger would arrive and carry me away somewhere. Anywhere." Then she laughed in a self-conscious fashion. "I don't know why I'm telling you this. I hardly know you."

"Please, feel free to tell me anything," I murmured reassuringly. "I'm a good listener."

As the weeks went by I was building a complete picture of the life that Dorothy and her father led – the grand house, the good furniture, the lovely ornaments, and the two lonely people, locked in a destructive relationship that made neither of them happy but to which there seemed to be no alternative and from which there was no escape. Not until her father chose to die, anyway, and that might be a long while, given his good health and his tenacity of spirit. It seemed as if I was the only person that Dorothy had to talk to; now it appeared that she looked forward to Tuesday lunchtime more for my accommodating ear than for the tasty hot meal and the opportunity to get out of the house. "No one else ever asks me how I am," she said one day. "It's as if I didn't exist, except as an adjunct to my father. I'm so grateful that you listen to me. It makes me feel like a real person, even if I don't have a real life any more."

I didn't want her gratitude; it only made me feel guilty. I'm not totally heartless, you realise – in a funny way I had begun to care about Dorothy, even though I'd entered into the relationship with nothing but my personal gain in mind. Not that that was going to stop me from carrying out my plans.

So when the day came that she invited me to visit her at home – diffidently, looking off into space for fear that I would reject her offer – I was ecstatic, and had to struggle to hide the enthusiasm of my acceptance. Now I could really begin to make some progress.

I've been to her house once so far, and it was much as she'd described it. She *does* have some beautiful things, and seeing her in her own surroundings brought her circumstances and her personality – and that of her father – so much more into focus for me. The visit was a success – she talked the whole time I was there, and invited me to return. I will, of course. For as many times as it takes to get what I want.

I don't think it will take too long. Dorothy is so trusting, so willing to take me at face value as long as I'll just let her talk. As I said earlier, when you know how, it's like taking candy from a baby. Of course it helps to have a well guarded pen-name. Dorothy knows me by my real name, the Christian name and surname bestowed on me by my parents and my husband respectively; there's nothing at all to connect me with Hildegard Hunter, the famous but reclusive novelist. And when my next book comes out, featuring a downtrodden spinster and her demanding father, Dorothy may find remarkable resonances with her own life, but I can guarantee that she won't suspect a thing. They never do. It's the perfect crime.

BITS

Mat Coward

An important purpose of a book such as Perfectly Criminal *is to introduce readers to up-and-coming authors – such as Mat Coward – as well as show – casing the work of well-established favourites. In the course of his brief crime writing career, Coward has experimented with a variety of types of short story, but humour is his trademark.* Bits *has a story-line and ironic conclusion reminiscent of that past master and long-time doyen of the CWA, Julian Symons.*

Many things led to the killing of Ian Unwin, but the beginning was when Tony Shaw's leather jacket was stolen in a pub near King's Cross. He'd stupidly left it unattended for about two minutes, while he crossed the uncrowded lounge bar to buy some cigarettes from a machine by the Gents. When he got back his jacket had gone, and with it his wallet, cheque-book, cheque guarantee card, ATM card, credit cards, union membership card – the lot, the whole pack.

Tony made all the right phone calls, cancelled everything, and so was very annoyed when his next current account statement showed that several of the missing cheques had been used.

He left the town hall half an hour early that afternoon, and asked to see the manager at his local bank. After a longish wait, a woman – a girl really, she looked about twelve – appeared

21

from behind a mirror-glassed door, wearing an expression which hovered between irritation and nervousness.

"Can I help you, please?"

"Are you the manager?"

"I'm your Personal Branch Banker," said the girl, her intonation suggesting that the words held no individual meaning for her.

Tony, wondering how she could be his Personal Branch Banker when she hadn't even asked his name yet, explained about the cheques which had been cashed after he'd reported them stolen.

His Personal Branch Banker took down his details, including home and work phone numbers, and then spent ten minutes fiddling at a computer which she had obviously not been trained to use. Eventually she must have elicited an answer of some sort, for she turned back to Tony and said, "Mr Shaw, is it?"

Tony said it still was.

"Um – actually, Mr Shaw, are you aware that your account currently shows an unauthorised negative balance of nine hundred pounds?"

"Oh, for Christ's sake," he groaned, and began explaining it all again.

A week later he'd heard nothing, and so flexitimed another half hour for a return match. The Personal Branch Banker had changed sex, was now a twelve-year-old boy, and had never heard of Mr Shaw or his fugitive cheques. Once more, Tony went through the story, but it wasn't until six weeks, eleven letters and seven phone calls to head office later that the stain on his account was expunged. The penultimate conversation included the following exchange:

Senior Account Supervisor (London): Mr Shaw, the cheques in question appear to bear the signature "D. Duck". Is that your normal form of signature, can you confirm?

Tony: My normal form of signature is "A.L. Shaw".

Senior Account Supervisor (London): Ah, right. OK, yeah.

Over the next few months, Tony thought about The Donald Duck Business quite a lot. Thinking about things quite a lot was one of the things he did most. He enjoyed thinking, sorting, planning, puzzling things out. He lived alone, had no noticeable family, either immediate or extended, and one of the reasons he liked living alone was so that he had time to think about things. He made a list, indexed it on his List of Lists, and filed it in his List Box. The list said:

1. Seeing the manager was a waste of time. No-one sees their bank managers these days – indeed, don't even have managers to see.

2. Everything is computers these days. Nobody actually knows anyone. Not like when I was a kid.

3. I have never met my landlord, Mr Chipping. I met his agent once, when I moved in, and all dealings since have been by post or by messages on answering machines.

4. I have never actually met most of the people with whom I am in regular contact at work. They work in different buildings, in different parts of the borough, and even many of those in the same building communicate by phone, fax, or internal mail.

5. Although I am only forty, the world I inhabit now is already a different planet to the one I was born on. What will it be like when I am sixty?

6. The world today exists in bits. The old cow was right when she said "There is no such thing as society". Modern urban life for the upper-working/lower-middle class (ie, most of us) is fragmented, automated, alienated.

7. From what I have heard, it is worse in the suburbs. Here in West Hampstead, people do at least occasionally say "Hi" to each other, in passing. Out in Metroland, apparently, nobody knows their neighbours, nobody talks to anybody, nobody notices anything – or if they do notice, they don't give a toss.

He named the file "Bits". He found what it told him of life faintly shocking, rather sad in a generalised way, but not personally discomfiting. Tony had given up on life – on LIFE, anyway – long ago; not out of bitterness or depression or frustration, but just because he had discovered that his wants and ambitions were modest ones.

He would be quite happy – really, perfectly content – to spend the rest of his days sitting in a comfortable armchair, with a book, a glass of whisky, a cigarette, and the knowledge that he would always have somewhere warm to sleep.

Not that Tony was a hermit. He lived a fairly solitary life, true, but he didn't actively shun other people – he just wasn't addicted to them. He preferred human company to be rationed, on his terms. Most of the time he was happy at home, listening to blues on his CD, watching the telly, or reading (SF or fantasy mostly, but only the good stuff). Once a week, however – or more, he was no slave to routine – he would visit a pub. There were several decent ones in walking distance.

And once or twice a year, in one of these casually cheerful places, he would get off with a woman. The last few had been, he readily acknowledged to himself, just a bit on the ropey side. He was no great catch, after all – an ordinary bloke, ordinary looking – and though at one time he had been able to impress young girls with his quiet, worldly maturity, he found that the present young generation had little interest in sex. They all worked in banks.

Never mind: he got by. He wasn't a superstud, and he wasn't celibate. He was fine, he got by.

Tony had no close friends, as such; had never seen the need for them. Instead, he had drinking companions – not rowdy, big boozers, more like playing-the-quiz-machine, doing-the-crossword-in-the-evening-paper, moaning-about-the-Tube companions. The sort of people who drift in and out of the margins of each other's lives, and only notice that one of their number isn't around any more during nostalgically drunken evenings of "Whatever happened to old Woss-is-name . . . ?"

Work didn't come into it. He'd been in the same department since leaving school at fifteen, so his salary and conditions of service were quite acceptable. He didn't mind the job particularly, it wasn't hard or dangerous or painfully boring, but he was always glad to get away from it. And he did have a dream.

Tony Shaw dreamed of ER/VR: Early Retirement/Voluntary Redundancy. As municipal government throughout the nation disintegrated, Tony dreamed of his fiftieth birthday, when his eternally cost-cutting employers would gratefully relieve him and themselves of the burden of his employment. At fifty, he would be free, with a pension and a small lump sum, and a reasonable expectation of enough remaining years in which to enjoy them. Quietly; securely.

Even the, though, at the back of his mind, was a sharp splinter of perfect self-knowledge: in common, he imagined, with many people whose ambitions were small, his ruthlessness in pursuing them could be, if necessary, unlimited. After all, he didn't ask for much – he was surely entitled to the little he did ask for?

Tony found that thought comforting; then, and later.

Five years after the Donald Duck Business, something terrible happened to Tony's plans. The council announced that the current round of ER/VR would be the last. Management had decided that their staff reduction exercises had reached a point where the cost of further redundancies would be greater than the cost of maintaining existing staffing levels.

Tony was still only forty-five. There was no way he could escape now. And, according to the memo he read and re-read, no way he could escape *ever*.

There had to be! That was all, there just had to be. One thing was certain, he couldn't carry on spending eight hours a day away from his chair, his book, his whisky, seven days a week, forty-six weeks a year, for the next twenty years!

Impossible. He'd been dreaming of early retirement for almost half his working life. If the realisation of his dream, his modest dream, was not to be given to him, then he would have to find a way to take it.

He'd have to, that's all.

Almost wild with anger – in a rare, scorching rage – Tony Shaw literally ran from his office. It wasn't quite half-ten in the morning, but he didn't tell anyone where he was going, he didn't leave any messages, he didn't open the rest of his post or switch off his terminal. He just ran: to the lift, out of the door, down the street, into the Underground.

And when he stopped running, he was in a pub near Hampstead station.

He was, at least, in sufficient command of his senses to have come to this pub, and not to the one he preferred, further up the hill, but which he had had to abandon a few weeks earlier. That was the pub where Michelle drank.

She probably wouldn't be there so early in the day, but he couldn't take the risk. Michelle had become a real nuisance, a one-night stand that had turned into something perilously close to "a relationship". That was what she called it; that was what she wanted.

Tony was always honest with his women. He never pretended to be looking for love, never pretended to be interested in anything but a brief interlude of mutually refreshing sex. It wasn't his fault, then, that Michelle had failed to understand the rules of engagement – or of non-engagement.

She was a good bit younger than him (mid-thirties, he guessed, though she didn't say, and he never asked) and considerably better-looking than he'd lately been used to. Tony had enjoyed being with her, once, even twice, but somehow she'd got it into her head that they were a couple. Michelle's skin was thick as well as pretty, and no amount of straight talking rid her of her troublesome illusions. When Tony would gently but firmly explain that, sorry, he didn't feel the same way about her as she apparently felt about him, she'd just smile and say, "That's OK. I know how hard men find it to talk about their emotions. It's your upbringing".

Thus it was that Tony now sat in a pub he didn't much care for, trying to find a way round a problem which was even more threatening than the Michelle situation.

It didn't take him long. All he had to do, after all, was give his subconscious a bit of a stir, and then decide if he could stomach what came to the surface.

Half way though his second pint, he decided he could.

Which meant that he had lists to see to: to begin with, one to steal and one to make.

The stolen list – the details of all those who had been accepted for the current, final round of ER/VR – was not hard to come by. In fact, he didn't even have to leave his office; just press a few keys on his computer, and make an educated guess or two.

When the system had been installed, the computer company

woman who trained the council staff in its use had told everybody the same thing: "Give yourself a password that isn't easy to guess, something random. Not your name, for instance". But she had taken a shine to Tony, who was a good pupil, and had added to him, confidentially, "Six months from now, ninety-five per cent of the passwords in this building will be user's names. It's always the same – people forget their original term, and end up thinking *What the hell, there's nothing confidential here, anyway.* You see if I'm not right."

She was right.

Back home, a printout of the stolen list safely in his pocket, Tony made another list. He headed it OPERATION POD, in honour of one of his all-time favourite SF films:

1. Male, obviously.
2. Roughly same age (few years either side might not matter).
3. Good deal – big pension and lump sum – so, long service.
4. Home owner, preferably paid off mortgage.
5. No visible family.
6. Suburban address.
7. Good sick record, so not visiting doctor etc. often enough to be known.

Comparing the two lists quickly eliminated most of the retirers, but left six possibles; six potential hosts, as Tony thought of them.

The next stage of selection required some footslogging, not just paper-shuffling.

In truth, Ian Unwin looked good to Tony right from the start, but he nonetheless worked methodically through his short list, with the aid, naturally, of another list of criteria:

1. Physical appearance: similar, or easily adapted to (ie, long hair doesn't matter, but baldness is no good; slight weight gain or loss would be feasible, but height must be close).
2. Position of house (definitely not flat or maisonette, bungalow best of all). As few neighbours as possible.
3. *Must have garden* – must not be overlooked by neighbours' windows.

4. Host's routine, weekends, evenings etc.: make sure, as far as possible, no regular visitors (including lovers, relatives), and no regular outings – hobbies, groups, church etc.

All this took time; he could have spent forever on it, of course, checking and double-checking, being ultra-cautious. But he didn't have forever. As it was, Tony used up his remaining fortnight of annual leave watching and eliminating. And in the end, as he had suspected at the beginning, it was Ian Unwin who passed all the tests most satisfactorily.

The clincher came on his third secret visit to the Ruislip cul-de-sac, bordering a park, in which Ian lived. Ian's only next-door neighbour had had a For Sale sign in the garden on Tony's first visit. That sign now read "Sold".

"Well then, Ian," said Tony to the silent street. "You're it."

Tony handed in his notice at work – having now, he explained to his boss, given up all hope of ever securing a decent ER/VR deal.

Sonia, the friendly, overworked young woman who had been his supervisor for the last eighteen months, was only too pleased to give him the reference he asked for, and to make it one that glowed like the sun above. A quiet guy, not very matey, but that was his business. He was always pleasant enough, and everyone knew he was a good worker.

"Got something lined up, Tony?" she asked, having made the appropriate noises about how much he'd be missed.

"Well, you know," he said. "Fingers crossed."

"Local government?"

He made a wry face. "No thanks! A book shop, as it happens. Old schoolmate, looking for a manager. While *he* takes early retirement, if you're into irony."

She smiled. "A book shop, how lovely! I quite envy you. Local?"

"No. Nottingham, in fact. Cheap property, clean air. Good beer. I fancied a real change." He grinned; he could quite fancy her, if it wasn't for the obvious complications. "Mid-life crisis, I expect."

Sonia laughed. "So it really is goodbye, then."

"Looks like it," Tony agreed.

He had to have a leaving do, of course. Avoiding it would have involved too much fuss. A photocopied note in the internal mail advertised his availability for farewell drinks in the pub opposite the town hall on his last Friday. Everyone attended – because he wasn't disliked – but none took their coats off, because none could really call him a friend. Souvenir photos were taken (and taken great pains with, by the office's resident camera bore), and a presentation cheque (topped up by Sonia, to prevent it appearing insultingly small) was duly presented.

Tony gave the same story about the Nottingham book shop to a few pub acquaintances, and, by letter, to his landlord. He was a little put out when the landlord rang to ask for a forwarding address, but couldn't very well refuse without seeming suspicious.

"Better make it care of the shop for now, Mr Chipping," he said, reaching for a guide to the second-hand book shops of England with his spare hand. "Hang on, I've got it here somewhere."

While working out his notice, he'd got to know Ian Unwin. This was essential, perhaps a little risky, but certainly not difficult. They turned out to have quite a bit in common. Ian, like Tony, was a loner. More so, if anything, really rather withdrawn, and Tony soon spotted one of the reasons why: Ian was an unadmitted homosexual.

"Great," thought Tony. "He'll be glad of some sympathetic company. Discussing books, playing chess." But he was careful to make it clear to Ian that he was a confirmed, if unprejudiced, heterosexual, so as not to arouse in the other any fears of being confronted with a decision about himself.

Their friendship proceeded very nicely, initially in lunch hour pub sessions, and later at the bungalow in Ruislip; and after a month or so, when Tony felt he knew as much about Ian as he was ever likely to learn, or to need, he killed him.

That too was delightfully simple.

"Look, mate, sorry about this, but I really think I'm too pissed to make that last bus. You do realise that's our second bottle of Scotch we're half way through?"

"No probs," said Ian – with some difficulty; though he didn't know it, he'd drunk at least four times as much as Tony. "Spare room, sofa, bath, whatever you like."

"Good man," said Tony. "In which case . . ." and he filled his host's glass to the top, one more time.

That was all it took. Getting Ian's unconscious frame through the hall and into the bath was hard work, but Tony was both fit and determined. Dragging the drowned body back out of the bath and out through the kitchen door was more exhausting than he'd anticipated, but in the end it was done.

As he dug the grave in the secluded, maturely-hedged garden (first place the police would look, of course, but in this instance they wouldn't be looking – no disappearance, no inquiry), Tony comforted himself with the thought that, from what he knew of his late friend, Ian would probably rather be dead, given the choice. He'd had no life to speak of, and seemed to harbour no hopes of ever finding one. Couldn't even admit what he was looking for, poor sod.

"So all I've really done," Tony thought, patting the earth back into place and covering the spot with a garden bench, "is put to sleep a sad old dog who had no use for his life, and in the process secure for myself – a deserving and appreciative person – everything my own modest heart has ever longed for. A comfortable house full of books, and nothing to do all day but read them."

The first potential crisis came quite soon: some kind of chesty, throaty thing that just wouldn't let go.

Well, why not? If anyone was entitled to be somewhat under the weather, it was him. He'd been through a lot. He'd been under a considerable strain.

Living as someone else was a little strange, Tony found, even though he had prepared himself for it so well. Bound to be, really. Not his fault, just one of those things. Even so, he eventually surrendered to the inevitable, and nervously, reluctantly, made an appointment with his – with Ian's – GP.

In the event, he could hardly contain his triumphant laughter as he left the doctor's surgery, clutching a prescription. *Bits!* The

Bits

whole world was in bits! Even if there had been any risk of the doctor spotting him as an impostor, the question hadn't arisen – because the doctor had *never once taken her eyes off her computer screen!* Not even when she'd asked him if he smoked, and he'd said, "Yes, if you must know".

All the same, he took the prescription to a pharmacist a couple of bus stops away, just to be on the safe side, but really: how could a scheme like his fail, in a world like this?

Other minor alarms, potentially tricky encounters with petty officialdom, came and went, but Tony didn't panic. He always kept an emergency plan in reserve, but never needed it; and, as time went on, he began to realise that he had actually done it. He had never wanted much from life, and now he'd got it all.

Got it, and held it.

Tony was aware of a slight change in his personality. Cautiously, always cautiously, but undeniably, he was . . . well, yes, he was coming out of his shell.

The suburbs, it transpired, were not as cold and unwelcoming as he had been led to believe. Or at least, not in this cul-de-sac they weren't. Not, anyway, since his – Ian's – next-door neighbour had been replaced by June Welsh.

Never having played the romantic role, it had taken Tony a while to realise that June's almost daily poppings-round, to ask about refuse collections, to get the name of a reliable newsagent, to borrow a screwdriver – were more frequent than might be considered normal.

After they had slept together for the first time – at her place; he hadn't completely abandoned his defences – thoughts of Michelle, the clinging nuisance from his former life, drifted into his mind. But this was different. Well, *he* was different: a different name, a different life. Perhaps it was natural that he should want different things now. Want more, even.

And June was definitely different. Not as obviously attractive as Michelle, older for one thing, about Tony's age; but more of a woman, in other ways. A woman of some refinement. Not posh, not stuck-up, but thoughtful.

Quiet, like him. She was a divorcee – of a few years' standing,

31

he gathered. Her husband had obviously hurt her (she didn't say how, and he didn't ask), and she had an air about her of emotional convalescence. And she was clearly keen on Tony.

He began to wonder if, after all, there was any real reason why he should continue to confine himself to one-night stands. Maybe, at his time of life, safe in his new existence, a steady lover might be just the thing.

He could even justify it on security grounds, without too much casuistry. A regular sexual outlet would certainly reduce the temptation to put his secret at risk through unwise pick-ups in local pubs where, for all he knew, someone might dimly recall that his face didn't fit his name. His sexual lifestyle had previously been a matter of choice, of personal taste, but now – in the post-Ianian period – other considerations had to take precedence.

And so June and Tony's second quiet, companionable coupling, a week after the less significant first, took place in Ian Unwin's handsome double bed (the bed in which Ian himself had been conceived, he had told Tony, by his now long-dead parents), and after that things took their course.

Life settled down. Marriage was never spoken of. No need, thought Tony, when the holy estate of next door neighbourness was already so ideal.

There were nasty moments, inevitably. He did not think of himself as a naturally dishonest man, and living a lie, in the most literal sense of the cliché, did not come easily to him. When June told him, her grey-blonde head on his chest, "Ian, you just can't imagine how happy I am we found each other," he longed to say: "It's Tony. Call me Tony".

The answering machine incident was unfortunate. He had left Ian's message on the tape, and kept the machine on at all times, as one more barrier against danger. The phone rarely rang. Tony did nothing to encourage calls, and clearly Ian – despite his, in retrospect, rather pathetic investment – was not the sort who had come home daily to a spool full of urgency.

When the phone did ring that time, just as he was letting June in through the front door, it made his heart jump.

She listened to the outgoing message (there was no incoming

message; a wrong number, or a frustrated salesman, presumably) with her head cocked, and then said, "Your voice sounds really weird on that. It's not like you at all."

He shrugged. "I bet even Frank Sinatra would sound like a prat on one of those things." They laughed, and the moment soon passed, but from then on Tony kept the machine's monitor volume set at zero.

Three-quarters of a year of growing happiness. Not just contentment; he was sure he knew the difference now – this was happiness.

He had his leisure, his security, his house to grow old in, his books, Ian's lump sum and pension. He had his whisky (here on the table beside him right now), he had everything he'd always dreamed of – and as if all the above wasn't more than enough, he had love as well.

Then, one night, Tony Shaw saw something on the television that revealed to him the shocking discovery that life wasn't only unfair, it was outrageously unreasonable. That no matter how modest a man's wishes, he could still never be allowed to enjoy them in peace.

There had been a row, a minor tiff. So minor, indeed, that it had ended not in shouting, but with a peck on the cheek, and the suggestion that "It might be better if we eat separately tonight, Ian, love. I'll see you in the morning."

Tony sat now, vaguely looking at the TV, planning the exact wording of the telephonic apology he would shortly make, when a face on the screen suddenly commanded his full attention.

It was unmistakably his face, in one of the photographs, the clear, professional-quality photographs, taken at his town hall leaving do.

It was quickly replaced by a moving picture of Michelle. Clinging, thick-skinned, telegenic Michelle. Tony zapped up the sound.

". . . leaving his fiancée, Michelle Knight, fearing the worst. Michelle: the most awful thing must be just not knowing?"

He killed the sound again. He didn't need to hear what had happened, it was already unfolding in his mind:

1. Michelle, convinced that he would never leave her without a word, had called at his flat. Somehow made contact with the landlord, been told that letters forwarded to Nottingham had been returned Not Known At This Address.

2. Had gone to his former workplace, where his puzzled boss, Sonia, had helpfully unearthed a copy of the farewell photo.

3. Had received little help from the police, who were not interested in disappearances of healthy, adult men when there were no suggestions of suspicious circumstances.

4. Had approached the production company responsible for *Lost And Found*, where her good looks, her obvious sincerity, and her romantic fantasies had struck a chord with a researcher bored with stories of missing dads and runaway teenagers.

5. And the rest was history.

And even as this list (file under *End of the World*) unfurled behind his eyes, the greater part of Tony's mind was filled with just two thoughts:

1. Is June sitting next door, watching this programme?

2. And if she is, what the hell am I going to do about it?

ABSTAIN FROM BEANS

Lindsey Davis

For Liza Cody,
Co-founder of the Milo Appreciation Society

Lindsey Davis seldom writes short stories, but Abstain From Beans *shows that she has a rare talent for the form. The tale is based on historical fact and has the famous athlete Milo of Croton solving the apparent murder of Pythagoras; the title derived from one of the weirder tenets of Pythagorean philosophy. Lindsey makes the point that the story has interesting links with the present day: "Pythagoras ran a Waco-style philosophy school, very secretive, and manipulating his students in what's now the typical cult manner. So Waco-like was it, that in the end the local citizens took against it, stormed the villa where Pythagoras was living (which belonged to Milo), burned the place down and apparently killed him." It is a perfect crime story so beautifully done that we do not even miss Lindsey's usual hero, Marcus Didius Falco.*

Dawn in the Mediterranean: sunlight twinkled to perfection on the Ionian Sea. Dolphins cavorted in the stinging blue waves. White marble glittered like a cliché on a dramatic seashore temple. On a promontory in the far south of Italy stood the little Greek outpost of Croton. It would have been idyllic, but for the nasty pall of black smoke hanging over the town.

The time was the Sixth Century BC. Not that the Crotonians would consider they were living *before* anything, or anyone. For them Croton was It. Top town. Top town in any league.

Its credentials were impeccable: founded by Achaeans, redoubtable Greeks despatched overseas by the famous Oracle at Delphi. They had established this jewel, with the only harbour on the hot eastern seaboard of the toe of Italy. It grew. It became home to the finest proponents of both athletics and philosophy. In the Greek world that covered almost everything. Then, to enrich their reputation further, the Crotonians proved themselves warlike as well, beating up the rival town of Sybaris so thoroughly that its very location would soon vanish from the map. For a small town which tended to smell of fish, Croton had done well.

That applied until yesterday. Something extremely unpleasant had happened at Croton last night.

On the outskirts of town, facing across pleasant fields and with a dazzling view towards the ocean, had stood a delightful villa – clearly built as the home of a major personality. There had been cool rooms, peaceful colonnades, and a courtyard with a fig tree. But this secluded location was the source of today's choking smoke. Last night rioters had caused devastation. Through the acrid fug which remained, fallen columns and roof tiles could be glimpsed in hot, haphazard piles. Doors and furniture, heated to charcoal, still glowed menacingly. Alone in the tragic wreck of his home stood its owner. As he surveyed the remains of the villa which had been gifted to him by a grateful town, his swelling anger made him inconsolable.

Rage was a dangerous emotion in a man of such strength. He was built on a colossal scale. Double the body-weight of most of his fellow townsfolk, or even the small-holders and fishermen nearby who earned their living by physical labour. None of his bulk was fat. His neck was as wide as his head. Little of the neck seemed visible, for a heavy scarf of muscle – where most men had none – buried the top vertebrae of his spine. Huge shoulders and arms strained the seams of this athlete's tunic. Compared to his shoulders' width and power his legs appeared normal. But these were the strongest legs in the world. When he kicked angrily at a scorched roofbeam, a whole tree trunk which had resisted the heat of the fire, it exploded under the blow, shedding its charred exterior surface like powder.

His name was Milo. He was a wrestler. The most famous wrestler ever. Milo of Croton had won both the Olympic Games and the Pythean Games, six times each. He came home, still seeking bigger and better trials of strength. When he helped destroy the rival town of Sybaris, Croton gave him this villa. Its gracious proportions and civilised amenities had seemed an incongruous setting; Milo had preferred to spend his time in the gymnasium in town, though he was generous and offered the use of his fine home to others. Even when he himself was absent, the villa had represented local recognition of his astonishing talent, and his high status in Croton. Now somebody had burned it to the ground.

After a long while standing silent in the ruins, Milo left the smouldering remains. He walked around the grounds, with the slow, purposeful movements of a powerful man who was holding his emotion under control. Milo was looking for a focus for his rage.

Eventually he came upon a failed philosopher, sitting in a beanfield, beside a corpse.

Somebody – a large group of people – had made quite a mess of the field. Out here in the open the tang from the low pall of smoke still caught in the throat. In addition a damp, sordid scent of crushed vegetation also hung in the warm air. Trampled bean haulms lay in huge tangles, like fishing nets after a violent storm. Amongst this horticultural disaster lay the dead body of an elderly man.

The corpse had a striking face and flowing white hair. His beard jutted boldly from the chin. He wore a long white gown, now stained by the wrecked bean haulms; it was the sort of robe philosophers wrapped themselves in while they aired their thoughts in the porticos of the gymnasia where athletes trained.

Lindsey Davis

At Croton, philosophers and athletes rarely deigned to notice one another.

Alongside the corpse the seated mourner cut an unimpressive figure: spindly legs wearing untidy sandals, knobbly knees beneath a tattered tunic, a mat of unwashed hair, a pathetic attempt at a beard. He was in his twenties, but had the pallor and pustules of adolescence.

The great athlete, who had always eaten well, who spent his days exercising in the clear open air, and his nights in deep sleep, surveyed this tormented human grub with amazed contempt. "What's your name?"

"Helianthos."

"Very pretty! I'm Milo."

"I was afraid of that."

Helianthos tried to forget the legendary stories of Milo's fabulous strength: destroying Sybaris almost single-handed, rendering an army unnecessary. And that famous tale about him carrying a heifer around the stadium on his shoulders, killing the beast with a blow of his fist, then eating it raw. That was Milo when he was happy and triumphant. Best not to think of such a man's behaviour if he was annoyed.

He was extremely annoyed now.

"Who has done this?" Milo felt dissatisfied with the question. He turned it over slowly then tried more informally: "Who did it?" Still not quite right, but closer. A combination of the two phrases came to his mind unbidden: *who done it?* . . . But to a son of a democratic Greek city this was unacceptable. Even athletes were taught grammar in Greek schools.

Any lad who was big enough and strong enough to look like a promising champion could generally find a place in a Greek school. And no one who went to a Greek school grew up afraid of asking questions: "Who is this man?" he boomed.

"That Man."

"What man?"

The mourner's voice sank to a horrified whisper: "*That* man . . ."

Milo considered the daft answer for a moment. Then he stared at the corpse. "Oh! Pythagoras. The *triangle* man."

38

His companion flinched. Everyone was supposed to know that the name of Croton's superstar mathematician and philosopher was never to be spoken by ordinary people. Mind you, Helianthos reflected, even the master would have allowed that the mighty athlete should not be called "ordinary". Not in a face-to-biceps confrontation anyway. Besides, Milo had been the great philosopher's landlord. He had a keen interest in the fire which ended the tenancy.

"So you were one of his lot?" Milo demanded.

Helianthos shook his head miserably. "Deemed unworthy," he squeaked. Milo could believe it.

Pythagoras' unworthy disciple had been grieving without tears, but now in the presence of another human being he sought to express his emotions in a wilder outburst: "Oh this is terrible! He's gone!"

Milo glared. "He's dead all right. That's the end of him."

"Oh not dead!" exclaimed the younger man. "Nothing ends. His soul has returned to the circle of life as a higher or lower being—"

Milo interrupted in a dry tone which gave the impression he had heard about, and did not support, the concept of reincarnation: "It had better not be promotion. It's due to him I've lost my house."

Helianthos looked up quickly, intending to retort that a mere house mattered nothing when the greatest mind in circulation had just been snuffed out and possibly reallocated to a slug. He realised he was looking up at a stomach that could flatten fences with a gentle nudge. Meekly he apologised: "I'm sorry about your house."

"You should be." Milo started complaining bitterly. "I was told your lot would be ideal tenants. A peaceful group. Thinkers who despise women, never drink, and don't even eat meat because you can't bear to kill animals. Dreamers, who would spend all their time meditating, and not break up the furniture. The reborn souls of lettuce leaves and butterflies."

Helianthos deduced that when Milo saw a fly he swatted it – and did not care whether in a previous incarnation it might have been his grandmother. He tried to win Milo's sympathy: "It was a beautiful villa. I can understand that you needed tenants. You wanted to prevent squatters—"

"Too right. Bloody goatherds – probably with their bloody goats."

"I'm really sorry about this."

"Thanks. Still nothing ends, you tell me. Perhaps at this very moment Pythagoras is being reborn as a stone-mason who can rebuild my place."

"He's already been the son of Apollo."

"Somehow I didn't think your great man would have seen himself as the son of a drain-cleaner."

Helianthos made no answer. Young people who attach themselves to unusual cults soon learn to ignore ridicule.

The followers of Pythagoras had once been welcomed to Croton as an educational sect who would raise the tone – or at least, as wealthy newcomers who would bring in business. More recently they had had to face unpleasantness. The trouble was that Pythagoras had raised the tone of his own parts of Croton so highly he tended to look down on the original inhabitants. The Greeks of Croton liked to sneer at the native Italians whom they had pushed back into the hills, but in their own agora they expected to swank. The philosopher's arrogance towards them was insulting. They responded with spirit. Some threw rocks.

To tell the truth, that was why the master had looked around for a secluded out-of-town villa where he could expound his great theories in private.

"I want to know who did it," Milo exclaimed. He held out a hand; Helianthos made the mistake of taking it. As he was pulled to his feet all the bones in his fingers were subjected to excruciating pressure. He had never felt such pain. "I'm a wrestler," said Milo. "I live by co-ordination and speed – and power, of course." Of course. "You're the man who has trained his brain. You'll have to help me work this out."

Helianthos, who had reckoned his best ploy was to run very fast to another area, found himself nodding obediently.

As the sun climbed, bees came to forage in the beanfield. Other insects were exhibiting a more doubtful interest in the fresh corpse of Pythagoras. The two men retreated to sit on a hurdle beside the dusty track. They made an incongruous partnership, the extremes of humanity: one triumphal body and one totally inadequate personality. "We need to establish what happened," Milo decreed.

Helianthos might have failed at philosophy, but he had mastered the unexpected reply: "I can tell you what happened."

"Oho! How? Were you here?"

"No. I was in a tavern in town."

"Were you drunk?"

"As drunk as I could get." Not very, Milo decided.

"Why?"

"Despair!" Noticing that this proud cry had failed to impress the wrestler, Helianthos continued shyly, "People rushed in shouting, *A gang of lads have gone up to Milo's house to see off Pythagoras!*"

"So you went with them?"

"No. I kept my head down and had more to drink. This morning I came up to see what was what. And I found him, lying here. He hated beans. He must have refused to cross the field with the others. He could have got away with them, but because of his principles he stood bravely to meet his fate. The attackers hacked him to pieces without mercy—"

"This hardly counts as an eye-witness report," Milo broke in, dismissing the sensational aspects. "It doesn't fit the facts. The man appears to have been killed with one efficient blow to the head. A hard one, which split his skull."

Helianthos looked surprised. "You're very observant!" Milo gave him a dry smile.

Time to get tough. Milo put it to the lad bluntly: "Was there anyone at your tavern who'll be able to confirm you were there all night?"

"I had nothing to do with this!" Helianthos was a realist; that was why he had been deemed unsuitable for Pythagorean philosophy. Even so, he felt put out. "Whatever are you suggesting?"

Unperturbed, Milo stated: "A rejected follower is the obvious suspect."

"I wasn't the only one!" Helianthos panicked. "And I don't know any gang of lads. Whoever destroyed your house definitely had help." Once he calmed down, Helianthos did possess basic good sense (in fact he was *completely* unsuitable for any sort of academic life). "Still, I'd better come up with an alibi. Well, the woman who runs the tavern will remember me clearly: I'm not used to drinking. I was extremely sick. Then I passed out for the rest of the night. I've got bruises from the people who stepped on me."

Milo stamped his foot with delight. A stadium's length away across the fields liquorice plants trembled. "So it's not you. Well, are there any other intellectual rejects hanging around the neighbourhood?"

"Once they're turned down as students they tend to slink off to their own cities. The people of Croton are very unfriendly."

"They get tired of being sneered at," explained Milo. "Don't blame us. It was your lot who looked down their noses. Who even refused to shake our hands."

The rejected pupil still clung to old loyalties. "You don't understand. The master was different from other people—"

"Oh yes! He was a demigod, the rest of us were dust. Says he!"

As an athlete, Milo naturally wished to keep sport separate from politics (except when he was asking for a civic contribution to pay for his training or his travel to sporting venues). He liked to pretend he had no idea what was going on in Croton, yet Helianthos was beginning to suspect that was a pose.

Milo spent his days relentlessly exercising and practising at the gymnasium. Even in the dry heat and cold rooms of the baths few people cared to engage Milo in casual chat. But when the spectators were standing on the raised walkways watching him, or while he silently scraped off the oil and sand which wrestlers applied as a protective second skin, other men talked to each other – and then Milo listened. He had heard the rumbles of unrest over the Pythagoreans' love of mystery and their snobbery.

One subject of the mutterings was the razing of Sybaris. Since he had helped to flatten the town (though not to put

its citizens to the sword), Milo particularly listened to that.
Attacking Sybaris had been strongly urged by Pythagoras. He
had convinced the civic elders of Croton that their neighbours
were too carefree. (The Sybarites were the kind of easy-going
folk who banned cockerels from their town to avoid being woken
up early.) The Sybarites had been glamorous, sophisticated – and
happy. Now there were people in Croton who whispered that
happiness was a feature of democracy which only barbarians
would destroy.

"Let's consider," said Milo, "who had a reason to go for
Pythagoras – a motive," he added, feeling pleased with the
terminology. It sounded businesssslike. "You lived in the commune. Tell me about it. If it wasn't an outcast who did this, the
next consideration must be an inside job."

"The whole community adored him," declared Helianthos.

"Explain it. What made him such a celebrity?"

"He was an extraordinary man."

"So what did he win his prizes for?"

Helianthos faced up to the question seriously: "His learning—"

"Such as?"

"His first study was how to perform miracles." At this
Milo showed a definite interest, but he made no comment.
So Helianthos continued: "Then he turned to mathematics. He
was taught mysteries by the priests of the great temples of
Egypt. He learned astrology, logistics, geometry and occult lore.
He travelled widely – Egypt, Phoenicia, and the Chaldees. After
that he turned his abilities to teaching, starting as tutor to the son
of Polycrates of Samos—"

"That old ruffian!" One of the perks of athletics was free trips
to Greece, sponsored by your home town. As a traveller Milo
had heard all about the piratical king of Samos. "How did your
prudish master fit in with riotous living amongst poets, girls and
pretty youths?"

"He was deeply offended. So he accepted an invitation
to cross the ocean to Croton and to found a school here."
Helianthos was remembering how he himself had been drawn
to it: "People came from all over the world. He accepted

about three hundred students, who were allowed to live with him in an exclusive school, devoting their days to his precepts—"

"Which were?"

"Oh that's an absolute secret! I couldn't possibly reveal them!"

"I think you'd better," Milo suggested, not even bothering to inflate his mighty chest.

Helianthos sighed. "I don't know much. Pupils at the school lived together, holding all things in common –" Milo knew most of the pupils had come from wealthy homes, arriving at Croton with well-stuffed travel packs. He was thinking how useful their money must have been for Pythagoras. Helianthos pressed on bravely. "They were divided into two groups: the mathematicians, who had a rightful access to knowledge, and the rest. I'm afraid I was in the second category. Our only duty was to obey the rules."

"What rules?"

"I am sworn not to tell."

"A man has been killed," Milo commented. "That may not be important of course. But property has been destroyed. That's *very* important. Tell me about the rules!"

"They won't make much sense to an uninitiate," Helianthos warned defensively. "Well, things like, not to leave the imprint of your body on the bedclothes on rising, not to look into a mirror beside a light – and the main one was, never to eat beans."

Milo breathed heavily. "I won't ask what the point was."

"Of abstaining from beans?"

"Oh I can see that! You don't want three hundred people farting all night." He could see *some* point in all of it: drilling the pupils with an unusual routine, so they could be controlled. Every fake demigod who ever lived – and some athletics trainers – knew that trick. It *was* a trick of course. He wondered how much else had been.

"Milo, every night we had to ask ourselves three questions: What evil have I done? What good have I done? What have I omitted to do?"

Milo gazed at him, giving Helianthos an uncomfortable feeling. "So while you were getting out of bed very carefully and watching your diet, what were the mathematicians up to?"

"I really can't tell you that. They had a secret language, devised by the master, based on symbols and codes—"

"Surprise me!" growled Milo. "So I suppose you have no idea what the great man was teaching them?"

At this juncture Helianthos began to look more sheepish. He was beginning to be interested in solving the mystery. "Well, I did keep my ear to the ground."

"Smart boy!"

"There were three main areas of thought being discussed: transmigration of the soul—"

"I think we'll skip that one," sneered Milo. A fly flew too close and he killed it: one rapid movement of his lower leg. A heel-kick that would have knocked the knee from under any other town's champion in the wrestling ring.

Helianthos tried not to quake. "His other principal interests were the theory of numbers, and cosmology – the universe."

"Numbers? You mean that stuff about the sides of the triangle?"

"Well, the Hypotenuse Theorem was one practical by-product. The main thrust of the master's teaching was more all-enveloping. He said that numbers are the essential element of matter. Where other thinkers have maintained that everything is composed of fire, or air, or water, the master taught that numbers have substance and everything is composed of them. Some are more powerful than others. The number ten is divine, and one, two, three and four have special qualities. Their sum equals ten, and they form the divine configuration." Helianthos risked drawing it in the dust:

$$* \\ ** \\ *** \\ ****$$

Seeing Milo's expression he erased it hastily.

Milo asked frankly, with a grin that said a lot, "You mean, according to Pythagoras, I could have saved myself bother if I'd known the right number? I could have walked out into the arena at Olympia, for example, and defeated my opponent just by shouting 'thirty two!' Or whatever?"

"Everything depends on the law of Harmony," Helianthos rushed on. "This controls the universe. The master observed that there is a relation between the length of a lyre string and the sound produced; that gave rise to his ideas about the Music of the Spheres – the ten heavenly bodies, or planets, whose continual sweet sounds mankind cannot hear—"

Milo whistled. It sounded derisive, though his manner was humble.

Helianthos paused, then began again: "The master said that in the beginning was Chaos, then numbers were created to give relationships between lines and points, and Harmony produced the Cosmos, which is Order."

"In this part of the Cosmos, Order seems to have broken down," Milo interrupted with one of his wry put-downs, waving an arm towards the smoking villa and the body in the beanfield.

"But we're here to reimpose Harmony!" Helianthos retaliated weakly. "If we ask the right questions we'll be able to draw a line straight to the culprits . . . Look, I'm not competent to explain it. I'm just illustrating what I secretly overheard."

"Was it convincing when *he* told it?"

"Oh absolutely!" The young man's face lit with remembered fervour. "His evening lectures were rivetting. People came from everywhere to hear him. He never let strangers see him – even initiates were not allowed that privilege until they had passed through all the mysteries. He sat behind a curtain expounding his doctrines, and it was—" He sought for words. "Magical!"

"Ah!" Milo said. "Well, he had studied under the Egyptians and the Chaldeans."

Helianthos felt Milo had something on his mind. "Whenever he taught his first words would be: 'I swear by the air I breathe and the water I drink that I shall never suffer censure on account of that which I am about to say'—"

"Big headed bugger!" Milo commented. "Hasn't got a lot to say for himself now." Pythagoras, being dead in the beanfield, for once proposed no argument.

Pythagoras would be known for centuries, even if his theories were discredited. Milo, as an athlete, would have no future once his strength started to fail, but he could enjoy a very decent present. When a wrestler had won the Pythean and the Olympic Games six times each he got a villa in the sun, free beef for life, more laurel wreaths than he could find space for – and a reputation that might also last for a couple of millennia. By then, even though he was famous for brawn not brain, Milo knew a thing or two. He reached the question he had been quietly saving: "Tell me about the miracles."

Helianthos blushed. "The master had a golden thigh."

"Is that the truth?"

"Well, it's a myth." Helianthos was catching the wrestler's sceptical attitude. "He killed a deadly snake by biting it. He held conversations with a bear, over many years—"

"I'd like to hear the bear's side of that story!"

"He persuaded a heifer to refrain from eating beans. He was seen at the same time in both Croton and Metapontium—"

"Don't go on."

"I'm just telling you what people said."

"No one can be in two places at once. Not even if they're composed of harmonious numbers and they reckon they were once Apollo's son."

Helianthos drew a deep breath. "Don't let's argue."

"I'm not arguing. I'm just thinking about those devious buggers, the Egyptians and the Chaldeans." The phrase "all done with mirrors" sprang unbidden to Milo's mind. He rebuffed it. Mirrors in those days – even the finest polished Etruscan mirrors – were not shiny enough for conjuring. Tricks had to be worked by sleight of hand, by deceiving the eye – or by the simple use of stand-ins.

Helianthos was worried by the sudden silence. "None of this is helping you decide who burned down your house."

"Or who killed Pythagoras! Tell me more about the cult."

"The school, you mean?"

"The school then. So what do you know about Pythagoras and his school?"

"Is this a time to be considering achievements?"

"Stuff his achievements. Tell me how he lived while he was at my villa. I want to know what he did to irritate somebody so intensely that they came mob-handed with torches, then smoked him out of his hidey-hole and kicked in his brains."

Helianthos shuddered. "Do you have to be so graphic?" Then when Milo merely shrugged, he found enough spirit to reprimand him with: "Those, Milo, were very particular brains! Those brains—"

"They're offal now," disagreed the wrestler. "And my house is ash! – So what was it like, at the commune in the final days?"

"Tense. Everything was going wrong. There was a terrible sense of approaching disaster. One student, whose name was Hippasus, had caused a lot of trouble. He revealed the existence of irrational numbers."

"Do I need to understand that?"

"All you need to know is that it strikes at the heart of the master's theories about numerical harmony—"

"Proves him wrong, you mean?"

"A blasphemer might say so."

"So what happened to the brave, outspoken Hippasus? Is he a suspect for the killing?"

"He's dead himself, Milo. The master cursed him. He was so terrified he fled, plunged into the sea, and was drowned a few miles from shore."

"Had word got out about what he had said?"

"Oh certainly. He was hopeless; he went around telling everyone."

"So he had thoroughly undermined the master's theory. Was it possible Pythagoras may have felt his term was up?"

"He had certainly considered relocating the school.

I believe there was talk of disbanding from Croton and moving – Metapontium had been suggested."

"It sounds as if the whole mystic edifice was on the verge of collapse. Were the pupils aware of this?"

"They didn't want to believe it. Sometimes there was hysterical talk. The main threat came from the town. There was serious opposition in Croton. People had begun to hate having mysteries on their doorstep. What happened at Sybaris alarmed them. That was when the pupils became agitated and even talked of all taking hemlock together – whatever had been decided, what was done last night overtook it. This came from outside."

"Well, it looks that way. Did Pythagoras have any particular enemies?" Milo felt pleased with this question. It had a sound feel; a rightness: order out of chaos. He liked it better than the one about who had done this.

"Oh I'm sure he didn't." Whenever Helianthos seemed to have grasped reality, his innocence and good nature had a habit of breaking through.

"So," commented the wrestler, in a rather facetious mood, "he was perfectly well liked – except by bean farmers, rejected philosophy students, and the entire city of Sybaris?"

Helianthos nodded.

"Well, we can rule out the Sybarites; none of them were left alive. So let's look again for someone who had reason to be jealous of the school. Somebody local, who could assemble a gang. Who was the latest would-be student to be shown the door?"

"Probably Chilon. He's from Croton."

"Was Chilon very upset at being chucked out?"

"Furious. He is of high birth and violent nature."

"Oh that Chilon!" Milo had remembered him. "He dabbled with weight training before his daddy bought him a set of philosophy lessons. Useless. No discipline. He's a spoiled thug. I can imagine his reaction if anybody told him that." Someone as arrogant as Pythagoras had probably had no qualms about telling him frankly.

"Does he have any friends?" Helianthos asked.

"He goes around in a group of other rich brats. They like to make a racket. Always pushing and shoving in the market-place."

"They sound the sort who might decide to pick on an unpopular group."

"Oh they'd love it! Especially if the unpopular group were ethereal types who could be relied on not to come out fighting. So you reckon when Chilon was turned down by the school, he went away, downed a few consoling drinks, then came roaring out swearing vengeance? I should have realised the obvious candidate was some crazy aristo."

"Why's that?" asked Helianthos.

"A poor man couldn't afford the drinks."

"Maybe he and his friends were just angry," Helianthos suggested.

"They were drunk," Milo insisted.

"No, it could have been high-spirits that went wrong." Helianthos still pursued the issue, now wanting the master's death to be more than a sudden act of violence in the midst of a drunken brawl. "They had to bring torches with them, as the night was dark, but maybe it was an accident that they burned down the house. Young men could be forgiven for carelessness."

"Not at *my* house!" Milo boomed. Helianthos fell silent. "You want me to believe Chilon's intentions were perfectly peaceful? He just intended to back Pythagoras against a wall and have a quiet word?"

"Explain that his opinions had become unwelcome in Croton, then show him the quickest route out of town?" Helianthos contributed.

Milo had become sarcastic. "Well, I wouldn't want to slander Chilon, if we've got it wrong!" Chilon's father was a big man in Croton. "But I might ask whether it would not have been more considerate to set Pythagoras on the road by daylight. And it's easy to envisage a scene where Chilon and his friends arrived at the villa in a bawdy throng, called for the philosopher who sensibly refused to emerge, then they torched the place to flush him out."

"His pupils fled for their lives across country," Helianthos now agreed sadly.

"Pythagoras himself refused to cross a field of beans. So he stood and met his death."

"That seems a logical explanation." Helianthos felt like a philosopher who was losing faith in logic.

The two men rose quietly and went again to survey the corpse.

"Just one more question," Milo said, as if it were an afterthought. "You identified the body. If no one was allowed to see him at close quarters, how are you so sure this is Pythagoras?"

Helianthos was taken aback. "I had glimpsed him from a distance. Initiates had described him. Who else could it be?"

Milo smiled. "Good question!" He was thinking again about the lore and the mysteries of the Egyptians and Chaldeans. Masters of cunning. Past masters of deception and fakery. "Put it this way, if by any chance you should hear in the near future that Pythagoras has reappeared somewhere else, you'll naturally assume it is another miracle."

"I will! – But you sound doubtful?"

"Oh far be it from me to dabble in mysteries."

"But?"

Milo made a self-deprecating gesture. "But it seems to me, something doesn't add up."

"Things always add up," the ex-student replied gravely. "The problem is they don't always add up the way you want them to."

"Maybe someone has deliberately decided how things should work out here."

"What are you suggesting?"

"Just this: that a man who kept his appearance secret, yet who made a practice of being seen in two places at once, might just have helped the myth along by employing a stand-in."

Helianthos discovered he was not as shocked as he would once have expected to be. "You mean the *stand-in* is dead?"

Below the promontory the Ionian Sea stretched to the bright

horizon, a blue so clear it hurt the eyes, variegated with mysterious swathes of darker hues. Dolphins played. Bees hummed in what was left of the beanfield. Helianthos seemed to have matured ten years. The effect was cheering. "But if you are right, Pythagoras escaped to safety after all. Chilon and the others found the poor old man dead and abandoned the chase—"

"Being a stand-in isn't much of a life. Maybe he had been promised his soul would be rewarded with a better existence next time," suggested Milo, in his scathing mood.

"Who killed this man?"

"What do you think?" asked Milo.

"I think –" Helianthos sucked his teeth then could not face the answer.

"It was perfect," said Milo. "A conjuring trick: the philosopher vanishes; yet he's lying here dead."

The two men walked slowly down the track, leaving the burned out villa and the fly-blown corpse. They were drawing near to Croton. Milo clapped an arm over the younger man's shoulders, causing him to buckle slightly at the knees. "So what will you do now?"

Helianthos managed to keep walking despite the pressure. "Return to my own people and try to lead a useful life."

"Good lad. If I was you, I'd try and get more exercise. And take care of your diet. Raw steak would fill you out a bit. But pulses are full of goodness," instructed Milo, with a comfortable smile. "You know – peas, lentils, that sort of thing."

Helianthos smiled back. "Are you recommending beans, Milo?"

Milo of Croton shrugged his massive shoulders peacefully. The failed student had really grown up. He had learned to make jokes.

"So . . . who killed the old man? Who stood to gain?" asked Milo quietly.

"Pythagoras." Helianthos had found an expression of wry acceptance which mirrored the wrestler's own. "But of course," he said, "we know that cannot be possible, because Pythagoras could not bring himself to kill any living thing."

"Philosophy's wonderful," Milo agreed.

THE SECRET

Eileen Dewhurst

Eileen Dewhurst is herself one of crime fiction's best kept secrets. For the past 20 years she has been publishing varied and intriguing novels which have earned much critical praise and yet not, perhaps, the breadth of readership that they deserve. Her short stories are few but, again, they are worth seeking out. Questions of identity evidently fascinate her and she explores them time and again in her work. The Secret is typical of her writing at its best, crisply written and distinctive.

The weather was so hot in Provence at the time Monica Millican drowned herself in her twin sister's swimming pool that her sister – the widowed Comtesse de Chameux-Periard – persuaded Monica's husband Roland via a telephone call to England that it would be prudent for his wife to be cremated where she had died. A memorial service, the Comtesse suggested, could be held later at home.

Not, of course, that the funeral could take place in either France or England to the usual time-scale, in view of the necessity for a post-mortem examination and an inquest. But at least the local morgue had the best freezing facilities in the area, and the Comtesse, with her unique local influence, was able to arrange the funeral for the day immediately following the body's release.

The Secret

In view of Monica's state of mind at the time of her death – she had had to resign from her teaching job and had already made an attempt to take her life in her own bathroom – Roland was required to be present at the inquest. As his French was so poor he was given an interpreter through whom he was able to explain to the satisfaction of the *coroner* that his wife's death was the tragically logical outcome of her behaviour over recent months. The *coroner* clicked his tongue sympathetically when Roland added that Monica had in fact been visiting her sister in an attempt to free herself from what had so sadly proved to be a clinical depression. A verdict was brought in of *Suicide alors qu'elle n'était pas responsable de ses actes.* "Suicide while the balance of her mind was disturb-èd", as the interpreter, seeing Roland's bewildered face, hissed into his ear.

"*C'était gentille, cette pauvre Madame Monica!*" sobbed the cook, when the Comtesse went into the kitchen on her return from the court. "*Et comme enfants, ces deux petites!* . . . *ont du être mignonnes* . . . *y a une photo, Madame?*"

The Comtesse found one after a search, and when she had shown it to the cook and to Roland she took it away and looked at it herself. At the two shyly smiling little girls who were Madeleine and Monica Thompson, clean, tidy and precisely alike.

Which they never had been, of course.

As she gave instructions to her staff, wrote the letters and made the telephone calls arising out of her sister's death, moved between the cool shade of the house and the dazzling sunshine of the terrace in intermittently successful attempts to avoid the brother-in-law she disliked but to whom she had been obliged to offer hospitality, the Comtesse found herself unable to stop thinking about those two little girls. Monica the one who had hung back, Madeleine the one who had led the way, the one who had been first to tell the time, tie her shoe-laces, write her name. Even when Monica turned out to be the academic one, Madeleine had continued somehow to outshine her – perhaps because academic achievement was not something by which Madeleine set much store. For her, it was more important to be quick-witted, lovely to look at, exciting to be with. And married to a man with wealth and influence.

By the time Monica went up to Oxford Madeleine was already establishing herself as a model. Whether she would have reached the top of her profession no one would ever know, because on a visit to Oxford to see her sister Madeleine met Félix Brion, elder son of the Comte de Chameux-Periard, who was on a postgraduate course in comparative estate management, and embarked very soon afterwards on her second career as his wife.

Monica, meanwhile, who had never developed charisma, drifted into a lack-lustre affair with a fellow undergraduate reading Mechanical Engineering, and married him a year after they had both gained Second Class Honours degrees.

Following her marriage Monica continued to teach, but following hers Madeleine, at her husband's request, ceased to model. Her father-in-law died soon after his elder son's wedding, and on inheriting the title Félix dedicated his working life to the extensive estate surrounding the family château in the valley of the Loire, an activity in which his wife had been gratified to assist him.

Neither marriage had been blessed with children. Monica had a couple of miscarriages and Madeleine never became pregnant – to the infinite disappointment of the Comte, who knew he had terminal cancer for some time before telling his wife, and had hoped to leave a son and heir behind him.

So when he died the *château*, the estate and the title passed to his younger brother. Not too much to Madeleine's chagrin: she was sole heir to *Les Pigeonniers*, the property in Provence, and to her husband's personal fortune, and although she had enjoyed assisting him in his running of the château and the estate she lacked the energy and the motivation to relish the idea of shouldering the responsibility of them on her own. And, as André showed no interest whatsoever in the female sex, there was unlikely to come a time when she would be obliged to insert the word *douairière* – dowager – into her title.

Madeleine had been the Comtesse de Chameux-Periard for fifteen years at the time of her sister's death, and Monica was

The Secret

in the thirteenth year of her marriage to Roland Millican. During their married lives the twins spoke to each other on the telephone every few months, sent each other birthday and Christmas presents, occasionally met. Over the years the Millicans spent a few holidays at *Les Pigeonniers*, but Roland was the only one who enjoyed them, and the sisters' regular meetings took place in London, where Madeleine went twice a year to shop and see friends. Monica, of course, always invited her twin to stay with her and Roland at their home outside Birmingham, but Madeleine regularly excused herself on the grounds that her time in England was short and the other people she wanted to see, the things she wanted to do, were in or near London.

Monica had always gone willingly to their meetings, the Comtesse mused as she moved restlessly about her house and garden. Partly, of course, because she enjoyed the rare break from Roland and the night at the Dorchester to which Madeleine always treated her. (*Poor cow!*, the Comtesse thought, with a rush of contemptuous sympathy, *pleased with so little. Poor weak, frightened, stupid cow!*). But also because of their tacit agreement that occasional meetings were necessary for the preservation of their Secret.

The Secret that, despite being identical twins, the sisters did not like one another.

Monica had always made it plain to Madeleine that she considered her shallow and superficial, while trying to hide her envy of her sister's place in the sun. No less obviously, Madeleine had no time for what she saw as Monica's narrow life, and pitied her for her dullness and her boring husband with the lascivious gleam in his eye on those rare occasions when he encountered his wife's glamorous sister.

But there was a social imperative with which both women had always felt it prudent to comply: twins were supposed to feel themselves in a uniquely close relationship, particularly if they were identical.

Not that that had been so obvious since they grew up, the Comtesse reflected as she sat in her black at the funeral luncheon, murmuring responses to the people who came up to her to commiserate – not a great many, as she had lived somewhat reclusively since her husband's death. Monica had met all the members of her sister's small circle during the couple of weeks of holiday that had preceded her death, and several of them had remarked on how unlike one another the twins looked, forbearing of course to put into words the most obvious reasons why this was so: Madeleine's fashion sense and Monica's lack of it; Madeleine's verve and Monica's troubled stare . . .

But today a few of them mentioned that stare.

"Yes," the Comtesse agreed. "Monica *was* troubled, I'm afraid. You sensed it? . . . Yes, I was aware of it too, but I never dreamed . . ." Here she paused, to raise a scrap of white lawn to her lips. "I hoped she was enjoying herself . . . beginning to recover . . ." That was where she choked to a standstill. Not really having to fake her distress, because she was so wary of her final evening with Roland.

He came over to her the moment the last guests had taken their leave.

"You must be tired, Madeleine."

She got to her feet, wishing he was not standing so close to her. "I'm tired of these clothes, and I'm glad it's all over." Almost all over. "I'm going to change. Don't forget this, Roland." She went to the side table where she had placed the urn when it had been delivered by an acolyte during the last stages of the funeral feast. Ashes were not usually presented to the relatives on the day of cremation, but the Comtesse was anxious to be rid of Roland at the earliest possible moment and had been financially persuasive.

She picked up the urn, which to her distaste felt slightly warm, put it into his unwilling hands. "Drinks on the terrace at half-past seven."

The Comtesse prepared herself for the evening with particular care, and in her most elegant manner. She did not wish to encourage the gleam in Roland's eye, but it was preferable to his other possible reaction.

Out on the terrace, where the brilliant colours of the day were paling to pastel under the darkening sky, she poured herself a stiff drink and sat down to await him, realising as she saw the glass tremble in her hand how everything since her sister's death had taken a toll of her – the early morning discovery of the body face down in the pool, the shock waves through the house and village, the questioning, the inquest, the effort to appear more upset than she was and preserve the Secret. Roland under her roof for a week had been the worst ordeal of all, but although the lustful gleam had appeared from time to time the Comtesse could not so far complain of his behaviour.

Tonight, though, was his last night at *Les Pigeonniers*. The last time he and she would ever have to meet.

"Ah! Roland! Come and sit down. After you've helped yourself to what you want." She waved her hand at the glass trolley with its array of bottles. "Have you been packing?"

A swift, keen look. "Not packing, no. Not yet. Not wanting to see the evidence around me that I'm on the way home, to tell you the truth. I don't suppose I should say this, Madeleine, but I've been very comfortable here."

"People usually are." She had made a nestling movement into her long chair before deciding it might appear provocative. "But you'll be glad everything's sorted."

"Yeah. Sure."

She watched him survey the bottles, select the scotch and generously pour, throw in two ice cubes. Swirling his glass so that the ice chinked, he strolled over to the nearest of the other long chairs and threw himself down.

"Ah! That's better! Old ticker been playing up a bit today. Has to be the strain, I suppose. But I'm bearing up."

"Good for you, Roland."

What a wimp! the Comtesse thought. Seeing himself now as a desirable male on the loose, but still the same pathetic Roland Millican using the excuse of his dicky heart to tout for sympathy. Still the same meagre figure with the stooped shoulders, round pink tonsure, small mean mouth and close-set suspicious eyes . . .

In which the lascivious gleam was back as he leaned towards the Comtesse's chair.

The Comtesse's desire to be rid of him was suddenly so strong she could scarcely contain it. Dinginess seemed to spread physically from his unlovely body, casting a film over the sparkling landscape beyond the terrace.

"You'll be glad to get home, Roland, get on with your life. I hope the memorial service goes well, I'm sorry I don't feel up to being there." The Comtesse had no parents alive to be distressed by her non-attendance. "And I'm sorry I failed to help Monica. I'll always feel that if she hadn't come to me she might still be with us."

"Forget it." Roland made a nestling movement in his turn. The Comtesse had never seen him so relaxed. "If she hadn't done it here she'd have done it somewhere else. She'd made up her mind."

"Weren't you afraid . . . Didn't you wonder when you came home from work that you might find—"

"She'd promised to pull herself together. So I hoped . . ."

Hoped she might have broken her promise? She wouldn't put it past him. "Yes, of course. Well, I'll try not to feel guilty. And if she wasn't happy . . ."

"She should have been!" Roland exploded indignantly. His drink splashed over the edge of his glass as his body jerked, and the Comtesse watched it spread like string across the creamy stone floor. "She had everything she wanted. A nice house – well, not on the same planet as yours, of course, but a nice house – and a nice garden where she enjoyed working. Things weren't so easy when she stopped earning, but we didn't have to count every penny and I never complained."

"You feel she's let you down, don't you, Roland?" the Comtesse inquired softly.

"I . . . Well, yes, in a way I do, you know." There was admiration too, now, in the pale eyes. "You're very perceptive, Madeleine. And very, very beautiful." The light of lust was growing into a powerful beam, and the Comtesse had to suppress a physical recoil. "You know, I'm beginning to think I chose the wrong sister. But you were always so busy with other people. Rather more than you are these days, it seems to me."

Now the Comtesse had to suppress a terrible desire to laugh. "What do you mean, Roland?"

"I mean . . . I don't have to go home, you know. Well, I do of course, for the time being, the memorial service and all that, and I suppose the look of things, but afterwards . . . I've a few weeks of holiday due to me." He was near enough to lean forward and place a hand on her bare knee. Her revulsion and disgust were so strong they made her choke, and she was able to move her knee without seeming to rebuff the hand as she searched for a tissue. "Oops!" he said. "Am I as bad as that?"

Roland in rare jesting mood made her think of a puppy panting its hope that a ball is about to be thrown for it to retrieve. "Look, Roland . . . Whatever I feel or don't feel doesn't come into it. How can I explain? I may look like a free woman, but I'm still a Chameux-Periard, and the Chameux-Periards guard their widowed family members. Ruthlessly. The way the Mafia guard theirs. You understand?" Grinning, the Comtesse drew a finger melodramatically across her throat. "I'm not saying my husband's family is on the wrong side of the law, but they have that in common with the first family of crime. Unless, of course," she went on, "a subsequent attachment is seen to be serious and honourable, when it can be approved by the family. This happens very rarely, and as you must realise, Roland, there can never be anything between you and me which could be seen in that light. All right?"

"All right, Madeleine, yes, of course." Roland drained his glass, looked at his watch, and rose to his feet. "Still half an hour before dinner, think I'll get my things together. It's an early flight."

"A good idea, Roland." And there was a chance he might follow it up by sending a message down to say he was having a bad reaction to the funeral, and would she mind if he missed dinner and had a tray sent up to his room . . .

Relaxing into her long chair, Monica Millican watched the disappearing figure of her husband and knew with relief and in triumph that the last and most dangerous hazard had been overcome.

She had always known she was capable of bringing it off, from the moment she had stood at her kitchen window that rainy morning in the school holidays, looking down the narrow garden and realizing that her life as it was was not worth living. For the

61

first time, from the lowest point even she had ever reached, she had squared up to fate and decided to bend it to her will. It had denied her Félix as a husband, but she would secure her place as his widow and his heir . . .

She had loved Félix and, she was sure, he had begun to love her. But then Madeleine had come to Oxford on a flying visit and swept him away with her: *You do understand, don't you, darling? We're made for each other. And it isn't as though you and he . . .*

Not quite then, no, but it would have been.

With Félix gone, it hadn't seemed to matter to Monica whether it was Roland or anyone else. But she had been married for only a few weeks when she had begun to wish it was nobody . . .

She threw her first wobbly that very evening. Not having the dinner ready when Roland got home from work, telling him she wished she was dead. She kept on telling him, and the following week she cut her wrists in the bathroom – crying so loudly as she did it that he was there to bind them up before she had done more than scratch them. Then she resigned from her job and went to a psychiatrist, and then it was on record that she was mentally disturbed.

She had never been tempted to let Roland into the Secret, so she was able to suggest to him that going to see Madeleine might be of help.

Roland had seized on the idea. It just might do the trick, she had seen him thinking, and even if it didn't it would give him a few weeks without her and the strain she was putting on his dicky heart.

Madeleine on the telephone had obviously found it hard to believe that her sister could want to visit her, but after a pause for thought she said she supposed that at least the sunshine, the idleness, and the absence of Roland might be therapeutic, and told Monica to come if that was really what she wanted.

It had continued to be as easy. Monica presented herself in France as even more dull and dowdy than she was in England, and was amused to see how Madeleine's wary sun-tanned face relaxed when they met at the airport and she was assured that her sister would not be her rival. Madeleine's relief, in fact, had

The Secret

made her generous, and she had let Monica help herself to her shorts, bikinis, slips of dresses – all of which fitted, as Monica had dieted discreetly to the specifications of her sister's most recent photographs.

After a couple of weeks Monica's skin, too, was a golden brown, and she wore Madeleine's emerald green bikini the day she joined her in the pool for her regular dawn swim and held her head under the water.

Changing the wedding-rings had been a fraught moment, but both had slipped off easily enough in the early morning cool. The hazard after that was to get back to her room and cut her hair the inches necessary to turn it into Madeleine's. But she had already worked out where the scissors had to go, and Madeleine – as she had seen initially from the photographs – had been content not to meddle with the natural ash-blonde with which nature had endowed them both. In case it should be observed that Monica's hair was a little shorter in death than it had been in life, she had left the clippings where they fell – on and around Monica's dressing-table – as evidence of a last pathetic attempt by the dead woman to look more like her sister.

As for the language . . . Monica had read Modern Languages at Oxford, and despite living so long in France Madeleine was lazy and had spoken English to her husband and as many other people as possible. Monica had listened to her with her staff, and quickly realized that her own knowledge of French still outran her sister's. But she had played it down, limping, stumbling, asking people to speak more slowly, apologising to Madeleine for having got so rusty. And even their own mother had been unable to tell their voices apart.

She'd been practising Madeleine's signature for as long as she'd been acting out her depression, and their handwriting had always been the same. And Madeleine had actually mentioned her intention of finding a local dentist now that her London wonderman was talking of retiring . . .

So that was it, really, apart from Roland. And Roland, now out of sight and so soon to be out of mind, had shown her that her crime had paid.

Getting slowly to her feet Monica followed him into the house and locked herself into her beautiful new bedroom. Even before cutting her hair after Madeleine's last swim she had taken the little bottle from Monica's handbag and hidden it at the back of one of Madeleine's drawers. Now she took it out and held it in her hand, reading the label. *Digoxin tablets: one to be taken once a day. It is dangerous to exceed the stated dose.*

She hadn't expected Roland to recognize her, but she had brought the pills with her just in case – the reserve bottle he kept at the back of the medicine chest. If he had been suspicious she would have put a lethal dose into the glass of scotch he always took up to bed with him and which Madeleine always put into his hand as they said goodnight, and no one would have known whether his unhappiness at the loss of his wife had made him suicidal or merely careless . . .

Reluctantly Monica threw the pills and the label down her sister's private lavatory and flushed them away. She would have relished killing Roland, punishing him for the years of sadistic belittlement, but that would have been to tempt the fate she had at last bent so successfully to her will.

And the second-best thing about a perfect murder was that it cut out the need to commit any more.

WHERE DO YOU FIND YOUR IDEAS?

Martin Edwards

For once, I can pinpoint where this story came from. The whole idea crystallised in my mind early one morning during a "Shots In The Dark" convention in Nottingham for crime writers and fans. I was having breakfast with an American friend, a knowledgeable and enthusiastic student of the genre and I began to speculate on the nature of the relationship between authors and their readers. The first session that day was a less than spellbinding interview with a much-lauded American author and I began to scribble furiously, much to the amazement of the fellow Northern crime writer with whom I was sitting: she could not imagine why I felt compelled to take copious notes of the speaker's pearls of wisdom and to this day I have not confessed the truth to her. Within 48 hours, the first draft was complete. It was fun to write and, of course, there is no resemblance between myself and that hapless veteran of crime-fiction, Gerard Babb . . .

Who would it be?

Looking down on the ground floor of the bookshop from his vantage point in the gallery, where he skulked in the aisle which divided Psychology and The Occult, Gerard Babb watched the punters drifting in from the street and asked himself which of them would put the question he had come to dread.

He checked his watch for the twentieth time. Five minutes to go. In reality, ten minutes, for the manager was sure to insist on delaying the start in the vain hope of a late surge of interest from the reading public of this drab Midlands town. Of course there would be no surge. All that was likely to happen was that two or three of the characters who now roamed the street in search of care in the community might wander in for a place to shelter and swig out of beer cans.

"Ready?"

Brian had appeared at his side. A squat and mournful fellow, Brian seemed to Gerard to be temperamentally unsuited to his job as a sales rep. He'd been made redundant eighteen months earlier from his job as marketing manager for a company which sold artificial bonsai trees and had kicked his heels in the dole queue for a year before taking a post with the firm which published Gerard. He'd confided that he regarded selling books as much the same as selling phoney miniature plants and he'd made it very clear to Gerard that he thought fiction a complete waste of time: why bother to read something that wasn't even true? Gerard couldn't help looking forward to the day when Brian, like a superannuated politician, was given another chance to spend rather more time at home with his family.

"As ready as I'll ever be."

"Not much of a crowd, I'm afraid." Brian prided himself on his realism.

"Better than Stoke-on-Trent."

Brian grimaced. They both knew that a turn-out of three would be better than Stoke-on-Trent.

Downstairs the manager was pacing up and down in the manner traditionally associated with expectant fathers. He at least had claimed enthusiasm for crime fiction of the type which Gerard wrote, although Gerard had noted his failure to have read any of the Inspector Dooley novels.

Not that he was alone in having denied himself that pleasure. Years ago Gerard had resolved that in future he would never, at parties, admit to being a crime writer. He could no longer bear the puzzled frowns of people he met as they struggled to remember if they had ever heard of him. The giveaway was that polite enquiry: "And do you write under your own name?" A civilised reminder of his lack of a public profile.

"Course," said Brian, "the weather will have kept a lot of people away."

"It's not rained all week."

"Exactly. People will be out enjoying themselves."

Gerard found himself envying them. Twenty years – even a decade – back, it had all been so different. Inspector Francis Xavier Dooley had achieved a modest following; if not in the Morse class as a puzzle-solver, at least he could claim a full complement of first names. Crime round-ups in regional news-papers usually included a mention of Gerard's books and smaller publications, whose reviewers valued a regular supply of free novels, had been known to describe them as "unputdownable". The posher Sundays, although more enigmatic, on occasion said things like "the mayhem quotient is as high as ever" and Gerard had been happy to take that as praise. In those days, he had been accompanied on book-signing tours by a young woman publicist and a couple of times the girl sent by head office had been sufficiently starry-eyed about authors to be persuaded to share his bed in the second-rate provincial hotels where they stayed. All that had changed now: he was expected to be grateful for the company of the local area rep, who was dying to dash back home at the earliest opportunity.

He gazed disconsolately down on his expectant audience. The usual crowd. A scruffy student with features cast in a permanent sneer; a bespectacled would-be writer thirsting for tips; an earnest young woman with a notepad and pencil; two old ladies who came to everything and never bought anything; and a tramp who could be relied upon to start snoring the minute Gerard began his talk. The manager had stationed his assistant next to the till while he gloomily contemplated the stacks of books which Brian had insisted on Gerard signing so as to avoid the risk of their being returned to the warehouse unsold.

How many minutes would pass before the question was asked?

He was sure he would not have to wait long. How would Inspector Dooley rise to the challenge? With his customary determination Gerard thought gloomily. Dooley was a loner, a maverick who was perhaps a little too fond of the bottle. No lover of discipline, he had a running feud with his boss, a play-it-by-the-book time-server who was always threatening to take him off the case. In his tyro days, when he had still fancied himself as a budding Graham Greene, Gerard had made Dooley a lapsed Catholic who wrestled with his own sense of original sin during each investigation. But his then editor, an unsympathetic atheist who refused to accept any novel over 180 pages in length, had urged him to concentrate on crime rather than character and although the editor had long ago found himself a better paid job in publishing computer manuals, Gerard nowadays never allowed his detective more than two paragraphs of introspection per sixty thousand words.

It was ironic, he mused, that at the point in his career where his reputation should have been secure, when his name should be cropping up with tedious regularity on the shortlists for all the genre's top awards, the kind of book he wrote should have fallen out of fashion. He regarded himself as an entertainer first and last, but it was difficult to entertain people who were unaware of his existence. Of course, he'd always suffered because of niggardly publicity budgets, but the last couple of years had been the most disastrous he'd ever known. His American publishers had ditched him and even in the UK, no paperback contract had been forthcoming for the last Dooley title. His agent was philosophical – "Trade's very difficult at present, darling" – but she could afford to be: she now acted for Mandy Deville, brightest new star in the criminal firmament (as *The New Statesman* had it), creator of Jess Valetta, the feisty Afro-Caribbean private eye who solved crimes in a tracksuit whilst jogging around Battersea Park and whose first two adventures had loped to the top of the bestseller charts.

Down below the manager was looking out of the shop's front door. With a sad shake of the head, he turned back inside and indicated to Brian that they might as well begin.

"Better get it over with, then, eh?" Brian suggested.

Where Do You Find Your Ideas?

They went down the stairs and the manager shepherded Gerard to the front of the sparsely occupied black plastic chairs. Against the back wall stood a showcard emblazoned with Gerard's name and the jacket of *Dooley Takes A Break*. Beneath it could still be discerned faint details of the previous week's bookshop guest – an alternative comedian who had written a novel which was at one and the same time a hilarious satire and a searing indictment of government policy. The comedian had attracted a full house, naturally, and the manager hadn't omitted to mention it.

In introducing Gerard, the manager said a few words – a very few, sixteen in fact, Gerard counted them – and the desultory clap of greeting from the two old ladies and the tramp scarcely qualified as even a ripple of applause. Gerard forced a smile and opened with his customary quip about the traffic cop and the crime novelist. Even in Stoke-on-Trent it had received a better reception.

As usual, he talked about his career to date. Increasingly, he thought, it had come to sound like an obituary composed by an unsympathetic rival. The early days of struggle; the joy of achieving published status; the naive dreams of glory; the years of decline. He had come to see a sort of parallel between the fate of his literary career and his relationships with women. His wife had finally left him for good after years of mutual infidelities. She had taken up with a solicitor who specialised in matrimonial law and wrote poems about cats in his spare time.

"He has more artistic ability in his little finger than you have in your whole body," she had spat in one of their final arguments. Her invective always compensated in ferocity of delivery for its lack of originality.

"Half a dozen bits of doggerel in a magazine for wannabe writers?"

"He's a successful professional man," she had said. "He doesn't *need* to write full time."

And, it was true, the lawyer had certainly proved good at his job. Gerald had been screwed so badly on the divorce settlement that he'd been forced to move into a scruffy furnished flat in the sort of urban area where old folk burned to death in their homes because they could not break through the security barriers when a fire broke out. Money was short and to pay the rent Gerard had even had to stoop to writing five minute mysteries for women's magazines. Under a pen-name, of course: he had his pride.

As he came to the Raymond Chandler Joke which always began his peroration, he turned his mind to his audience. Who was going to torment him this time? The student was composing his sneer with some care and the aspiring writer had scribbled furiously throughout the entire talk. They were the likeliest to ask the question Gerard feared most, but neither of the old ladies could be ruled out of contention. One was fiddling with her false teeth as if making ready to put him on the spot, whilst her friend had finished the packet of humbugs she had been guzzling from the moment he first opened his mouth.

Why was he so keyed up, why bother about the reactions of a small group of people about whom he had no reason to care? Even when he was starting out, surely he had not felt as tense as this? Even though he was saying nothing he had not repeated a hundred times before, it seemed as though the words were sticking to the roof of his mouth. He paused and, giving the audience a tight smile, poured himself a glass of water.

For God's sake, pull yourself together, he instructed himself. *Soon it will be over.*

Yet even as the words echoed in his head, he realised that they applied with as much force to his writing career as to this latest unimportant talk. How could he go on, when he couldn't answer a simple question to which even a first time novelist can respond with a smug smirk?

He stumbled over the last few sentences in his notes and it was plain when he had come to the end that those present had not even realised he had finished. After an expectant pause the manager clambered awkwardly to his feet and said, "Well, thank you, Mr Babb for a most, er, interesting insight into the literary life. And now, I'm sure, everyone will be bursting with questions . . ."

His reedy voice trailed away as every hand in the audience remained resolutely on its owner's lap. This was Brian's cue. With every sign of resentment, he raised his arm and Gerard gave him the nod.

Where Do You Find Your Ideas?

"I wonder if you could tell us what the future holds in store for Inspector Dooley?"

Dead easy. But Gerard bumbled on inconclusively in reply and Brian's expression made it clear that he wished he had kept his mouth shut. At least the ice had been broken, however, and the student had thought of something to ask.

"What do you see as the novelist's function?"

Gerard gave him a chilly look. "To make money," he replied and the sight of the student's face gave him a thrill of pleasure almost reminiscent of the days when writing THE END on the last page of his manuscript had given him a sense of achievement rather than making him tremble at the thought that he might never finish another book.

The would-be author was next. "What's your writing routine each day?"

Maybe things would not be so bad tonight after all. Gerard reeled off the standard nine-to-five answer with a fluency he had thought beyond him these days. He said nothing about the long hours spent in the cubbyhole he now dignified with the name of study, staring at damp patches on the walls and seeing in them, like ink blots, the scornful faces of people he knew. His wife; his agent; his new editor, a sweet-looking girl with a foul tongue who was already casting round for an excuse to drop him from her list.

Timidly, the old lady with the false teeth lifted an age-spotted claw. "Can I ask, please, who is your favourite detective story writer?"

Gerard didn't see it as his job to promote the competition. "Agatha Christie," he said promptly. Bloody woman, she'd been dead thirty years and she still outsold him by a hundred to one. But at least you could never describe Miss Marple as feisty.

"Why did you set your last book in Cornwall?" asked the young woman sharply. "I missed the Lancashire setting."

God, a regular reader. They were thin on the ground these days. And she had a point. In the early Dooleys, Gerard had traded on the rugged Northern background against which the Inspector carried out his investigations. On his last outing, Dooley had been suspended for cuffing a teenage yobbo round the ear and had spent the time before his case came to court touring round the South West. In the time-honoured tradition of all holidaying sleuths, he there stumbled across a mystery crying out for his special deductive gifts. Gerard was uncomfortably aware that the puzzle, which hinged on an unbreakable alibi, and Dooley's solution (the murderer conveniently had an identical twin brother) owed more to guesswork and cliché than to ratiocination. Yet it was a novel which, as authors so often say, *had* to be written. In his present straitened circumstances, Gerard could only afford a few days away if he could claim tax relief on the expense and the Inland Revenue demanded that he justify his outlay by producing a book. Besides, the homicide rate on the western slopes of the Pennines had already reached Miami standards and Gerard had been desperate for a change. But he gave the girl some flannel about pushing out the boundaries of detective fiction and she nodded sagely as if she understood what he was talking about.

"When are your books going to be on the telly?" demanded the humbug-eater, evidently one of those who believed that anything of merit would sooner or later find its way to the small screen.

Gerard grunted. Years back, an independent production company had taken out an option on the Dooley series. He'd allowed himself to be seduced by the notion for a year or two, mentally casting. Anthony Hopkins as the Inspector and worrying about whether he would have a right of veto if the script editor decided to marry Dooley off to a blonde bimbo with a view to boosting the ratings. In the end he had not needed to fear that his artistic vision and integrity might be compromised by the demands of commercial television. The option had expired without being renewed.

Still, one could dream. He gave the woman an enigmatic smile and said, "These things are very delicate, you know. I do have hopes but I'm sure you'll appreciate that I can't say anything at present. I have to respect confidentiality."

At the back of the room, Brian choked back a snort of derision and checked his watch. Gerard began to breathe easier. It looked as though he would be spared the question.

And then the tramp stirred. He had seemed half asleep and he did not bother to raise his hand, perhaps assuming that life on the road entitled him to disregard the conventions. To Gerard's surprise, he spoke in a rich and resonant tone. Evidently a man of education.

"I wonder if you would enlighten us about one thing, Mr Babb?"

Gerard gave him a cautiously encouraging smile.

"You see, I have done a little writing myself over the years . . .''

Ah, Gerard reflected amiably, that would explain the long straggly beard and the unkempt appearance. He was just one more author awaiting an overdue royalty cheque.

". . . and although I fancy I have an elegant enough turn of phrase, I struggle to put together a full-length work of prose. So I wonder, can you tell me this: *where do you find your ideas?*"

Gerard banged his glass down on the table, spilling the water over his notes so that the ink began to run. The manager frowned. Brian gazed at the heavens.

"I. . . . er . . ."

It was no good. He could not form the words of his reply. For this was the question that terrified him, the familiar enquiry to which he could not bear to respond. To admit the truth would be impossible.

Quite simply, Gerard had not had an idea in years. The last half dozen Dooleys had recycled the plots and themes of all the early books in the series. In *Dooley Takes A Break* he had even found himself plagiarising large chunks of his own dialogue. Fortunately, the Inspector was so gruff and monosyllabic that no-one – certainly not his foul-mouthed editor – had noticed. It had occurred to him that no-one cared whether he repeated himself or not. And yet he cared. He, Gerard Babb, still wanted desperately to write novels. There was nothing else he could do. He could not claim to be a successful novelist, still less a success as a human being – and yet the urge to write was as strong within him as ever. The only trouble was that he could not think of a single new thing to write about.

Everyone, he realised, was looking at him. Experimentally,

he opened his mouth a couple of times, but an answer would not come. *If only I knew where and how to find a few ideas,* he felt like saying, *I wouldn't need to be stuck up here in front of you lot, trying to give a civil response to your bloody stupid questions.*

Brian was shaking his head. The manager coughed nervously. The student had begun to snigger and the would-be writer still had his pen poised over a virgin page in his notebook. Gerard realised he must say something. Anything.

"I wish I knew," he croaked.

It was more than an admission, it was like a tidal wave breaking down a harbour wall. Awareness of his own desperate inadequacy began to flood through him as never before. He could no longer hide from the truth that he had for so many years suspected yet never had the courage to confront: he was finished as a writer. His fictions were as dead as last autumn's leaves. Brian had put his finger on it after all. Who in their right mind would bother with a story that he, Gerard Babb, had clumsily made up, when it had never actually happened?

And as he stared out, unseeing, beyond the puzzled faces of his audience, he forced himself to face reality. He had told lies for a living for far too long to have a hope of finding another trade. His whole existence had become as pointless as his work. So why go on?

"Why go on?" he said, his voice still hoarse.

He was vaguely aware of the manager blundering to his feet and saying, "Well, yes, perhaps we have slightly over-run our time. As a result, of course, of all the interesting questions. And perhaps we'd just like to show our appreciation to Mr Babb for sparing the time from his busy schedule to be with us this evening."

The old lady with the false teeth clapped quietly, as if she had been so programmed that she could do nothing else, but the rest of the audience appeared to be baffled that the proceedings, though never more than desultory, had finally come to an unsatisfactory end. Gerard heard the student snort and the would-be writer murmur with disapproval. Brian's emotions appeared to be mixed: he seemed annoyed by Gerard's performance, but glad that he now had the chance to escape.

"Mr Babb will be available to sign copies of his latest . . ." began the manager, but he realised he was speaking to rapidly retreating backs. Even the tramp had hauled himself to his feet with a show of disappointment, as if he were accustomed to much better fare.

Brian came over to Gerard and muttered in his ear, "What d'you think you were playing at? After I'd been to such trouble, too. I'll have to report this to Carol-Jane, you know that, don't you?"

Gerard shrugged and turned towards the manager, whose mouth was beginning to set in a petulant line.

"Well, Mr Babb, I won't pretend this has been the most successful event Porlock and Macdonald have ever hosted."

He did not offer his hand and Gerard lumbered towards the door. He was turning his mind towards death. Funny, he had written so much about it and yet he had so seldom contemplated it. How should he proceed? Whisky, aspirin and a polythene bag offered one popular escape route. He did not care if it upset his landlady: the old cow deserved a bit of a fright. Finding the wherewithal to purchase a decent bottle of whisky might prove more of a problem and doing the job with the aid of a few glasses of Sainsbury's finest somehow seemed like too much of an anti-climax.

What would it be like, death? As he stepped into the cold night air, he trembled at the prospect of the unknown. Would there be pain? He realised his pulse was racing and the ironic notion occurred to him that suddenly he felt more alive now that he was facing the end than – oh, for as long as he could remember.

Fifty yards ahead of him, the tramp was ferreting in a litter bin. Who was he? That cultivated voice had suggested a man with a past, someone who had fallen on difficult times. What was his story? A marriage gone wrong, a vengeful wife? A gambling addiction that had caused his downfall? The jealousy of work colleagues who had conspired to make sure that he lost his job?

Funny, Gerard was using his imagination again for the first time in years. And okay, it was rather like taking a huge old machine out of mothballs, cranking it up and hoping for a smooth response. But at least he was doing it.

Gerard walked towards the tramp. Might it help to approach the man, learn a little about him? It was possible the chap might make a good character in a story.

Catching his breath, Gerard realised that he had begun to think as a writer should. The creative urge had caught hold of him again. He was only a few yards behind the tramp now. The man was absorbed in an old newspaper he had fished out of the litter bin and was oblivious of Gerard's approach.

Gerard looked around. Although it was still only early evening the street was deserted apart from the two of them. The bald spot on the crown of the tramp's head glinted under a yellow street light. It fascinated Gerard, drew him on. And yet, somehow, it offended him. Must get rid of it, stop the bloody thing shining in the night. A broken bit of paving stone lay in the gutter. Gerard picked it up and raised it briefly to the heavens before dashing it down on the tramp's head. The man gave a shocked gasp and collapsed to the floor. Gerard lifted his foot and began to kick at the blood-oozing bald patch.

And as he delivered the fatal blow, the germ of a story came to him. A killer, driven to savage and motiveless murder, stalking the streets of dreary English towns. Forget about Inspector Dooley, this would be a non-series suspense novel, searing and bleak. A story about a truly perfect crime.

Gerard could not help exclaiming with joy. He was saved. He knew the secret now and he need never again run short of inspiration.

At last he had discovered where to find his ideas.

THE PERFECT IMPERFECT

Gösta Gillberg

Membership of the CWA is predominantly British, but overseas writers are welcome to join and Gösta Gillberg is one of a number of Scandinavian crime writers who belong to the Association. This story, translated into English by the author himself, has a well-evoked rural atmosphere and a clever plot, but above all an idiosyncratic charm which made me keen to include it in this book. Gillberg's name will be unknown to most readers; I hope we hear more of him before too long.

"The perfect crime," said my uncle, "is the crime that is never detected, when nobody knows a crime has been committed. Consequently nobody can say if it happens often. But they do happen, I know, on the operating table. Sometimes from carelessness, sometimes it's called euthanasia. You know, a few times it may be plain murder from the usual motives: greed, hate, love or fear. But nobody ever finds out.

"Then there is, shall I say, the semiperfect crime. The crime is detected, but the culprit isn't apprehended. But in that case the culprit will live in constant fear, fear of being detected. Well, perhaps he lives in fear when he has committed the perfect crime, too.

"When I come to think of it, the perfect crime is, of course, the crime that is detected, the culprit apprehended – and acquitted. Then he has nothing to fear. That has happened, you know. In fiction, of course, but also in real life. For instance . . ."

He settled back in his easy chair and lit a long, fat and green cigar and blew smoke towards the ceiling.

"For instance, there was Arvid Högman."

And he blew more smoke.

Arvid Högman bought the little island called Heron Isle just off the mainland. The island was big enough to feed a cow and a few sheep. It held a small house and some sheds. He moved in there with his wife and a two year old son, three sheep, two pigs and a red-and-white cow which mooed mournfully as he rowed across the waters between the small fishing village on the mainland and the island. For six hours he rowed there and back before he had transferred the last of his things.

Next day he entered the general store in the village to introduce himself. He was a big, broad-shouldered man with rust-red hair and sunburned hands. A plug-chewing old-timer perched on a herring keg in the store remembered having seen him one evening a few weeks before. That was when he bought the island. He didn't tell them why he had come here or where he came from. In fact, he didn't tell them anything at all and he didn't make a favourable impression. The old-timer spat after him when he left and the storekeeper shook his head. They regarded strangers with suspicion. Tongues wagged among their women for a few days and then a busybody found out, somehow, that Arvid Högman had killed a man up North. In self-defence. They discussed this too, of course, but finally he was accepted – accepted as being there but not admitted into their inner circles.

A fortnight after his arrival, he and his wife sculled over to the mainland and he walked the two kilometres to the nearest railway-station and bought a one-way-ticket to one of the coastal towns.

His wife entered the store to buy some victuals and this was the first time they got more than a glimpse of her. She was tall and lean; her hair was turning grey and her hands seemed grey, too, with blue veins. There were bruises on her arms and

The Perfect Imperfect

when she opened her mouth to order in a whispering, scared but shrill voice they saw that a front tooth was missing. She seemed self-conscious and afraid and she kept looking over her shoulder as if she wanted to shake something off. She left the store with a short, hesitant nod and at the door she stopped as if she had something to say – and then she opened the door and rowed back.

Next day at noon Arvid Högman returned in a new motor launch, a fact which naturally set them speculating on where he got his money and what he wanted the boat for. And when they heard him late one night setting out to sea they speculated still more. But in their heart of hearts they knew. Twice a month they heard his launch starting late at night and coming back in the morning. Rumours reached the little customs station on Seagull Island and one night the customs boat surprised him and his launch was searched. Nothing was found.

In late October the first autumn storm broke. It lasted three days. Big white-crested waves crashed against the little island. The wind howled and screeched, the days were as grey as a bad conscience and the nights as black as the devil's riding boots, as someone put it. It was Sunday when the sun broke through the ragged clouds and the green waves grew tired. Arvid Högman rowed over to the mainland with his dead wife. She had drowned, there was no doubt about that, though there were bruises and wounds on her body, most of them caused after death.

But people talked.

She was buried two days later.

Arvid Högman ran an advertisement in the bigger papers and every day he came over to the store, which was also the post office, for replies. He received a few but before he had time to decide he had a reply in person.

She was big-hipped and heavy-bosomed and had a small moustache. She spoke explosively, as if she had little time to waste. Would somebody please take her over to the island.

She was rowed over and Arvid Högman accepted her. She seldom came over to the mainland and when little more than a year had gone by they noticed she was growing big. Two years after she had arrived they became aware that they hadn't seen her for a long time. Tongues wagged again. They remembered Arvid Högman's past, the manslaughter, his wife's sudden death and the bruises on her arms and the missing front tooth. They sent a small delegation to the vicarage.

The vicar listened to them and the following day he went over to the island. Even if he didn't believe what they believed it might be a good thing to visit Arvid Högman, who seemed to lead an ungodly life and had never been to the small white church behind the grey and black rocks. The vicar disregarded the NO TRESPASSERS sign that Arvid Högman had put up and moored his dory beside the big motor launch.

Arvid Högman met him outside the house. His four year old son hung back in the doorway, grimy and pale.

"What do you want?"

"Good morning," said the vicar.

"Can't you read?" asked Arvid Högman; his red-haired hands were clenched.

"Oh yes," said the vicar, "but as you haven't come to my church I felt obliged to come to you."

The tension in Arvid Högman's face disappeared and he laughed good-humouredly.

"You must pardon me," he said, "but much as I admire your work I have no use for you. Not yet, anyway. And I would be grateful if you left this island now. Good morning."

He turned round and, petting his son's head, went inside. And the vicar returned without having seen anything of the so-called housekeeper or having had the opportunity of asking Arvid Högman about her.

They waited for the vicar on the other side of the sound. And they talked. When a new housekeeper arrived two weeks later, they were convinced.

History repeated itself. She, too, seldom visited the mainland and she, too, in time grew bigger and they suddenly didn't see her any more across the sound. And Arvid Högman found another housekeeper.

They discussed what they could do about it. They dared not visit the island, not even when he was away on his nocturnal voyages. One of the fishermen had tried landing on the edge

The Perfect Imperfect

of the island but had been warned off by the scowling Arvid
Högman and a double-barrelled shotgun.

One summer night the storekeeper watched through his field-
glasses as Arvid Högman and his housekeeper set out in the
motor launch. The son was evidently asleep in the house. The
storekeeper sat all night by his window, waiting, watching,
nodding and napping. When the dawn turned red, Arvid Högman
came back.

Alone.

They gathered that day in the store and talked and talked. The
long and the short of it was that in September Arvid Högman
was summoned before the assizes at Tolskepp to answer some
questions about the disappearance of one Sara Fager, who had
been his third housekeeper.

Now the situation was this. The names of the two first
housekeepers were unknown and no missing persons could
be identified as having been on Heron Island. Consequently
the official summons related only to the third woman whose
name had become known by some chance (I never heard how,
my uncle said). Neither could Arvid Högman be arrested and
indicted for murder as "they" wished since strictly speaking
nobody knew a murder had been committed.

The small courthouse was crammed and Arvid Högman
stood, big and broad and with a derisive smile, before the
district judge and the jurors. Naturally he understood what they
were after and he knew they had no proof. When asked where
Sara Fager, who had been his housekeeper, was he said he
didn't know. When had he seen her last? He thought for a
moment.

"On July 16th," he said.

The storekeeper burst out: "That was the night you murdered her!"

The judge's gavel banged and Arvid Högman took a step
towards where the storekeeper was seated. Fires of anger
flickered in his eyes.

"Say that again!" he roared.

The gavel banged anew and everybody in the room rose
believing they would see and hear better. The storekeeper

81

looked shamefacedly at the judge but Arvid Högman repeated, "Say that again!"

The storekeeper seemed hypnotized and whispered, "That was the night you murdered her."

Arvid Högman looked over the court and then turned to the storekeeper again.

"I just said I don't know where Sara Fager is and I don't, but if she is where I hope she is, you'll regret those words."

The judge was about to bang his gavel again when the door opened and there was a new sensation.

A woman with a small red-haired baby in her arms stood there.

"Are you in trouble, Arvid?" she said.

She was Sara Fager, of course.

It was wonderfully well staged.

After that there was nothing they could do to Arvid Högman. He had committed the perfect crime, the perfect murders, but if you care to listen a little, I'll tell you (my uncle said) how he made them imperfect.

When I met Arvid Högman, I was the medical officer of the district to which Heron Isle belonged. Among my sordid duties were those of inspecting sewers and privies and outhouses etcetera, so even though Arvid Högman allowed no trespassers, I landed on his island one evening and went up to his house. He met me at the door and I expected a gun but he carried no weapons. Instead he bid me welcome.

"You couldn't have come at a better time, Doc," he said and I noticed a cloud of anxiety on his face. "My son is ill. I fear he is dying."

The boy, who must have been about twelve then, was in bed in a room behind the kitchen. I examined him and did what I could for him and then returned to the kitchen, where Arvid Högman sat at the table staring into a tall glass of liquor. He was half drunk.

"Your son is out of danger now," I said. "He has had pneumonia and the crisis is over."

He looked at me with bloodshot eyes.

The Perfect Imperfect

"Thank you, Doc. Sit down and have a drink."

"No, thanks. I have to look at your outhouses before it gets dark."

"Sit down and have a drink."

It was an order and as he was intoxicated and I was young and green and people said he had committed more murders than one, I sat down.

He fetched another tall tumbler and filled it to the brim with a yellowish liquid.

"Drink!" he ordered and I drank. It burned all the way down and brought tears to my eyes.

"Estonian export. Smuggled personally," he declared with a laugh and then his eyes darkened again.

"You must stay awhile, Doc," he said. "I'm getting old and I am lonesome when the boy is sick. I have had visitors these last nights."

He refilled his glass and took a big gulp and looked at me as if he didn't see me clearly. I also felt the effect of the liquor. Dusk filled the kitchen with gloom.

"Ghosts," he continued drunkenly. "I have murdered, you know."

I suppose I said yes to humour him for his eyes suddenly focused.

"You do?" he said sharply.

"That's what they say," I explained.

He stared into nothingness again.

"And they're right, too," he said in a low voice. "I murdered them. Couldn't have the house full of brats. My wife. I hated her though I've always loved the boy and I'm glad to know that they'll take good care of him at the vicarage, if something happens to me. They're nice people really and he'll make out. I killed her that night, my wife that is, that night in the storm. And the others. They were such a nuisance. Wanted me to marry 'em." He was very drunk now. "Of course they," he made a contemptuous, half-failing gesture towards the mainland, "suspected me but I fooled 'em."

He looked up at me suddenly. For a brief moment his eyes were clear.

"And there's nothing you can do about it," he said and his eyes dimmed again. He rose and staggered and stumbled over the floor to fetch another bottle. He refilled his glass. I stood up. The room whirled and its shadows danced but I managed to get into my boat and over to the village on the other side.

My head was heavy next morning but I went back to the island to look to the boy. Arvid Högman was slumped over the table and when I lifted his head I saw that he was dead. He had died with a wide grin on his face. I signed the death certificate myself. *Trombos cordis. Mors subita.*

My uncle leaned back in his chair and lit another cigar.

"So, you see, Arvid Högman had committed the perfect crime but made it imperfect by telling me."

"But he himself," I said, "pointed out that there was nothing you could do about it, so it was still the perfect crime, disregarding the ghosts, of course. There was only one witness to his confession and even if his son had been well enough to listen Arvid Högman could have said he was only making it up when he was drunk. Or that the witness, you, lied. No, there was nothing you could have done about it."

My uncle looked at me.

"But I did," he said.

We were silent. My uncle waiting for his words to sink in and I remembering what he had said about Arvid Högman grinning widely. Of course, *risus sardonicus!*

"Oh!" I said. "Strychnine?"

"Yes. I committed the perfect murder."

"But just now you made it imperfect," I said. "By telling me."

He smiled at me.

"Yes? But what can *you* do about it?"

84

THIS WAY NOBODY GETS THE BLAME

Lesley Grant-Adamson

Lesley Grant-Adamson is one of crime fiction's restless experimenters. She is constantly trying something new; even more impressive is that, whatever type of story she tackles, she usually succeeds. Recently she wrote a teach yourself guide to writing in the genre; it not only contains helpful tips to aspiring authors but also offers satisfying insights into her own work. Her novels include such hefty books as Curse The Darkness, *but here she shows an equal mastery of the short form. To gauge Grant-Adamson's skill, one need only compare* This Way Nobody Gets The Blame *with the many examples of relatively banal "coffee break fiction" which appear in magazines. Here, every word is made to count and although the story is brief, Grant-Adamson's way with words guarantees the reader disproportionate pleasure.*

"This way," he said, "nobody gets the blame."

Ella gave him a teasing look, which he missed because he was striding along, quite quickly considering how much he had to carry. But he'd sounded so proud she couldn't resist saying: "It was very clever of you to work it all out, Phil."

He took the remark seriously. "You too, Ella. It's just as much your plan as mine."

"Well, whoever it belongs to, let's hope it works."

This time he stopped and looked hard at her. "You haven't spotted a flaw? I mean, if there's anything not quite right now's the time to . . ."

"No, no, it's perfect."

"You're sure?"

"Honestly. It's foolproof."

"And it's as good as done." He began to walk on again, his waterproof jacket rustling.

The path narrowed and Ella trailed behind. Over to the right the sea heaved against a rocky shore. For the rest there was an empty hinterland, with sunlight fading on granite walls enclosing salty fields.

Philip urged her on with an impatient toss of his head, but she thought it added a touch of normality if she were dawdling, so she didn't hurry.

"Come on." He took up a studiedly relaxed stance while waiting for her. He was a terribly unconvincing actor, his irritation undisguised. She'd experienced a lot of it lately. Nobody would have dreamed the whole mess was his fault and not hers.

"*I am the innocent victim,*" she thought, dreamily, as she watched the waves rushing to destruction.

She turned the dreamy look into a smile as she drew nearer to her husband. "I'm trying to look natural, Phil. We shouldn't dash as though we expect every wave to be the last."

"I don't remember rehearsing this dithering when we did our trial runs."

She winced at the unfortunate word, trial, but Philip appeared not to notice and strode on. After a few paces he ushered her past him so that from then on he was following her, or rather he was shepherding her down the path.

They passed the kink where a big stone had broken free and the surface was slippery. Ella skipped swiftly on but she heard her husband's boots slide on the scree. He was fond of those boots, he'd had them for years, but there'd been too many slips for her to believe they gripped well.

This Way Nobody Gets the Blame

Philip hadn't proved sure-footed in other, figurative, ways either. He'd made a mess of his business and a worse one in borrowing to wriggle out of trouble. And then he'd done the very silly thing.

Like everything else about him his mistake, his crime, was unoriginal. It used to be called borrowing from Peter to pay Paul, but now there were bleaker ways of describing it. Misappropriation, fraud, or embezzlement. They came to the same thing: he'd stolen money.

"We're in a fix," he'd admitted to Ella the day he told her about the huge debt, the investor who'd been plundered, and the sham their lives had become.

"You mean we'll have to sell Silver Acre?"

She loved the old house, its cosy position in a hollow overlooking the sea, and the status that being its owner conferred on her. She'd never been comfortable before. Her childhood had been poor, and in the years when Philip was building his business they'd scraped by in a bungalow on a modern estate. At Silver Acre she felt truly at home for the first time in her life.

When he didn't answer her question, she'd asked another one: "Who else knows about this?"

"Nobody."

"Not even Heidi?"

"Not even her."

Heidi was his assistant, an Austrian woman with bright blue eyes and a singsong accent. At one time Ella had suspected she was rather closer to him than that, but Philip had persuaded her not.

"Is there nothing else we can do?"

He gave a bitter laugh. "Not to save the house. We offered it as security and the bank will take it."

"Are we going to be bankrupt?"

He spoke flatly, as though explaining to someone especially dim. "*We're* going to be bankrupt and *I'm* probably going to be in prison."

"But . . ."

"But what? Don't you think I've thought all around this, before I decided I had to tell you?"

87

"Yes, I'm sure you did."

It had always been his way to do things and tell her afterwards. She used to protest at him shutting her out but it made no difference because it was his nature.

For a second she was so angry with him that she didn't care whether he went to prison or not. It would be what he deserved for wrecking her life as well as his own, she thought; but the thought was very brief. "There must be a way," she said.

And she saw from his face that he thought so, too. Before long they were plotting.

The path turned into rugged steps. Ella climbed down easily. On the first visit she'd found it tricky but they'd tramped this route half a dozen times since that evening of plotting. If anyone had cared to look they would have noticed that the couple from Silver Acre liked to go fishing below the cliffs some evenings.

But no one would have guessed that one evening their car was to be abandoned where they usually parked it, near the start of the path. Or that a van had been bought especially for them to flee in and lay hidden in a barn on the edge of their land. Or that in its glove box were false passports. Or that Philip had rounded up what was left of the money, a substantial amount as long as no debts were honoured, and had transferred it abroad.

Where the steps met the rocks Ella paused once again and gazed around. A wave frothed towards her. The lower step was awash, her boots and ankles drenched.

Behind her Philip said: "You see? If you hadn't been hanging about we'd have been over without getting wet."

He splashed past her and hoisted himself up on to the rocks. "Come on," he shouted back. "Give me a hand with this."

Ella leaped across while the water was receding, perched on her usual toe hold and reached the top of the rock. A buffeting wind was coming from the west. Waves were jagged white lines when they were far out, but whisked into fury near the shore. With a terrible sucking, the water snatched what it could from the land.

While Philip battled to position their rods, she stayed where she was. They'd hoped for a lively sea, to give credence to the idea that they'd been swept away and drowned. So far, luck was with them.

She couldn't just stand there, watching him. He seemed to be having trouble with her rod, and he gestured for her to help. For a moment she was rooted. Then she darted forward, keen to get it done.

Ella sprang at him and sent him over the edge. He had no chance, in those slippery boots of his. She didn't hear him cry out, but she saw his astonishment. In the instant before she made contact, he'd been turning towards her, arm outstretched. Her first thought, as he disappeared into the spray, was that she was fortunate to have avoided his clutching hand. If he'd moved more quickly, or if she'd been slower, he would certainly have got a grip on her sleeve and she could have plunged into the sea.

Alone, she followed the escape route along the cliff top. Rain was blowing on the wind and the light was as poor as she'd hoped. Any lighter and she might be recognised, any darker and she'd need a torch. Soon the waves were turbulent ghosts on a black sea. She cut inland.

At last she drew close to the barn. Its door was rattling in the wind. "*Philip ought to have made it secure*", she thought crossly. "*Supposing it had blown open and someone had noticed the van?*"

Inside the barn it was totally dark. She felt the van's bumper against her leg and squeezed round to the driver's door. As she opened it, everything collapsed in a whirl of confusion.

A woman in the passenger seat was gabbling at her in a singsong voice, pawing at her. "Oh, Philip, I thought you'd never come! How did it go? Did she suspect anything? It must have been absolutely terrible for you . . ."

THE PERFECT MURDER CLUB

Reginald Hill

When I first started work on this anthology, I was keen to gather together stories linked by a common theme. But what should it be? The theme had to be relevant to the genre, yet broad enough to liberate writers' imaginations, rather than to stifle them. Then I had the opportunity to look at the manuscript of this story – and the problem was solved. Hulbert's idea of the Perfect Murder Club is appealing and the tale is told with Hill's characteristic verve. Yet Hill, like most writers, admits that he cannot resist tinkering with his work. He experimented with a number of different endings to this story and the version of it which appeared in Ellery Queen's Mystery Magazine *earlier this year differs from the first, which is presented here. But I was keen to retain the flavour of the original and the author readily agreed. Perhaps comparing the two will give some future PhD student researching Reginald Hill's writings something extra to chew on . . .*

I switched on the news.

Starvation in Africa. Earthquake in Asia. War in Central Europe. Bombs in Belfast. And so many murders only the most gutting merited a soundbite.

Life was cheap.

One of the bodies lying by a roadside looked a bit like my bank manager. No way it could be. Nothing to do with him ever came cheap.

But it got me thinking. All these dead people and I didn't know any of them. What a waste!

I found a sheet of paper and started making a list of everyone I wouldn't mind seeing dead. I drew three columns; the first for the name, the second for the offence, the third . . . I wasn't yet sure what the third was for.

It turned out to be a surprisingly long list, even though I limited myself to those I knew personally. Once start admitting people I didn't know, like those neanderthal yobs rampaging round the Arndale, or this horse-faced telly-hag now droning on about the Health Service, and the list could have gone on for ever.

Finished, I read through it slowly, excising one name (gone to live in Provence which surely must be regarded as some sort of sanctuary for the unspeakable) and adding two more.

On the box a weather forecaster was being brightly facetious. I studied her vacuous smile and was tempted. But no. Rules are rules.

So I turned to the problem of the third column. No problem! It was obvious what it was for. Mode of dying.

I had a lot of fun with this, making the death fit the life. Thus *he* whose halitosis had nauseated me these many years should choke on a pickled onion, while *she* whose voice had cut through my sensibility like a buzz saw should swallow her tongue.

But eventually the game palled. It was more interesting than TV but just as empty. What I needed was a strong shot of reality. I took another look at Column 3 and soon saw where I'd gone wrong.

It wasn't for mode of dying, it was for method of killing.

Now fancies fled away. Now there was only one real consideration. How to do it and get away with it.

I had to devise the perfect murder.

An hour later I was still staring at a blank column. Perfection I'd discovered was surprisingly difficult. Or perhaps what was surprising was that I should have been surprised. After all I'd never come close to achieving it not even in the things I used to do every day. Perhaps if I had I might still be doing them. But it was no use brooding over what had gone for ever. What I needed was expert assistance. But there was no Government Re-training Scheme in this field, and it was pointless turning to the Yellow Pages. One obvious condition of the perfect murder is that you don't advertise.

I let my mind go blank in the hope of enticing inspiration and suddenly I found it being invaded by that most ephemeral of messages, a Radio 4 *Thought For Today*. It had been uttered by one of those bouncy bishops who like to be known as Huggable Henry or something equally expectatory. After the usual mega-maunderings, he had cast the following already soggy crumb of philosophy upon the morning waters.

Sometimes what looks like an insurmountable barrier can turn out to be an open door.

On the whole you'd be better off pulling Christmas crackers. But this time, in this one respect, it struck me that Bishop Henry might unawares have come within hugging distance of a truth.

Think about it. If you've committed a perfect murder the last thing you do is go around shouting about it. But what's the point in perfection without appreciation? It must be like running a mile in under three minutes, and no-one knowing about it. Of course, some people would probably be content to hug such knowledge to themselves. But if even a small fraction of the probable total of perfect murderers were as eager to talk about it as I was to listen, then all we had here was the classic marketing problem of how to match supply and demand.

Now this was something I *was* quite good at. I'd already established that *they* couldn't advertise. But there was nothing to stop *me*.

The next morning I went down to my local newspaper office. The young man I spoke to first proved singularly stupid and I found myself wishing I knew him well enough to put him on my list. But finally the advertising manager appeared and after I explained to him that I wanted to place the ad in connection with a TV programme I was researching, all went smoothly. You could persuade people to show their arses in public if they thought it was for the telly. In fact I believe if you're tuned to the right satellite, you can see it happening already.

My advertisement appeared that very same evening. I read it with a certain complacent pride.

HAVE YOU COMMITTED THE PERFECT MURDER?
If so, you've probably felt the frustration of
not being able to tell anyone about it. But relax!
Your troubles are over. A new organisation has
been formed to exchange information on method
and technique. To complete your job satisfaction
and enjoy at last the applause which is your
due, contact
THE PERFECT MURDER CLUB
Confidentiality guaranteed. Ring now.
You won't regret it!

After some debate I'd given my home number. It was pointless running the ad unless people could get in touch. I knew it also opened access to undesirables like the police and the usual pranksters and cranks. But not having committed any crime myself (yet!) I had nothing to fear from the law. And as for the rest, I was pretty sure I could sort out the wheat from the chaff with a few pertinent questions.

The first call came within half an hour of the evening edition hitting the streets.

The caller was male, slightly adenoidal, and, I soon deduced, not very bright.

"Hello," I said.

"Hello." Pause. "Is that the . . . er . . . Perfect Murder Club?"

"Depends," I said. "How can I help you?"

"I dunno." Another pause. "Look I saw your advert . . . what's it all about?"

"It's about what it says it's about."

"Yeah . . . well . . ."

I could almost smell his desire to strut his stuff.

"Are you interested in becoming a member?" I asked very businesslike.

"Yeah . . . well maybe . . . it depends . . ."

"It does indeed," I said. "It depends on whether you are qualified. You're not a time-waster, I hope? Ringing up out of curiosity or for a giggle?"

"No!" he replied indignantly.

"OK. How about a few facts then just to establish you qualify for membership. No names, of course. Nothing to give yourself away. Just an outline."

"Yeah? Well, all right. It was my wife. She fell down a cliff. Everyone thought it was an accident. It wasn't. I pushed her."

"I see. And where was this?"

"Scar . . . on holiday!"

What a twit!

"And that's it, is it?" I said.

"Yeah. Why? What's wrong with it?"

"It's not exactly perfect, is it?"

"What do you mean? She's dead. I'm married to a woman I really love. I got a hundred thou insurance. If that's not perfect, what is?"

"I'm glad things worked out so well for you," I said patiently. "But there was no guarantee she was going to die when you pushed her, was there?"

"It was a hundred foot drop onto rocks!"

"So? There was a Yank fell five thousand feet when his parachute didn't open. Landed on a hypermarket roof in Detroit. Only injury came as he sprained his ankle climbing down the fire escape. No, your wife could easily have survived to give evidence against you. Was it daylight? Good weather?"

"Of course. You don't go walking along that path in the dark when it's raining!"

"Right. Then suppose a birdwatcher had spotted you through his binoculars? Or another walker? Or maybe a farmer? Where would you have been then?"

"But that's the point! Nobody did!"

He was getting very agitated. Time to close.

"No," I said. "The point is this, Mr . . . sorry, I didn't catch your name?"

"Jenkinson . . . oh shit!"

The Perfect Murder Club

"Precisely, Mr Jenkinson," I said. "You are clearly not a perfect murderer, merely an extremely lucky murderer. Word of advice, Mr Jenkinson. Use some of that insurance money to have a mouth bypass or you could end up in real trouble. 'Bye now."

I chuckled as I replaced the receiver. Poor sod. Preening himself on being the undetected Maxwell of murder when all the time he was merely its John Major, in the right place at the right time and probably too wimpish for anyone to suspect he could have given the monstrous woman in his life a fatal shove.

I settled down to wait for more calls.

They came steadily over the next couple of hours. There were two clear cranks, one confessing to the murder of Marilyn Monroe, the other claiming to be Lord Lucan, plus a few pranksters, sadly unimaginative in their tall stories. I was entertained by an indignant lady who told me I was a symbol of the moral corruption of our society and invited me to repent at a charismatic pray-in she was holding in her house later that evening. I excused myself, but compensated a little later by sending along a couple of men who'd mistaken my advert for a coded signal of the next meeting of their sado-masochist group.

And as anticipated I heard from the police. Of course the mastermind who called didn't say he was police but pretended to be a punter. It was like listening to some village thespian stumbling through Hamlet. I let him ramble on, till finally, thinking he'd got me fooled, he said, "Look, I'm sure I've got something that would interest you, but I'd rather not discuss it on the phone."

"Perfectly understandable," I said. "Do drop in any time you like. I'm sure you've traced my address by now."

Pity we don't have video phones. I would have liked to see the expression on his face as I rang off.

Now all this was good fun, but as yet there'd been nothing to help me in my serious research. Then finally just as I was giving up hope, I got a call which sounded like it might be genuinely useful.

It was a woman's voice, youngish, rather nervous, but with

95

an underpin of determination that made me feel this wasn't just a time-waster.

Not that she gave anything away. I liked her caution. The urge to share a triumph is one thing, the kind of stupid gabbiness displayed by the idiot Jenkinson quite another.

For a long time we just waltzed around the subject, but I soon became aware that I wasn't doing all the leading. In the end I felt myself being steered into the first steps to openness.

I said, "So what is it I can do for you, Miss . . . er . . . ?"

Not even acknowledging this clumsy attempt to get her name, she said, "I would like to be able to talk in safety."

"The Samaritans are said to be very discreet," I said trying to regain the initiative. "And sympathetic."

She fell silent for a while, then said softly, "It's not sympathy I want. It's empathy. And appreciation."

Gotcha! I thought.

"I think the Club can guarantee both of those," I said in my strong serious voice. "If you could perhaps just give a flavour of what you would be bringing . . ."

Another silence. Then speaking very carefully she said, "It's to do with a person who had the power to injure me. I was not able to continue under this threat. So I worked out a method for disposing of this person without leaving any clue to link the death to myself."

"A method?" I said, perhaps too eagerly. "Poison? Accident? Can't you give a hint?"

"I think I've said enough," she said, her nervousness returning. "Perhaps too much. The compulsion to talk is strong, but the instinct of self-preservation is stronger."

I was terrified I'd lost her. This was the genuine article, there was no doubt in my mind. This was someone who had the brains to work out what had to be done and the will to do it.

I said, "I understand, believe me. You who have already had to extricate yourself from someone's power will be more reluctant than any of us to risk recreating that situation. This is precisely why the Club has been formed. Nobody will hear your story who has not a similar story to tell in return. When secrets are exchanged, their power is cancelled. Believe me, any confession made here is as safe as any ever heard by priest in the confessional."

I stopped myself from saying more. I could feel her being tempted, but it was her own desire which would bring her to me, not anything further I could say.

She said, "I would need to see you face to face before I could decide whether to trust you."

"No problem," I said. I could still sense her hesitancy. This was no time for making rendezvous with copies of *The Times* and white carnations. To bring her into the open I had to put myself there first.

"My name," I said, "is Hulbert. I live at Bullivant House, Flat 36. I shall be here all evening."

"Alone?" she said, suspicious still.

"I promise. And of course you may check before you as much as open your mouth."

"I will, be assured. If I come."

The phone went dead.

After that it was a case of sitting and waiting and hoping. The phone rang again a couple of times. One was a pushy young fellow who said he hadn't committed a murder but would really like to try. I told him it was like a good golf club, you needed an official handicap before you could join. The other was my ex-wife, one of whose ferrety friends had recognised my number in the ad and passed the information on. She pretended concern for my mental health, but I knew that all she was really worried about was whether I'd hit upon some money-making scheme I wasn't revealing to her solicitor.

I knew better than to offer a simple denial but told her, yes, I was collecting material for a book and all I needed to get lift-off was a little financial backing to help me hire a top PR firm and could she see her way . . .

She'd rung off by now so I turned to my list and promoted her from Number 4 to Number 3, above my ex-mistress. Equal first remained my ex-accountant who'd mishandled my finances and run off with my ex-wife, and my ex-boss who'd made me redundant and shacked up with my ex-mistress.

I was debating further revision when the door bell rang. She'd come! I dropped the list onto the coffee table and hurried to let her in before she could change her mind.

A man stood there, square jawed, red haired and built like a rugby league forward. I'd never seen him before but I recognised his voice as soon as he spoke.

"Evening, Mr Hulbert. You were right. No problem tracing your address."

It was the cop I'd spoken to earlier. With my nervous murderess on the way, this was a nuisance.

Deciding the quickest way to get rid of him was to cut through the crap I said, "Good evening, Inspector."

"Sergeant, actually," he said, producing his warrant card. "Sergeant Peacock. All right if I come in?"

He pushed by me as he spoke. Hamlet he might not be, but when it came to acting the heavy, he was clearly well rehearsed.

He said, "It's about this advert of yours, sir. We found it . . . intriguing."

"But not illegal," I said confidently.

"Not in itself maybe. But it could be a channel to illegality."

"I'm sorry?"

"Taken at its face value, this ad invites people who've committed murder to confide in you. If anyone did confess murder to you and you didn't pass on the information to us, that might be an offence. If after making that confession, this person or any persons privy to the confession went on to commit a similar offence, that too might make your advert an offence. Or if . . ."

"All right," I said impatiently. "I get the picture. All I can do is assure you that I placed the ad on a frivolous impulse, nothing more. It's a joke, a mere squib. Naturally, which I much doubt, if any of those replying should rouse my suspicions in any way, I would of course immediately contact the police."

He wasn't so easily satisfied.

He said, "So you've had replies?"

"A few. Cranks, mostly. Nutters. Nothing to worry you with."

"We worry quite a lot about nutters, sir," he said significantly, his gaze drifting down to the coffee table.

Too late I recalled that my death list lay upon it, difficult but not impossible to read upside down. This put paid to any immediate implementation. Even if my nervous murderess did turn up with the perfect method, I'd be mad to start knocking off people whose names might have registered on Peacock's suspicious mind.

I said, "There we are then, sergeant. Now unless there's anything else, I have a heavy day tomorrow and would really like an early night."

"Of course, sir," he said. "Work, is it?"

"Indirectly," I said. "Looking for it. I'm one of the three million, I'm afraid."

He didn't look surprised. He probably knew already. Once he'd got my name and address from the telephone company, it must have been easy to check everything else from my health record to my credit rating. I could feel all my exes getting safer by the second.

"Good luck, sir," he said. "A job's important. I've seen what not having one can do to the most sensible of people. Leads them into all kinds of stupidities. Like putting silly ads in the paper."

"Yes, I'm sorry. And if anything in the least suspicious turns up . . ."

The doorbell rang.

I suppose in that brief moment my expression must have flickered from faintly-embarrassed-honest-citizen to guilty-thing-surprised and back, for he was on to me like a claims clerk.

"Expecting someone, sir?"

"No . . . well, not exactly . . ."

"Wouldn't be someone who answered your ad, would it, sir?"

I could only shrug helplessly. I mean, I was sorry for my nervous murderess, if that's who it was, but after all I had still committed no crime.

Peacock said, "I think maybe I should deal with this. What's through that door?"

"The kitchen" I said.

"Right. You duck in there and don't come out till I tell you," he said.

What could I do but obey? I went through, leaving the door just a fraction open behind me so I could hear what was going on.

I heard his footsteps cross the tiny hall, then the front door open.

"Yes?"

"Mr Hulbert?"

I recognised the voice instantly as belonging to my nervous murderess.

"Yes."

"We spoke on the phone earlier."

"Oh yes."

He really was a terrible actor. He couldn't hope to get by on monosyllables for ever!

"You are the Mr Hulbert who spoke to me on the phone?" insisted the woman. "About the Club?"

"Yes I am," declared Peacock, at last getting some conviction into his voice. "And what might your name be?"

I strained my ears for her reply, but all I heard was a noise like a kitchen knife cutting through an iceberg lettuce followed by a sort of bubbly sigh and a gentle thud.

Then silence. Broken by a man's voice – not Peacock's – saying thickly, "Oh my God."

"Shut that door," said the woman. "You want everyone looking in?"

"No. Let's get out of here! What are you doing?" The voice was spiralling into panic.

"Just checking in case he made any notes."

The woman's voice was unexpectedly close. She must have moved silently into the living room. Fortunately when startled, I tend to freeze rather than jump. I held my breath as I listened to her rustling through the pad on the telephone table and searching through its single drawer.

"Nothing," she said.

"Sylvie, please hurry," pleaded the man in vaguely familiar tones. "God knows who else he's got coming round here!"

"You reckon the world's full of idiots like you who want to shoot their mouths off to strangers?"

Her tone was tinged with affectionate exasperation rather than real scorn and her words triggered the memory which the man's voice had primed. This was Jenkinson who'd pushed his wife off a cliff at Scarborough. Sylvie must be the lover he'd referred to. And perhaps his accomplice? No. That wasn't likely. In the first place from what he'd said, the murder sounded more like a sudden impulse than a thought-out plan, and in the second place, if he'd confided in Sylvie even after the event, he wouldn't have felt the urge to ring the Perfect Murder Club.

Her next words confirmed this.

"If only you'd told me what happened, there'd have been no need for this."

"It didn't seem right to tell you somehow," said Jenkinson unhappily.

I could see his point. When proposing marriage it can't strengthen your case to reveal that you pushed your last wife off a cliff. But once it dawned on him that he'd been stupid enough to give a complete stranger the means to identify him, he'd gone running to her.

How marvellous to have a woman whose reaction to such a revelation was neither outrage nor recrimination, but direct action to clear up the mess. I felt quite envious. Dim wimp he might be, but Jenkinson must have something I didn't to inspire such loyalty, even if it was only a hundred thousand quids' worth of insurance money!

"Right," said Sylvie. "Nothing here. You haven't touched anything? OK. Let's go."

I stood with my ear pinned to the kitchen door till I was sure they had left. Then I waited another five minutes to be absolutely certain.

My relief at not being discovered had been so great that it didn't leave much of my mind to speculate on the possible connection between Sergeant Peacock and the noise of a kitchen knife slicing through a lettuce, so when at last I peeped through the door into the hallway, I could still pretend I wasn't sure what I was going to find.

I saw at once that I'd been right about the kitchen knife but wrong about Peacock not getting away with monosyllables for ever. They'd seen him into eternity, no bother. He looked quite peaceful, slumped against the wall with the knife sticking out of his throat. His eyes were still open and seemed to be staring straight at me. Suddenly I felt a surge of hope that perhaps after all he wasn't dead. I stooped over him, took the knife handle in my fingers and with infinite care drew it out of the wound.

That was how his driver, coming up to tell the Sergeant he was wanted on the car radio, found me.

At my trial he testified he'd seen no-one either entering or leaving the building after Peacock went in. But of course he wouldn't have been able to see the side door I'm sure my careful little murderess used. Naturally I told both the police and my lawyer about the man called Jenkinson who'd pushed his wife off a cliff at Scarborough. They both checked independently and both discovered there was no record of anyone of that name dying of any cause in that area in the past ten years.

Only later did it occur to me that I'd deduced Scarborough from a single syllable. It might have been Scafell in the Lakes, or the Isle of Scarba in the Inner Hebrides, or Mount Scaraben in Caithness, or simply Scar in the Orkneys.

But by then it was all over. I was sure that once Sylvie Jenkinson realised what had happened, she had set about covering their tracks too deep for pursuit. Besides, I found I didn't really want to pursue them. If a perfect murder is one you get away with, they've managed one each. That's a record you've got to respect. If they have kids, we may yet see something really spectacular.

And really spectacular is what it will have to be to make the headlines. I still watch the news every night. Life in here isn't all that different from life outside, not if you've been unemployed for a year or two. And life out there hasn't changed much either.

Starvation in Africa. Floods in Asia. War in Central Europe. Bombs in Belfast.

Now they've gone over to *Today in Parliament* where they are all bawling and yelling and bickering about whether kids today spell better or worse than kids twenty years ago.

Suddenly I see where I went wrong. What do I know about perfect murder? I was playing outside my league. I had set up in competition with the multi-nationals!

No wonder I ended up in here. A man should stick with what he knows.

There's always the prison magazine.

I take a sheet of paper and start constructing another ad.

FITTED UP? WRONGLY CONVICTED?
If so, you must have felt the need for a sympathetic
ear. Now's your chance! To get the credulous
and creative hearing you deserve, contact
THE PERFECT INNOCENCE CLUB
Maximum publicity guaranteed.
Memoirs ghosted. Rights negotiated.
Apply to Cell 24
You won't regret it.

I wonder if the Chaplain's got Dickie Attenborough's telephone number?

AN (ALMOST) PERFECT ALIBI

H.R.F. Keating

*One of the pleasures of putting this book together
has been the opportunity to include a story by Harry
Keating. Of course, the author of that celebrated
novel* The Perfect Murder *simply had to be asked to
contribute to this volume. He has in the past himself
edited CWA anthologies, including the non-fiction
collection* Blood on My Mind *and this year his work
in the genre received due recognition with the award
of the CWA Diamond Dagger. He is the consummate
professional, and when I asked him for a perfect crime
story, he produced one within a matter of days. Like
all his work, it is insistently readable.*

Lord Frampton, Billy Frampton, needed to murder his wife.
Money came into it, and besides he hated the woman. But he
had been altogether unable to work out how he could get away
with it until one warm evening in early Spring, in the notorious
Walletjes quarter of Amsterdam, going into one of the *bruine
kroegen* bars, he met himself coming out.

He had gone over to Amsterdam from Brussels, where his
business interests took him for the inside of most weeks. He was
a director of a number of companies, none of them particularly
thriving, and during his working week he generally managed to
make the short trip across at least once. Having on one occasion

been seen by one of his Brussels acquaintances coming out of a well-known *maison de tolérance*, he had been made the butt of a long continuing joke which eventually had begun to get on his nerves. So he had transferred his recreational visits, as he thought of them, to the Dutch city, to one or another of its many *kammer te huurs.*

Just as he approached this particular rather grotty *bruine kroegen* to get himself a drink and a bite to eat before driving back to Brussels, someone came up to the other side of its glass door. It was the man he took, for one long instant, to be himself. The fellow was exactly his own height and build. His features were altogether of the same cast, a ruddy, drink-enhanced complexion, dark hair beginning to be flecked with grey, sharp blue eyes, a fleshy prominent nose, a just-kept-in-check double chin. He was dressed much as he was, too. For these Amsterdam excursions he habitually put on some fairly indeterminate clothes, plain dark trousers and, in the welcome warmth of this late March evening, no more than a plain-coloured woollen shirt. And his extraordinary lookalike was at first sight wearing just the same outfit. He was even smiling in the same way he himself had been, a mild reminiscent grin reflecting his recent activities in the *kammer te huur.*

When he realised how he had been momentarily deceived into thinking he had seen himself coming towards himself on the other side of the bar door, he had intended simply to step aside and let the lookalike stranger pass. But something in the fellow's way of carrying himself, or perhaps it was only that faint, contented grin, gave him a glimpse, even then, of what use might be made of this extraordinary coincidence.

"I say, old boy," he said as the man pulled back the door and stepped into the soft, neon-garish night, "did you happen to notice how absolutely alike you and I look?"

He spoke in English, somehow confident that anyone who so closely resembled him must be at least able to speak his own language.

The fellow at once gave a roar of laughter.

"I did," he said. "I bloody well did. Gave me a hell of a shock for an instant. Thought I'd really had a bit too much this time."

It was evident that, although he was speaking English fluently, he must in fact be a Dutchman.

"Well, since it turns out you're well within your limit," Billy said, "won't you come back in and join me in something in the gin line."

"Nothing nicer."

They sat on either side of one of the bar's little tables, generous drinks in front of them, contemplated each other with wonder, exchanged forenames – even as early as this Lord Frampton took care to make himself no better known – and began to talk.

Soon it became clear that, though they did indeed have a good deal in common, their paths in life had been very different. Jan was a drop-out. It was now that Billy saw that the trousers he had thought, on the far side of the glass door, to be much like his own dark pair were in fact jeans. Jeans that had not been in the wash for many a week. And his own plain green shirt had been echoed not by its fellow but by a greasy-looking sweat-shirt.

But, as this became clearer to Billy, the notion he had just had a glimpse of at the bar doorway did not diminish. In fact, it grew firmer. And when in the course of chatting it transpired that Jan, like himself, was a confirmed practical joker – his own troubles with his wife had begun when she had flatly refused to fall in with his plan of getting married on All Fools Day – he began to set in motion the plan half-formed in his head.

He ordered two more gins.

"You know," he said, "I think there's something you could do for me. A little joke I'd rather like to play on some friends of mine."

"If it's a joke, that's just my liking."

"Well, let me explain what I have in mind. I told you, didn't I, that I come over to Amsterdam for the delights of the *kammer te huurs*?"

"Which, alas, I am tasting not too often."

"Well, the reason I come here – besides the quality of the ladies – is that my friends in Brussels, ever since I once happened to be seen by one of them coming out of a certain notorious house, have made it their greatest pleasure to keep reminding me of it."

An (Almost) Perfect Alibi

"Must all of them be tremendous – is it? – progs?"

"The very word. Well, prigs, actually. But you clearly know the sort of clever-clever guys they think they are."

"Too many of such I know, my friend. Much too many."

"You're right. And, the trouble is, they've now taken to speculating about what I come here for when I miss out on the little dinners we hold near where we all live. Now, this is what it's occurred to me you might do, seeing that we look so very much alike."

"Wait. I guess it. I will be you. While you are coming here to Amsterdam."

"A man after my own heart."

"Yes, yes. I'll dress up in some clothes of yours and join all your friends in a damn fine dinner."

"Well, I don't think we can quite go that far. But what we could do, I'm sure, is for you to drive past the restaurant – we always eat outside at this time of year – in my car and slow down and hoot, or tap on the window or something. And we'll carefully time that so I can get back from here and show myself to them in the flesh just half an hour or so later. Then they won't be able to believe I've been out of Brussels at all."

"Well, okay. Okay, of course I'll do that. But—"

A note of doubt had entered Jan's voice.

"Now, don't be offended at this," Billy said hastily. "But I will, of course, pay your expenses and add on, if I may, a bit more."

"Oh, yes. I'm not so rolling in the bread that I could do it without that."

If only you knew, Billy thought, if only you knew. You may be able to do no more than look longingly at the ladies in the lighted windows, but, if the truth were told, I'm miles further than you down on the minus side.

"No, no," Jan went on, "but what it is is this. I want to do something better than just show my face like that. Do something really good. Really damn, damn funny."

"Yes, I know, old boy, it does all seem a bit tame. But, believe you me, when I think that I've put one over on those

107

guys I'll really hug myself. And I'll make that plain when we
come to settle up. Promise."

By this time he was well in the grip of the whole plan. Or
rather in what he already thought of as its Stage Two. The night
he would murder his wife.

If the fellow ducks out now, he said to himself, I'll bloody
strangle him.

But Jan did not duck out, and in another half hour they had
arranged every last detail of Stage One. The try-out.

Except that Billy did not reveal his determination not to go
anywhere near Amsterdam on the chosen evening. With as much
at stake as there was – or was going to be in Stage Two – he
intended to keep a very beady eye on this Dutch joker for every
minute of the dummy run.

He did. Standing well back in a doorway opposite the block
where he had his flat, he watched Jan, dressed as instructed in
a long, clothes-concealing raincoat and wearing a jammed-down
hat, enter and pass, apparently unnoticed, the ancient crone of a
concierge still employed at the old-fashioned place.

Then he moved a little further along the street to where he
could look up at his own windows. In due course a light showed
in them.

Right, he thought. He's used the key I lent him and now, if
he's obeying instructions, he ought to be changing into those
rather good leisure clothes I left out for him. Then down he'll
come and stand with his back to that idiot old woman of a
concierge and do as I almost always do. Check myself, himself,
in the long dingy mirror there.

So next time, in Stage Two, there'll be yet another witness to
say I was here in Brussels at the very time some stranger was
murdering my wife in London.

And, yes, lights out in the flat. Now, round to where I told
him the car will be parked. Keys tucked under the driving seat.
Will he be able to cope with the right-hand drive? He said he
would. But I'm not sure I altogether trust him. Rather too ready
to jump at whatever comes along.

Well, we'll see.

An (Almost) Perfect Alibi

He saw. Jan came, easily strolling, up to the car, slid in, started up without any trouble, drove off. A little too fast. But not really dangerously so.

Quick. My waiting cab.

God knows how much all this is costing me. But I suppose you could call it an investment. And one that, if all goes well, should pay off more than handsomely.

Cab to a spot not far from the restaurant. Yes, the boys all grouped outside round the same put-together tables just as usual. Plus two or three other similar groups. So he'll never know who he's supposed to be cheating. Bonus, there.

And here comes Jan. Driving by on the near side of the street, after coming round the long way to get here, as instructed. So far so good. And slowing down. Hope there's no bloody impatient taxi driver behind him. But, no. No trouble there.

Hoot, hoot, hoot.

Don't over-do it, you fool. But at least all the diners outside looked up. Hardly could help it. All that row.

Now, drive on. Drive on. Do as you were bloody well told.

Yes. Yes, he's obeyed orders. I do believe it's on. Really on. This day week, Saturday, if I can line up all the other circumstances, he'll be doing this for real.

And I'll be hopping on to the Eurostar to London. Thank goodness, virtually no passport control in the good old European Community. Get in to Waterloo about quarter to four. Tube to Kensington. No cabbie to identify me. Do the business. Tube back. Train leaves Waterloo just before half-past five. Time enough. Then here in Brussels join the boys at the restaurant round about nine. When, to all intents and purposes, I've been seen by the concierge looking into that long mirror in the hallway at five o'clock or so and at about seven I've been seen when the gang were beginning to arrive at the restaurant as I drove by and hooted.

Train straight away now to Amsterdam. And meet Jan after he's driven there – my old motor won't beat the train, however hard Jan puts his foot down – at the *bruine kroegen* with the glass door. Where else?

And so he'll never suspect that I haven't been all this time enjoying the pleasures of a *kammer te huur*. And it won't ever occur to him that all this business means much more to me than playing some ridiculous, feeble joke on my friends.

Then for Stage Two.

But the next week, when Stage Two was under way, it did not seem quite so easy. Not that anything had appeared to be going wrong. Jan on the phone had accepted without fuss his doleful-sounding statement that it had turned out his group, for once, had failed to gather outside their favourite restaurant. He had, too, been every bit as enthusiastic as before about playing the whole joke over again in exactly the same way the following week. Especially when money had once more been mentioned.

No difficulty either in telling Fiona she could have her 'serious talk' about divorce this Saturday – April the first, wedding anniversary that never was, that's ironic if you like – at about four o'clock. So she'd be safely there, waiting.

Nothing at all to go wrong.

Except, he found as he made his way to the Midi station, a certain unexpected squeamishness. But, damn it, he said to himself, I hate the woman. And then there's the money aspect.

And, though the trip went exactly as he had imagined it at that moment when he had watched Jan drive, hooting, in front of the restaurant, he still felt as if something must be going astray.

But how could it be? The dummy run had gone absolutely as he had hoped and Jan had agreed, eagerly, to repeat it. There had been no difficulty in getting on to the Eurostar. And, now, in London no strike on the Tube. No bomb scare at Kensington High Street station. Everything just as he had planned it.

Then, when it came to it, the actual business had gone beautifully. Just like dealing with unwanted puppies as a teenager in the stables at home. Don't think about it while it's actually happening and there's nothing to it.

Return journey all okay. Back in plenty of time to drop in on the boys in the restaurant before they split up. There'll be no snide remarks now about the joys of Amsterdam's *kammer te huurs*. And then there's the comforting feeling in the back of my mind that the money troubles are all over. And the wife troubles.

Plenty of taxis at the Midi station. Get myself dropped just round the corner from the restaurant.

And – me voilà – here I am. The boys all there.

And me.

But not me. Same colour of hair. Same build. Same clothes. My clothes. My best leisure outfit.

But not me. But Jan. My lookalike.

And the grin on his face.

Jumping to his feet. Pointing at me. The others getting to their feet. Laughter. Glasses raised.

"Bienvenu le poisson d'avril."

And Jan. Bloody, bloody Jan.

"Welcome home, Mr April Fool."

SCOTS BLUID

A Philosophical Investigation after L.W.

Peter Lewis

Peter Lewis is best known amongst crime buffs as the author of critical works about Eric Ambler and John le Carré and as the husband of Ngaio Marsh's authorised biographer, but his occasional forays into fiction writing are conspicuous for their flair and originality. There are a few in-jokes in Scots Bluid, *but I have little doubt that all readers will relish the humour of the story as well as its ingenuity of construction.*

Stuart knew who had sent the letter as soon as he saw the distinctive envelope among the pile awaiting him on the doormat. He also thought he knew what was in it, but as we shall soon see he was completely wrong about this. Envelopes addressed to Stuart were usually of two types. The long pristine white ones signalled business of some sort and demanded immediate attention, which he rarely gave unless they were likely to advance his literary ambitions. Frequently these were addressed to Mr Campbell, causing him to explain irritably, "the name's Aiken Campbell, unhyphenated double-barrelled like Vaughan Williams, but the other end of the alphabet". The others, the recycled and re-recycled ones from friends, acquaintances and

Scots Bluid

impoverished editors of poetry magazines run on budgets with exceptionally short shoestrings, came in all shapes and sizes. Torn and tattered, more often than not, they tended to be held together by Friends of the Earth address labels and assorted bits of sellotape. A surprisingly high percentage were as fragile as the wimpiest damsel in medieval distress and reached their destination only because the Post Office came to their rescue, sealing the contents in waterproof plastic wrapping. Someone more capable of embarrassment than Stuart (a pre-postmodern emotion, he once explained) would have been embarrassed at the amount of trouble his correspondents caused the Post Office.

The large, heavily textured red envelope consequently announced its presence with the authority of a major-domo bellowing out the names of guests about to meet the receiving line at a state banquet. Some months earlier an identical envelope had contained an acknowledgement for the story Stuart submitted to the editors of a new collection of Scottish crime stories, two well-known members of the Scottish Chapter of the Crime Writers' Association. *Scottish Blood*, its provisional title, was being sponsored, modestly, by a flash design firm recently set up by a couple of whizz-kid products of the Glasgow College of Art eager to establish themselves in the Scottish arts world. This explained the sumptuous envelopes, since the sponsorship offered was mainly in the form of secretarial and administrative services.

Stuart had noticed an announcement about this book in one of the circulars he regularly received from the Literature Department of the Scottish Arts Council, his main source of information about the numerous poetry competitions run all over Britain, sometimes by the most unlikely organisations ("nobody wants to read the crapping stuff unless you pay them to judge it," groaned Stuart). These days he was more discriminating about which he entered, but he had always achieved a considerable degree of success, whether writing in English or Scots. When he had a number of prize-winning poems to his credit, a new small press of Lilliputian size in Glasgow brought out an ultra-slim collection of his work ("it hasn't enough volume to call it a volume," he observed). It had a spine you could slice onions with, according to the Waterstone's poetry buyer in Edinburgh who claimed she needed danger money for handling copies.

The comparative success of this flimsy publication on almost transparent paper ("no sense of anticipation because you can see what's coming next," he commented at the launch) encouraged a somewhat larger and better subsidised press in Edinburgh to do a more robust book for him, again slim but not knife-edge sharp. Even the Waterstone's buyer couldn't complain, especially as it sold much better than most poetry by young writers. Stuart, always highly competitive, prided himself on keeping up with the leaders in the Scottish literary stakes for the under-thirties. He had now reached the good-quality bog-paper stage, he observed, marking a real advance on the reject stuff of his earlier collection ("the only disadvantage is that critics can wipe their arses on this one whereas they wouldn't have risked it with my first unless they were sufficiently coprophiliac to enjoy having shit all over their hands").

Since his undergraduate days at St Andrews, Stuart had occasionally written stories, but with a busy though officially part-time job in BBC Radio Scotland as well as regular reviewing to do for *The Scotsman*, he found poetry much easier to fit into the spare corners of his life. He could work on poems in his head while walking or driving or shaving or even watching TV. Prose was different, a laborious effort, requiring sustained concentration over a period of time, as he was finding at the moment. Against his better judgement, he had recently been talked into contributing a short book about the novelist J.G. Farrell to a new series of student monographs being edited by an old friend who lectured at St Andrews.

However, Stuart's discovery that the editors of the new crime collection were urgently seeking contributions by Scottish writers was a challenge that appealed to him. Apparently the Scottish Chapter of the Crime Writers' Association did not want to miss out on the current interest in regional crime anthologies south of the border, such as *Northern Blood* and *Anglian Blood*. Stuart wouldn't have described himself as a crime fan exactly, because he had too many dislikes ("I'm very discriminating, you know" – indeed we do), much preferring the American hardboiled private-eye tradition to any other variety of the genre, while not warming to its abduction by feminists on both sides of the Atlantic. Since many of his readers were women, he was careful not to say so in public.

Near the top of his top drawer, Stuart happened to have the draft of a long, complicated mystery story which he could easily modify to enhance its crime potential. He was sure that this was the best piece of fiction he had written, the only problem being its length. The announcement for the first *Scottish Blood* did not rule out the possibility of including long stories of exceptional merit ("or by the editors and their CWA cronies," Stuart added) but made it clear that preference would be given to brief ones. After rewriting the story as he wanted it, he made several attempts to condense it substantially, but these seemed considerably inferior to the full-length version, which he called "First Time Lucky". With the deadline for submission imminent, Stuart decided to risk the long version but explained in a covering letter that he could provide shorter though, in his opinion, less satisfactory alternatives if they liked "First Time Lucky" but couldn't accept it for reasons of space. He even made a suggestion about the book title. Wouldn't *Scots Bluid* be punchier and more dynamic than *Scottish Blood*? Admittedly this was much better than some possibilities, like the appallingly twee *Tartan Shorts* used for a recent anthology of Scottish stories, but didn't it sound a bit too anglo?

Apart from the acknowledgement he heard nothing, so when the second luxury red envelope eventually arrived, Stuart was convinced that his story had been turned down. He opened the other letters and a package of new books for review, but put the red one aside for the time being. He had received his share of rejection slips from poetry magazines when first submitting work as a precocious teenager, and usually felt desolated, not just disappointed; but by persevering he succeeded in placing a poem here and another there, until he became a fairly familiar name in the small world of Scottish literary magazines. Acceptance, not rejection, became the norm, and one editor in particular even solicited him for new poems. So the prospect of rejection for a story he had laboured over much more than any single poem brought back that experience of dejection familiar from his early attempts to become a published poet.

He decided to complete some urgent work for a Radio Scotland interview he was doing on the afternoon show, and leave the letter until the evening when he could soften the expected blow with a large glass of Macallan ("mega-mega-tot" in his postmodernist jargon). Yet even put out of sight ("get thee behind me, Satan"), the letter continued to torment him, preventing him from concentrating on his immediate task. He regretted the excess of self-confidence which had prompted him to submit only the long version of "First Time Lucky". That had been presumptuous of him and he would now pay the penalty. It was obvious that he would have stood a much better chance if he'd sent one or other of his abbreviated versions, weaker though he thought them. They weren't *that* bad. He could imagine the editors chuckling as they agreed that a would-be contributor pushing his luck with a title like that was certainly not going to be rewarded. And why had he suggested altering the book title? This bit of interference might have really annoyed the editors, especially if one or even both of them had been included in *Tartan Shorts*. He'd meant to check before posting his letter but forgot. But there was no point in kicking himself now. It was far too late for might-have-beens. After wasting an hour in spasmodic self-flagellation, he could resist the lure of the letter no longer and gave into temptation without even a tot of Macallan.

Not only did the editors accept "First Time Lucky", they enthused about it. If this was the first time one of his stories was to achieve publication, they said, there was certainly no luck involved. It was an outstanding debut, subtle, thought-provoking and highly polished. They would take it as it stood even though substantially longer than their suggested word limit, but they didn't mind including a few long stories if the quality was high. And his was ("I don't need them to tell me," thought Stuart). Furthermore they appreciated his proposal to Scotticise the title ("I wanted to 'Scotch' it in every sense," said Stuart) and actually preferred *Scots Bluid* to *Scottish Blood*, but pointed out that the publisher couldn't risk alienating readers in England since there was such a big market for crime among southrons. Only once before, when his first poem was published, had Stuart experienced something like levitation. When he left home to record his studio interview, still not fully prepared, he didn't just go, he lifted off.

It wasn't until shortly before the publication of *Scottish Blood* that Stuart discovered who all his fellow-contributors were. Most were unknown to him, but then he was much more familiar with poets than prose writers, except for such big names as Alasdair Gray, James Kelman and Irvine Welsh. What he noticed immediately was that he would be second in alphabetical order, not first, as he almost always was in poetry magazines. Indeed virtually throughout his entire life, from kindergarten to St Andrews, he was first in every group he belonged to. It wasn't inevitable, of course. In Scotland or Britain as a whole, "Aiken" wasn't the equivalent of "aalii" in the plant world or "aardvark" in the animal kingdom. If he were a novelist he would be trailing behind Peter Ackroyd, and in Finland with all those "aa's" he might be an also-ran. He didn't have to be first, but it had come to seem that way. It was his privilege, almost his right, despite the close shaves. At one school, he was in the same class as Ainslie and Ainsworth, the verbal equivalent of Siamese twins. The only time he was pipped at the post, so to speak, was when he'd joined a mountaineering club in the Cairngorms. One of the members was called Adams. Stuart resented this deeply, and was surprised at the irrational force of his own resentment. There wasn't much he could do about it. Or was there? Fortunately, or unfortunately, depending on your point of view, Adams had a bad fall when climbing with Stuart and didn't return to the club when he'd recovered.

In a recent anthology of new Scottish poets Stuart once again led the way ("quite right too," he told his arch-rival David Aird, "the first *should* come first and the least should come last"). Stuart always took delight in being just ahead of David, who had been with him at St Andrews where the competition between them would not have disgraced a pair of heavily spurred fighting cocks going at each other hammer and tongs. This had been exacerbated by a widely distributed poster for a "new generation" reading they'd done together in Edinburgh, putting Stuart after David as "Aitken", an error he was convinced David had deliberately engineered.

What Stuart found so reässuring about leading contemporary Scottish poetry from the front was that even readers of anthologies and magazines who didn't get far were likely to read him. Did anyone reach tailenders like Sandra Urquhart, Flora Wallace, Perdita Wycherley and ffyona Young (he called her "f. fyona Young" and quipped "if you want to know what the first 'f' stands for, use your imagination")? Actually, with female domination at the end of the alphabet, some readers probably did begin there. For once, the last might indeed be first. Women, even heteros, had all the literary advantages these days. There were anthologies of Scottish Women Poets, New Scottish Women Poets, and Scottish Lesbian and Gay Poets, which did of course include some men but not WASSMS (White Alive Straight Scottish Men) like himself. If the WASSMS of the world failed to unite, they would soon be driven to extinction.

The writer who had squeezed ahead of Stuart in *Scottish Blood* by the merest whisker was Graham Agnew. He couldn't have been much closer ("without gross indecency involving penetration," quipped Stuart). Graham Agnew wasn't even a name to Stuart, who had to wait for his one free copy of the book ("a splendid example of Scottish generosity and an example to others," he told the publishers) before learning more from the Notes on Contributors. He took one of his reviewing days off to read *Scottish Blood* from cover to cover as soon as it arrived, and there was no doubt in his mind that "First Time Lucky" was the outstanding contribution, although to his literary pals he claimed only that it was one of the best three or four. Most reviewers of the book, none of them his friends, agreed with his verdict, as he knew they would. But reviewers, he insisted, were very different from readers. Would readers recognise his superiority? Or were they too conditioned by trash to see brilliance even when it hit them in the eyes, let alone between?

Graham Agnew's paltry effort about James Boswell, on the other hand, was one of the weakest and most derivative in *Scottish Blood*, as was the pseudo-Peters medieval story following "First Time Lucky", which was therefore sandwiched between two stale slices of historical crime. Except for Umberto Eco's *The Name of the Rose*, Stuart generally disliked this mode. Historical fiction by someone like J.G. Farrell was one thing, even though it was taking up more of Stuart's time than he had time for, but most mysteries set in the past, including the ones surrounding "First Time Lucky", struck him as tweely unhistorical.

Some writers would have considered that the inferiority of the adjacent competition only served to make their own work shine ever more bright, but not Stuart. He felt his story was diminished, even contaminated, by the company it kept, whereas he didn't mind being cheek-by-jowl with David Aird in poetry publications since he recognised David's prolific talent despite being locked in literary combat. Indeed it was the threat posed to his own comparatively meagre output by David's poetic abundance that caused Stuart to trigger the feud in the first place, unforgettably declaring during a workshop in St Andrews attended by several prominent Scottish writers that David was by far the *wittiest* person around, as long as you spelt the word not with *w* but with *sh*. Had *Scottish Blood* begun with "First Time Lucky", Stuart wouldn't have minded so much what followed. His story would have been in the clear. It was the sandwiching that did the damage.

There were several launch events for *Scottish Blood* in large bookshops throughout Scotland, allowing all the contributors to be involved somewhere. To meet as many as possible ("you can never tell who might come in useful"), Stuart made a point of turning up at Edinburgh, Glasgow, Perth and Dundee. It was at the last of these that he finally met the writer he thought of as the usurper of his rightful place ("he stole pole position from me"), Graham Agnew, a schoolteacher in Fife and a keen angler, according to the *Notes*. As the son of a dedicated angler, Stuart knew plenty about the sport although he detested it ("the silent in pursuit of the silent", "the unspeaking in pursuit of the eatable"). In revenge for the many childhood hours of dreary

119

nothingness in the company of his father and his fishing friends, Stuart normally took every opportunity to "take the piss out of the piscatorial" ("show me a compleat angler and I'll show you a complete cretin"), but with Graham he controlled himself. When they were introduced, it was Stuart who raised the topic of fishing, after which there was no stopping Graham, who thought he had found another enthusiast. By the end of the evening, Graham was proposing a fishing trip together despite Stuart's insistence that, however much he regretted it, he no longer had sufficient time.

"All the more reason to make time," replied Graham, "since you must be in real need of peace and relaxation."

Partly owing to good reviews in London as well as Scottish newspapers, *Scottish Blood* was a moderate success. The publishers' caution over the print-run on the grounds that short stories, even crime, were much harder to market in Britain than novels, proved unfounded. But the crucial factor was the unexpectedly large American demand, seemingly a direct response to the relatively high proportion of historical narratives, mainly by women ("typical," moaned Stuart, "but it's not an ill wind if punters also read the really good ones – if there is more than one"). Historical crime, whatever Stuart thought of it, was very much in vogue, providing a much needed antidote to the glut of supposedly authentic police dramas on TV and nihilistic gangster movies. Without trying to, *Scottish Blood* turned out to be a winner. It contained an amateur woman detective in Victorian Aberdeen ("elementary Shirley MacHolmes," suggested Stuart), a lesbian Jekyll and Hyde responsible for mayhem in Glasgow at the height of Charles Rennie Mackintosh's career ("Roberta Louisa Stevenson, I presume"), the Burke and Hare story told from Burke's point of view, an erotic mystery involving James Boswell and some independent-minded and physically versatile Edinburgh whores, part of Mary, Queen of Scots' life cast as a spy thriller, and an investigation carried out by a medieval nun in the Lowlands ("Sister MacCadfael, God help us!").

To feed the American market, there had to be an immediate reprint, with a large-print edition to follow for the UK. Without waiting for the iron to cool, the publishers asked the editors to

Scots Bluid

proceed with *Scottish Blood* 2, and another large, red envelope
dropped on Stuart's doormat. He, like other contributors, was
being given first bite of the second cherry. If interested, would
he send a suitable story, soonest. Half-expecting this request
since the editors' strong hint about a sequel, even an annual
series, at the Glasgow launch, Stuart had already given it some
thought.

To his own amazement the outline of a complex mystery
during the 1745 Jacobite Rebellion had occurred to him when
reviewing some new books about Bonnie Prince Charlie (Stuart's
insistence on referring to him as King Charles III provoked many
complaints), but even Stuart felt it wouldn't be easy to live that
down after what he'd recently said about historical crime to his
friends. Not without adopting a female pen-name ("Charlatan
Brontë?"), but that wouldn't do for *Scottish Blood*. Instead he
rapidly transformed the imaginings of a disgruntled academic
friend into the hard reality of fiction as "Second Attempt", taking
as his epigraph a recent, controversial statement by the historian
and poet Perdita Wycherley ("part part-time poet," according to
Stuart): "There's nothing wrong with killing people, as long as
you kill the right people, and 99.99% of the time that means
men." She went on to point out that exactly the same percentage
of the human race responsible for the Bible, the epic literature and
the entire philosophical tradition of the West, not to mention all
the wars, atrocities and genocide throughout history, were men.
Wasn't that a coincidence? Or was it?

If you wish to proceed immediately to Stuart's own summary of
"Second Attempt", feel free to jump over this paragraph and the
next, returning after his résumé if you feel the need for illumination.
Not that you're likely to get much. But Stuart himself has insisted
on the need to explain the intellectual position of his generation,
especially for older readers ("give those thirty-something codgers
and geriatrics something to rouse them from their senility," he told
me). So here goes. You may find this too philosophical, but in that
case it is difficult to understand why you're reading a philosophical
investigation in the first place. Unless Stuart's right and you're too
senile to know what you're reading.

121

Stuart belongs to the first generation for whom the absurdity and meaninglessness of life is a *donné*, a starting point, not a painful discovery involving prolonged torments of existential angst. Preceding generations in the twentieth century and even the later nineteenth endured a disorienting sense of spiritual deprivation and the loss of all moral bearings, as first God disappeared, to be followed by the foundations on which every certainty rested. Hence the history of pre-postmodern art, literature and music. One widespread though illogical response to this condition of confusion, fragmentation and uncertainty was to complain bitterly about His absence as though it were a personal affront. Now all this is behind us. We have come of age. We have even freed ourselves from the delusions of freedom. We know that all ethical imperatives and pronouncements, even something like "The Holocaust was evil and wrong," are nothing more than linguistic gesturing and rhetorical assertions. We inhabit a world in which all our legal, moral, political and religious beliefs, values and institutions can be seen to depend on traditions which have "melted into air, into thin air," to quote Prospero, who knew how insubstantial all our pageants are. Not only are the Emperor's new clothes non-existent; no longer is there anyone who would hesitate for a nanosecond to point this out. Clear? I hope this approximates to what Stuart wanted me to say. Now on with the show.

"SECOND ATTEMPT" BY STUART AIKEN CAMPBELL: AUTHOR'S SYNOPSIS

The title of my own *second attempt* at crime fiction refers, as we shall soon see, to the action perpetrated by my main character in pursuing a grievance, but also to the alternative endings I have provided. One attempt at closure was not enough. In what I consider *my* ending – the first – disappointment leads to a blissfully ecstatic revenge ("vengeance is mine, I will repay without any help from the Lord, saith the avenger," p.9 of my print-out of the story for *Scottish Blood* 2). To the armies of the benighted still clinging to the long-discredited relics of Western morality, the revenge will appear totally disproportionate, but not to the avenger, Morag Sinclair MacLeod (unhyphenated double-barrelled). A post-Christian post-feminist, Morag is a temporary lecturer in the Philosophy of Religion at Glasgow, just completing her PhD. In response to a circular announcing that two senior Edinburgh professors are soliciting material urgently for a new collection of essays in her field, she submits a proposal, despite the warning that there is likely to be fierce competition for space because a number of academic superstars from around the world have been invited to contribute.

With her proposal given strong encouragement by the editors, whose letters always arrive in large red envelopes, Morag comes under considerable pressure from her Department to write a substantial essay for the proposed book. She has other priorities, but the prospect of being within the same covers as the superstars leads her to concentrate on the essay. She postpones her holiday plans, causing a serious rift with her loyal, long-distance lover in Caithness, and overworks herself to the edge of breakdown. However, the editors' immediate response to her submitted essay is so favourable that Morag feels just about justified. She goes to Wick in an attempt to patch up her life.

The next news is that the book has been put on hold in the hope that the superstars may still agree to produce something for it, but there is no suggestion that Morag will not be included. Her love affair enters a hostile phase of mutual recrimination. The final news is that the superstars have sadly declined the editors' invitations because of their heavy commitments, and that without them the publishers have asked the editors to produce a much shorter book than originally planned. Among the casualties is Morag, whose love life goes from worse to even worse. The list of those included in the book comes as no surprise to her: mostly men in senior positions like the editors themselves – pillars of the academafia. The editors try to soften the blow by lavishly praising her work, but this is no consolation.

Her instinct is to let rip, firing verbal warheads by the dozen via the Internet and e-mail, but she wills herself to stay calm – after visiting her university library and shredding with her bare hands every book and publication she can find by the two editors ("Hell hath no fury like a husband horned with one exception –

a writer wrongly rejected," p.14 of print-out for *Scottish Blood* 2). Morag feels much better for the exercise.

Her first attempt to right the wrong done to her takes the form of a long letter to the editors asking them to change their minds. Having aroused her expectations, led her to expend a great deal of energy, and brought her to a state of excitement, they should not deny her the ultimate satisfaction of publication. Why not ask all the original contributors to condense their material so that everyone can be accommodated? Put succinctly their reply is "fuck off", but it is couched in orotund sentences of syntactic tortuousness befitting men who receive professorial salaries for their linguistic legerdemain.

Her second attempt is different. Demurely appealing for their help and advice about her future, she politely requests a meeting with them one evening when she is in Edinburgh. How about dinner in a good but cheap place she can recommend in Leith, near where she often stays with a friend? She knows they can't refuse and they agree to collect her, enabling her to put her thoroughly researched plan into effect. With some time before the restaurant booking she has made, she suggests a tour of the nearby industrial dock complex. With her love of everything to do with ships and the sea, she finds this vast area fascinating but, as she suspects, they have never visited it. Sitting in the front to act as navigator, she directs the driver to a remote and usually deserted corner well off the official public route. Releasing her seat belt as they approach the dockside, she suddenly lurches into the driver, wrenching the steering wheel, forcing his right foot down on the accelerator and preventing his left foot from reaching the brake. The car speeds up, swerves and, as Morag opens her door, pitches into the dock. Everything happens so quickly that the two men are paralysed by surprise, then panic, as water rushes into the car, trapping them.

In the first ending, *my* ending, Morag escapes from the car just as it hits the water. This makes it much easier than she expected since she was fully prepared to extricate herself from inside the car at the bottom of the dock if necessary. As a strong swimmer and experienced scuba-diver, she has the lung capacity of a pearl fisher and is known in her diving club as "the mermaid". Water holds no terrors for her. She also knows to wait for the equalisation of pressure before attempting to open a door under water, but she doesn't have to use her knowledge. While the two men drown, Morag reaches safety, feeling both relief and satisfaction that it has been so easy. Almost too easy, she fears. As the only eye-witnesses of the incident are too far away to see what was really happening, the only testimony of significance is Morag's. No-one questions for a moment the story she tells of getting lost in the docklands and skidding on an oily surface because of the rain. At the inquest she blames herself for suggesting the pre-prandial drive, but everyone assures her that it was a tragic accident and that she has no reason to feel guilt. Indeed she achieves her fifteen-minutes of fame when the media dub her "the miracle survivor" and celebrate the coolness and quick-thinking, together with her fitness and athleticism, that saved her life. Morag sends wreaths to the funerals of both men but decides not to attend, explaining that she is still emotionally traumatised by the accident. Meanwhile she becomes fully reconciled with her lover and they celebrate in the time-honoured, multi-orgasmic way.

In contrast to this realistic, happy-ever-after outcome, the second ending – my spoof one – is dictated by the conventions of crime fiction and by the demands of those many older devotees of the genre who still believe, however irrationally, that assertions about "morals" and "justice" still mean something, when it is self-evident to all except the mentally deranged and deluded that they don't. As the car hits the water Morag is still inside the car but is confident that she can escape underwater, especially as the car is almost certain to come to rest on its wheels, according to the statistics about such accidents. But this is where the malevolent fates intervene. Very much against the odds the car turns over on impact, and then even more unpredictably rolls onto its side, the passenger side, making Morag's door unopenable. She had allowed for the remote possibility of ending upside-down and saw no problem in coping with this, but tipping over sideways seemed as unlikely as winning the National Lottery. Once the car is full of water, she is able to manoeuvre herself into the back, but the body of the man still strapped in blocks her access

Peter Lewis

to the openable door or window. He runs out of oxygen long
before her, but by the time she moves him out of the way, even
her lungs are empty. When the car is raised, it contains three
bodies. How's that for being hoisted on your own petard?

By the time Stuart sent "Second Attempt" to the editors of
Scottish Blood 2, repeating his earlier regret that it wasn't *Scots
Bluid*, the sad death-by-water incident shortly to be narrated had
occurred. The slight delay in bringing you this dramatic episode
was recommended for two reasons by the publishers responsible
for the publication you are currently reading. They required me
to move material around, something not demanded of Stuart
himself, it should be noted. The first reason was that you might
prefer to hear the response by the editors of *Scottish Blood 2* to
"Second Attempt" when the synopsis is still fresh in your mind
rather than after your immersion in the forthcoming account of
death by water on the next page or two. The second reason was
that delaying the disclosure of information in order to create
suspense and tension is a sine qua non of mystery and crime
writing, and should be employed at every opportunity. If unable
to stand the suspense, please skip the next paragraph, returning
to it – if you think it's worth it – at the place indicated.
   Accepting "Second Attempt" without changing a single comma,
the editors congratulated Stuart on the stylistic and formal originality
of his fine achievement ("stylistic, I hope," said Stuart, "but
formal! I ask you. *Genesis* begins with alternative accounts of
Creation, so what's new about alternative endings? Where have
these dinosaurs been living since God didn't create the universe
twice?"). At the same time they expressed uncertainty as to how
Morag's behaviour should be interpreted, while acknowledging
that this was presumably Stuart's intention since, they gathered,
the uncertainty principle was as much a sine qua non of
contemporary writing as building up suspense was of mysteries
and thrillers. Initially they felt that Stuart was presenting Morag
sympathetically as a justified non-sinner since she belonged to a
generation for whom the concepts of sin and evil had ceased to
have even metaphorical meaning. But mightn't radical feminists
look for disguised misogyny in such a story by a man? Could

126

Scots Bluid

Stuart be accused of a devious ironic ploy to subvert Morag, defining the female principle as essentially destructive? "Who can tell?" replied Stuart. "Anything's possible. Untruth like ugliness is in the eye of the beholder."

if you didn't skip the above paragraph, sincere apologies for the delay, but you know how tyrannical the rules of this genre are. While still putting the finishing touches to "Second Attempt", Stuart had to visit his alma mater, St Andrews, to give a poetry reading. As usual he topped the bill. The only time he hadn't since the substitution of "Aitken" for "Aiken", allegedly by David Aird, was when he read with the British-Guyanan writer Fred D'Aguiar, but this didn't count as it was a mistake. Fred should have been down among the D's but had been erroneously elevated to the A's, ahead of Stuart. Recently Stuart had shared several gigs with David Aird, the organisers hoping that the flyting match the pair often indulged in would attract good crowds looking for the literary equivalent of all-in wrestling. On these occasions both poets put on a most entertaining performance, laying on the abuse as thick and fast as any medieval flyter. "Who needs friends when you have an enemy like me?" Stuart once asked David, who replied, "Having someone you love to hate can be much more satisfying than having someone you love."

On this occasion, however, Stuart was teamed up with two women who, from past experience, were likely to find disguised misogyny in everything he wrote, Perdita Wycherley and ffyona Young. Perdita greeted him with her most ladylike smile, saying, "So what's a non-buggering wanking WASSM like you doing in a place like this?" as though St Andrews was the gay and lesbian capital of Northern Europe. It was a bit of a coincidence, he thought, to be sharing the platform with Perdita when he was writing a story owing something to her celebrated quip about the desirability of killing men. But was it? Perhaps the prospect of reading with her had given her some power over his imagination. It was sometimes said that she wasn't an expert on the witch mania of the seventeenth century for nothing.

The audience included Graham Agnew who lived in nearby Cupar. He had invited Stuart to stay with him overnight and even to make a weekend of it, fishing. Stuart declined the offer

of accommodation because when in St Andrews he couldn't not
stay with some old university friends living in Crail, but agreed
to meet Graham on the Saturday. A-fishing they would go, but
not for long because Stuart had to return home later that day.
Work called. The arrangement was that Graham would collect
Stuart from Crail and then, since time was short, drive the
very short distance to Fife Ness. Stuart suggested a remote and
usually deserted piece of coast he knew well from his student
days, though to angle for girls not fish.

Graham was astonished that Stuart had already drafted his
story for *Scottish Blood* 2.

"Blame radio," said Stuart. "Doing programmes to rigid
schedules doesn't half speed you up. Anyway 'Second Attempt'
is a good bit shorter than 'First Time Lucky'. Even so, I did
burn the candle at both ends for a couple of weeks."

"I haven't begun writing my story yet," explained Graham,
"but I've got an idea I'd like to try out on you. See what you
think. It helps me to talk about what I'm working on."

So he did, enthusiastically, while they prepared to fish. To Stuart,
it seemed even worse than the earlier story – a similar historical
lemon, involving what sounded like the same independent-minded
and physically versatile Edinburgh whores whose excesses had
whittled away Boswell's manhood, but this time it was Robert
Burns's turn. Stuart didn't mind Boswell being given a fictional
going-over, since the man was so adept at fictionalising himself,
but Burns was another matter. The editors couldn't possibly
accept this *dreck*, could they? Somebody needed to stop Graham
in his tracks, and this time the editors would, surely. But how
could one be sure? Perhaps they would include it, not because
they wanted to but to avoid alienating other contributors to the
first *Scottish Blood*. Group solidarity. The team spirit.

Dropping Graham *might* well cause offence, but including
Graham *would* certainly cause offence to Stuart. The prospect
of rubbing literary shoulders with Graham for a second time was
intolerable, especially as he would almost certainly have to follow
in Graham's wake again. The chance of a new Scottish crime
writer with a name between Agnew and Aiken suddenly arriving
on the scene to cushion Stuart from Graham was less likely than

winning the National Lottery. There was decidedly more chance of someone intervening between him and that Boyd woman who wrote the "Sister MacCadfael" tosh. Stuart listened to Graham without saying much apart from the occasional "yes" and "h'm, h'm", but eventually he had to make a response. He pointed out resemblances to the Boswell story and queried a number of points of detail but otherwise remained non-committal: "Better to see how it develops once you've got it down on paper. Or up on the screen. You know how much these things change once you get going."

The report in *The Scotsman* of the tragic manner in which Graham Agnew died pointed out its striking resemblance to the accident which caused the death of the famous novelist J.G. Farrell in Ireland. Like Farrell, Graham had clearly slipped on wet rocks while fishing, hit his head in falling, and then drowned while unconscious. There were no eye-witnesses and the only testimony was Stuart's. Feeling cold, he had gone for a walk on his own to warm up. He met a couple of locals walking their dogs (they confirmed this) but saw no-one else, and when he returned to the place where they were fishing there was no sign of Graham. Stuart was a bit surprised but assumed that Graham had also gone for a stroll or was having a pee. As time passed Stuart became increasingly alarmed, and began a search along the coastline, frequently calling out for Graham. Only then did he consider the possibility that something had happened to Graham – a heart attack, perhaps, since even young men can have cardiac conditions – and he had fallen into the sea. By the time Stuart was able to contact the emergency services, a couple of hours had elapsed. Wanting a day without any disturbance for once, he had deliberately left his mobile phone behind. It was a tragic coincidence that he didn't have it with him when he needed it most. Graham's body was found fairly quickly, before dark, but there was no possibility of resuscitation.

Stuart attended the funeral and sent a wreath. It was the least he could do. In the circumstances it might seem odd, he thought, if he didn't put in an appearance. Morag hadn't, but there remained a few situations in what was expected of men wasn't expected of women. Funerals still tended to be masculine affairs, and it was considered well beyond the call of duty for her to attend two. She obviously couldn't go to one and not the other. In any case Morag was a fictional character whose actions were determined by the narrative conventions he had adopted, not by the pressures of real life.

If you are one of those readers with sufficient initiative to have skipped the delaying paragraph a couple of pages back, this is a suitable breathing space for you to return to it, if you feel you've missed something. You probably haven't.

After Graham's funeral Stuart made a point of writing to the editors of *Scottish Blood 2*, suggesting that they dedicate the collection to his memory and include a tribute to him in their introduction. They would know the things to say: what a great loss he was to the new wave of Scottish writing, not just crime, and how regrettable it was that his untimely death happened just as he was about to put down on paper the story he had thought up for *Scottish Blood 2* – again opening up the eighteenth century for crime fiction with characteristic daring by inventing a narrative about another great Scot of the period, none other than Robert Burns.

It wasn't until Stuart received proofs of "Second Attempt", with the usual request for them to be returned the day before the day before yesterday at the very, very latest, that he finally learned whose company he would be keeping in *Scottish Blood 2*. He couldn't believe it. Were his eyes deceiving him? When the editors had replied positively to his suggestions about Graham, they had indicated that the line-up this time would be substantially different. A couple of contributors to the first collection were travelling abroad. Several were struggling to meet deadlines for contracted novels, biographies and TV or radio scripts, and couldn't afford to take time off to write even one story. Stuart noted with relief that some of the drop-outs belonged to the historical camp. He knew that Perdita Wycherley was joining him this time because in St Andrews, the evening before Graham's death, she had told him about the seventeenth-century witch story involving James VI (a.k.a. James I) she was writing, one of the fictional offshoots of the historical research which had made her internationally famous.

But the last thing Stuart expected when he eventually saw the full list of contributors was that he had been pushed into third place by two new women, Kathleen Abbott and Margaret Adair, whose titles established them as historical crime writers, like Perdita. What was more, Margaret's title, "Retreat to Culloden", suggested that she had somehow appropriated the story he had thought up about King Charles III and the '45.

What was going on? Was reality itself going out of the window? Not that reality was anything other than a figment of the collective imagination, as even the dimmest first-year philosophy student could demonstrate, Q.E.D. But even so. Had the Hyde in himself, unknown to the Jekyll, actually invented these two women and written their stories? Was the Hyde so desperate to be the front-runner – indeed first, second and third – that he had somehow succeeded in implanting more authorial A's into the book? Stuart couldn't very well ask the editors if Kathleen and Margaret were real or merely figments of his own imagination, now could he?

To retain his sanity – or was it "regain"? – Stuart told himself that they had to be real, but their presence still struck him as highly improbable statistically. Was it coincidence? Or more than coincidence? Pure chance? Or conspiracy? Did their AA surnames perhaps indicate that Kathleen and Margaret were a pair of avenging angels sent by Graham? He remembered the myth of the Hydra, which grew two new heads for every one cut off. Was Hyde battling unsuccessfully against this nine-headed monster? Or was he the sorcerer's apprentice, who tried to stop the magic broomstick by cutting it in half only to find that he then had twice as much chaos? Magic broomsticks reminded him of Perdita and all her witch stuff. Could she be involved? She was said to be capable of anything. Lady Macbeth's words after the killing of Duncan brought him back to some semblance of reality, whatever that was: "These deeds must not be thought After these ways; so, it will make us mad." Indeed. Quite so.

Stuart willed himself to stay calm – after visiting the National Library in Edinburgh in a vain search for any trace of Kathleen and Margaret. Nothing. He would have to wait for an advance copy of *Scottish Blood 2*, expected before long, to learn something from the Notes on Contributors – if they could be trusted and were not the work of Hyde. The real clincher would be the launch events. The two women were bound to turn up for one or more of these, weren't they?

Apart from his radio work, Stuart busied himself with a crime story he had promised one of the two women editors of a "Best of New British Crime Writing" collection, *Be With the Dead*, which, if he remembered correctly, was a phrase from that source of innumerable titles, Shakespeare's Scottish Play. Stuart broadcast a long interview with this particular editor, Lesley Aaron, when she was in Glasgow and Edinburgh doing readings and signings to launch her latest novel. She knew of "First Time Lucky" because it was on the shortlist for the CWA Short Story Award, and asked if he had anything she and her co-editor, Jill Abercrombie, could consider for *Be With the Dead* as they were still short of really good stuff. He didn't, but he didn't tell her that. He wanted to be in the book, but why did every other crime writer he came across, it seemed, have a name beginning with A? Coincidence? Or was there a conspiracy, especially by women?

"I certainly have one story you might like," he told Lesley, "but it needs a bit of polishing."

"In that case, apply plenty of grease to your elbow and polish fast," she replied. "We're approaching our publishers' final, final, final deadline – if you know what I mean. The one they really do mean. What's the story about? What's the title?"

What indeed? Both questions were as yet unanswerable. "Untitled" came to mind as suitable for a non-existent story, but whereas painters could get away with that, a crime writer could not. The words he heard himself say were "The Third Policeman", although he didn't know where they came from.

"You're really into numbers, aren't you?" she said. "But you can't use that."

He looked blank.

"It's that postmodern Flann O'Brien novel well before post-modernism. You must know it."

He didn't, but he said he did. She'd nearly caught him out. "It's only one of my working titles. What I had in mind was some ironic intertextuality between my narrative and his, but I suppose you're right. I'll probably end up with something else."

"Such as? What are your other provisional ones?"

Lesley was a one-woman inquisition. Why did she have to grill him? He was not St Lawrence nor was like to be. Because they were discussing *Be With the Dead*, he blurted out some remembered words from the Scottish Play: "When shall we three meet again?"

"Longish but better," she said. "Perhaps you'll come up with something snappier."

Stuart should have been trying to complete his overdue book on Farrell but instead worked as he hadn't done since the last couple of weeks before his St Andrews finals to provide her with a story. He had inadvertently committed himself to featuring one policeman, if not three, and there had to be three somethings even if they weren't policemen. How's that for freedom of the imagination. When she phoned to remind him that he only had a few more days, his story was still incomplete, but he said, "Just a few minor revisions then off by e-mail or fax or even, if you prefer, the pre-postmodernist post."

"Always polish, polish, polish! Eh, Mr Aiken scribbling Campbell," was her reply.

"WHEN SHALL WE THREE MEET AGAIN?": AUTHOR'S SYNOPSIS

This story is about an Edinburgh policeman, Detective Inspector Nolan, who suspects that he may have come across a perfect murder. But is he deluded, the victim of his own fiction-nourished imagination? That is the question. Nolan's favourite reading and viewing is, not untypically for a policeman, crime fiction. To an outsider this might seem like a busman's holiday, but to a professional there is something fascinating in the almost total lack of resemblance between his everyday working life and fictional representations of crime and policing. In Nolan's experience the harder such fiction tries to attain naturalistic authenticity, the more conspicuous becomes the gap separating it from the real thing. Paradoxically this desire for total credibility only serves to advertise its essential artificiality. He finds that fiction parading its artifice can carry more conviction because it acknowledges its own limits.

At the insistence of his wife Nolan has reluctantly been trying out American feminist and lesbian crime, which he reluctantly has to confess is much better than he expected, but his current bedtime reading is that comparative rarity, a mystery set in Scotland. Hot off the press, this novel is by an Edinburgh author who, according to the blurb, has just contributed to an entire anthology of Scottish crime fiction, *Scottish Blood*. As Nolan progresses with the narrative in nightly instalments, he discerns remarkable similarities to a recent double disappearance he helped to investigate.

All the signs in this case indicated a runaway husband who fled abroad with his mistress, leaving plenty of clues as to their plans but nevertheless successfully vanishing without trace. It seemed straightforward enough, if unusual, but there were a couple of unexplained and possibly suspicious aspects. Without any tangible evidence, Nolan speculated to his immediate superior about the remote possibility that the absconding lovers may have been killed just as they were about to depart, the result being an almost perfect murder, presumably by the man's wife with or without assistance. In no uncertain terms Nolan was told that he wasn't Reginald Wexford or Adam Dalgliesh and that he should keep his exceptionally large feet – even for a policeman – firmly on the ground instead of indulging in daft fantasies. If he had to read himself to sleep, why didn't he try this Booker Prize stuff that was on TV the other night? That would have anyone snoozing in no time and guarantee a good night's sleep.

The plot of the novel is much more intricate than the actual case itself, but at its centre is the double disappearance of a lesbian and her secret foreign lover whose elaborate plans to perform a vanishing trick are discovered at the very last moment by her long-term, long-suffering partner, who kills the other two women in a jealous rage. As she does so, she shrieks, "When shall we three meet again?" Being a doctor, she finds a way of disposing of the bodies, and before reporting the disappearance goes to considerable lengths to ensure that the trail of evidence will establish a meticulously planned and executed flit. The police are perfectly satisfied with this explanation. After all, quite a few people manage it.

Still only halfway through the novel, Nolan is perplexed. Crime fiction frequently draws on real cases, but this novel was published too soon after the actual disappearances he investigated for it to have been influenced by them. So, an example of life imitating art, since the writing must have come first? Pure coincidence? What else could it be? With such an abundance of crime fiction, this must happen from time to time. A statistical probability, even. If Nolan suggested re-opening the issue on the grounds that he'd read it in a novel, he wouldn't be back on the beat. He'd be out of the force and into community care. Still, he decides to risk a little private eyeing ("playing Marlowe") to satisfy his curiosity about the author, whom he assumes wrongly to be a man because of the use of initials. The Notes on Contributors in *Scottish Blood* would have put him right but he doesn't have a copy. When he discovers his elementary mistake, he sentences himself to repeat "Remember P.D. James" a hundred times as a penance. However, the important discovery is that the author is at least acquainted with the family involved in the disappearances and has been in touch with the abandoned wife. Could *they* be lesbian lovers, Nolan wonders? Or has his recent trawl through American feminist crime fiction over-sensitised him to such possibilities?

Pressing on to the conclusion of the novel, which has been the opposite of a relaxing, escapist read, Nolan finds that there is a policewoman who has a few residual doubts about the pair of vanishing dykes. Could they have been murdered? However, for fear of ritual disembowelling by her superiors led by the Chief Constable, she dare not raise her doubts officially about a closed case. Instead she decides on some off-duty snooping. At this point in his reading Nolan feels queasy. Should he abandon the novel and return it to the library without finding out what happens to the policewoman in her pursuit of the doctor? Curiosity, however, gets the better of him and he reads the remaining chapters in a burst to learn that the opposite of justice is done and the villainess, as he calls her, does not receive her deserts. When the policewoman begins to close in, the doctor kills her and successfully disposes of the body. Another mysterious disappearance remains to be explained, but there is nothing to link the doctor with the policewoman. The story ends with Nolan pondering his own future. Will he continue playing Marlowe or forget about the whole thing? As in my "Second Attempt" there are alternative endings, but this time they are implied. Everything is left to the reader's imagination.

Stuart did finish his story by the final, final, final deadline – just. The day after faxing it to Lesley, Stuart received a copy of *Scottish Blood 2* and turned immediately to the Notes on Contributors to read about Kathleen Abbott and Margaret Adair. The entries were brief but seemed to confirm their reality. Both lived in the Highlands, he gathered, Kathleen in Wick and Margaret in Inverness. Stuart checked with the publishers about the launch events, which were virtually identical to the previous year. Margaret, unfortunately, was believed to be in New York and therefore unable to participate; but Kathleen was available, but only for the one in Aberdeen, the only northern launch.

Stuart hadn't intended to drag himself all the way to Aberdeen, since he was expected to show up at three or four of the more southerly do's, but now there was no choice if he wanted to meet Kathleen in the flesh. If she existed, then it was safe to assume that Margaret did too. The publishers were delighted that Stuart was going to Aberdeen because most contributors would not be there. In fact when he reached the bookshop, only one other contributor apart from the editors was there, and it wasn't Kathleen. A message had arrived, however, saying that because of an unexpected problem following the arrival of her friend Morag from Edinburgh she wouldn't be able to make it, considering the length of the journey from Wick and the necessity of an overnight stop in Aberdeen.

Scots Bluid

Finally Stuart took the opportunity to quiz the editors about Kathleen and Margaret, something he had so far refrained from doing, despite his desperate curiosity, for fear of drawing the wrong sort of attention to himself.

Had the editors ever met the two authors? No.

Had they had much communication with them? No. Only the bare minimum. First, the stories, then the contracts, and then the corrected proofs. Not even a phone call. It was a little unusual for new authors, but they were Highlanders, remember, and more than likely to be reticent. Only speak when spoken to. Stuart returned home a sadder and a none-the-wiser man.

The messages awaiting him on his answerphone included one from the police. It was such a shock he didn't take it in properly the first time. Before daring to replay the tape he reached for the Macallan. A mega-mega-tot. It had to be about Graham, didn't it? What other contact had he had with the police recently? A second mega-mega-tot was called for. When Stuart found sufficient Dutch courage to listen to the message again, it seemed that his panic was unjustified. Whatever the reason for the police call it was most unlikely to concern Graham. The number he was asked to ring was in Edinburgh, not somewhere in Fife. And the message continued reassuringly about there being no need to worry since it was a purely routine matter. There was a remote possibility that he might be able to help Detective Inspector Campbell.

All this could, of course, be a deceptive ploy designed to put him off his guard but he didn't think so. Still, he would have to be cautious. You couldn't be certain of anything these days. When Stuart phoned, Campbell said: "So we'll have a meeting of the Campbells, won't we? Bit of a coincidence, but it happens. Scotland's not short of Campbells." Stuart was about to launch into his "I'm not Campbell but Aiken Campbell, unhyphenated double-barrelled like Vaughan Williams, but the other end of the alphabet" routine but thought better of it. The last thing he wanted to do was rub this policeman up the wrong way. Stuart settled for a meeting of Campbells.

Peter Lewis

SUMMARY OF POLICE INTERVIEW WITH
STUART AIKEN CAMPBELL

As I am sure you will agree, to reproduce the complete transcript of the interview here is unnecessary. It would seem wordy, repetitive and tedious – the kind of thing you are familiar with in realistic fiction in which the author is trying ever so hard to create an illusion of everyday reality and convince you of its authenticity. But if you are taken in by that sort of verbal prestidigitation, you'll be taken in by anything, won't you? What you will find here is a brief summary.

Inspector Campbell explained to Stuart what it was all about: the messy car accident in Leith involving two senior professors from Edinburgh University (Sinclair of Philosophy and MacLeod of Divinity) and a young woman, which had been widely reported not long ago. Stuart was bound to remember it, perhaps had even covered it for Radio Scotland. After all he had been one of the last people to talk to the driver, Professor Sinclair, before the accident. Stuart had recorded an interview with him that afternoon, only an hour or so before it happened. The accident, in which both professors were killed, had seemed an open-and-shut case, and there had been no reason whatever for the police to talk to Stuart.

Now, however, there was a suggestion that what occurred might have been something other than an accident. Stuart jumped to the conclusion that this meant murder, but Campbell went on to hint at the possibility of suicide by Sinclair. Not necessarily premeditated. More likely a spur-of-the-moment act. For people in a certain mental state, even a trivial thing can momentarily throw them off balance, and if they're driving, the consequences can be tragic, not only for themselves but for others too. So what the police were now trying to establish was the mental state of Professor Sinclair at the time, since he did have a history of depression.

Because of the circumstances Stuart remembered the interview well enough and admitted that he found Sinclair odd, but wasn't that how professors came? Especially philosophers. Several of his professors at St Andrews shouldn't have been allowed out.

Indeed by being in St Andrews they effectively weren't. That may even have been the reason for their appointments, since it was such a hard place to get out of. Compared with some of them, Sinclair didn't seem particularly eccentric. His behaviour hadn't suggested a man at the end of his tether or about to blow his cylinder head gasket. Stuart took it for granted when he heard of the man's death that it had been accidental. There was nothing else he could add.

Stuart couldn't remember what had happened to the young woman in the car but he didn't want to ask the policeman in case that unleashed more questions. Had she survived or been a casualty? He couldn't remember her name. Something beginning with "M", perhaps? Margaret? No, not Margaret. He was thinking of the invisible contributor to *Scottish Blood* 2 from Inverness. The press had concentrated on the two eminent men, the loss to Scottish intellectual life, that sort of line, not the young woman. Had she been working for an escort agency rather than for her PhD in the Philosophy of Religion, she would have attracted every bit as much attention as the men.

Among the pile of post awaiting me on the doormat this morning is a large, heavily textured red envelope. It's so distinctive that I know at once who sent it. I am also pretty sure what's in it. I received an identical envelope a little while ago, acknowledging receipt of my story, "Scots Bluid", which I submitted under the pen-name Hilary Aal (a surname I found in the local telephone directory) for a new collection of crime writing by Scottish authors being edited by two members of the Scottish Chapter of the Crime Writers' Association. Names of uncertain gender seem appropriate today when uncertainty about everything, including gender, is *de rigueur*, and I previously used Evelyn Adie, although if you are going to be that close to the front of the dictionary, why not go the whole hog? I deal with all the rest of this morning's letters but can't bring myself to open the red one. I hate even the possibility of rejection, let alone the probability – this time, downright certainty, I'm convinced.

After sending my story I learned that one of the editors had had to drop out and that the last-minute replacement was Perdita

Wycherley. This was a surprise since I thought of her as a poet and historian rather than a fiction writer, although as an expert on witchcraft in the early modern period she has, I suppose, done plenty on what she calls "crimes against womankind" or "femocide". It was also embarrassing, or would be if I were capable of embarrassment. By coincidence, I borrowed a sentence from one of Perdita's books as an epigraph to "Scots Bluid". I nearly dropped it before submitting my story because it seemed a bit pretentious to use an epigraph, but in the end I didn't bother. Inertia, probably. How was I to know she would end up as one of the editors? She won't see it as coincidence but as a deliberate ploy.

"Scots Bluid" is certainly Scottish enough for anyone, but it is well over the recommended word limit. This doesn't rule it out automatically since the editors stated that long stories of exceptional merit might be included, but I have severely restricted my chances. The trouble was that I was dissatisfied with every attempt I made to cut this story down to the expected length. Finally I sent the full version, while indicating my willingness to condense it if they liked the story but not the length. Afterwards I regretted my decision not to send a shorter version. It isn't *that* bad. I shouldn't have been so self-confident and blasé. I also made the mistake of expressing my opinion of the proposed title for the book, *Secret Murders*, a phrase from the Scottish Play. Why didn't they go for something straightforward like *Scottish Blood?* As well as pointing out that *Secret Murders* didn't sound sufficiently Scottish, despite its source, and that Shakespeare's play had been so overfished for titles that it had been *done to death* (a good title, I observed, but already used by Sara Woods), I also argued that crime fiction did not necessarily feature murders. The title implied narrow parameters. My own story, for example, depends heavily on the conventions of the genre, but how far it is about murder is up to the reader to decide. Later I couldn't believe how arrogant I'd been. Of course, some people not only get away with this sort of behaviour but are actually congratulated for it. It's a funny old world – if it exists.

I put the letter aside unopened and try to get on with some urgent work, but I can't concentrate. Even out of sight the letter preoccupies me. In the end I give in and fetch it. I tear open the red envelope.

THIS IS THE END

Or is it? If you are still not satisfied and require an alternative, how about this?

EXTRACT FROM A NEWSPAPER REPORT, 1ST APRIL
One of Scotland's leading young poets, Stuart Aiken Campbell, has been fatally wounded by a letter bomb. According to Inspector Nolan who is leading the police investigation, a large red envelope, probably containing a small amount of Semtex, exploded as he was opening it at home. On hearing the news, his exact contemporary and another prominent poet, David Aird, said: "Campbell – now he's dead we can call him by his real name instead of that ridiculous unhyphenated double-barrelled label he insisted on – always had to be one step ahead of the rest of us. It's therefore no surprise that he's won the race to the grave. Wherever he is now, and it's easy to guess, he'll already have elbowed his way to the front."

Perdita Wycherley, another of Campbell's contemporaries and co-editor of the forthcoming *Secret Murders*, commented: "This really is a red-letter day. For my generation, notions like justice and morality have lost all credibility, but his death does give us an inkling about what people meant when they said that there was some justice in the world after all. The only downside is the horrible feeling that Campbell will be the winner in the immortality stakes, simply because poets who die young appear to have an enormous advantage over the rest. Just think of what being dead before he was twenty did for Chatterton. Campbell was hardly a boy poet, of course. More like Marlowe and Keats and Shelley and Rupert Brooke, but you see what I mean. There's an old Greek saying, 'Those whom the gods love, die young.' All I can say is that either the Greeks were hopelessly wrong or the gods were incredibly bad judges of character when it came to dispensing their favours."

DISPOSING OF MRS CRONK

Peter Lovesey

Peter Lovesey is not only one of the world's leading mystery novelists but also a master of the short story and says, "If I have to offer something to St Peter as mitigation for a mis-spent life, it will be a collection of short stories." He uses the form to experiment with things, ideas and settings. He once even wrote a story (Youdunnit) *in which the reader is the murderer.* Disposing Of Mrs Cronk *is a story from a seasoned mystery writer on top form and offers witty dialogue, sharp characterisation and an excellent perfect crime plot.*

"Foolproof."

Gary shook his head. "Too simple."

"The simple ideas are the best."

"What if he susses us?"

And now Jason shook his cropped head. He made you believe in his wild ideas, did Jason. Those pale blue eyes of his, as still as the stones in a mosaic, watching you. The mouth like a crack in the earth.

"What's my action, then?" asked Gary, weakening.

"Collect the readies."

"Five grand?"

"More if we like. We set the fee."

"Five is enough," said Gary with the measured calculation of a young man behind with his rent and trying to subsist on unemployment benefit of forty-two pounds a week. "And all I do is collect?"

"And look the part."

"How?"

"Suit. Tie. Shades."

"What do I say?"

"Not much. You just collect, I said."

"Alone?"

"I can't hold your bleeding hand, Gary. I'm doing all the heavy stuff, aren't I?"

There was a pause for thought.

"All right, Jay. You're on."

"How's it going, Mr Cronk?" Jason asked, grasping the crowbar he used to strip the casing from the frames of the wrecks that were brought in.

"Same as usual."

"Mrs Cronk still giving you grief?"

"Don't ask, Jason."

Jason hauled on the crowbar and exposed the burnt-out interior of a Vauxhall Cavalier. "Not much here worth keeping."

"Pity. Try the engine, son."

With two or three expert stabs at the front of the car, Jason forced up the bonnet. "Battery looks all right. I'll have that out."

His employer prepared to watch the swift dissection of the mangled vehicle. In other parts of the yard, other beefy youths were dismantling derelict pieces of machinery, fridges, cookers, lawn-mowers, for scrap metal. It was not a bad living in these grim times. There was money in scrap. Call it waste disposal, recycling, totting, what you like, it paid. Not many overheads. Low wages. These were young lads straight from the dole queue, glad of anything. With the basic tools, a breakdown lorry, a second vehicle to cart the good stuff down to the dealer and fly-tip the rest, you were set up. Cash for trash.

If only his domestic life worked as neatly as his business.

Disposing of Mrs Cronk

Jason leaned over the bonnet, peering at the way the hoses were fixed. Then he ripped them out with his large hands. He was the pick of the bunch, in spite of his aggressive looks, the nearest thing to a foreman on the site.

"I knew a bloke had grief from his old lady," Jason said, turning to pick up another tool. "Funny business. She couldn't get enough of it. Know what I mean, Mr Cronk? Big, healthy woman. Soon as he got into his pit, she was on him, regular, and when I say regular I mean three, four, five times a night and coming from all directions. Too many hormones, I reckon. No bloke could have stood it. Knackered, he was. His work suffered. His pecker was in permanent shock. He gave up going out with his mates. Got the shakes. Anyway, he faced facts in the end. It couldn't go on. So he went to the Fixer, paid the fee, and slept soundly ever after."

Mr Cronk reflected on the matter while Jason lifted out the battery.

"What do you mean by the Fixer?"

"I thought you'd know about the Fixer, Mr Cronk."

"I don't mix in your circles, Jason."

Jason applied himself to the heavy work, his biceps rippling.

"He takes care of problems. This geezer's problem was his old lady, so the Fixer fixed her."

"How?"

"Disposal." Jason ripped out the radiator and slung it onto a heap of rusted metal. Unlike the others, Jason never confused ferrous and non-ferrous.

"You mean he . . . ?"

"Yup. It wasn't crude, mind. The Fixer's a pro. No comeback. This bloke is free now. Free to marry again if he wants, but I don't think he will. Once bitten . . ." Jason gave a coarse laugh and picked up the bolt-cutter.

"What happened to the woman?"

"Accident, they said. She didn't know nothing about it, that's for sure. Drove her car off the road. The thing was, this road was next to a two-hundred foot drop. The coroner reckoned she fell asleep at the wheel."

"Accidental death?"

Peter Lovesey

Jason grinned.

Mr Cronk gaped.

"The insurance paid up, easily covered the Fixer's fee."

He severed a bunch of cables and wrenched them out. There wasn't much left of that engine.

"What sort of fee does he charge?" Mr Cronk eventually asked.

"Ten grand."

"As much as that?"

"It sounds a lot, but it's like cars. You pay for a decent motor and you get value. Believe me, he's the Roller of his profession. He don't let people down."

Towards the end of the afternoon, Mr Cronk passed Jason again. The parts worth keeping had been stripped from the car, sorted and stacked neatly nearby. He was already sledgehammering another vehicle. He was a lad you could depend on.

"Er, Jason."

"Mr Cronk?" He rested the sledgehammer on his shoulder.

"You're feeling hot, I expect."

"What do you expect? I ain't picking daffodils."

"How would you like a cool swim? I've watched you working. You deserve it. Come home with me. I've got a thirty-foot pool."

"What, now?"

"Now's the right time."

"I'm covered in muck."

"You can take a shower at my place. We do have soap, you know."

Mr Cronk's house and garden were so palatial that Jason wished he had put the Fixer's price higher than ten grand. The pool had a glass roof that retracted at the push of a button like the sun-roof on a posh car. The bottom of the pool was lined with blue, green and gold tiles. There was money in recycling, more money than Jason had dreamed was possible.

He took a slow shower, soaping himself thoroughly in the shower gel Mr Cronk had provided. He watched the grime go down the chromium plughole. Then he dried himself with the

146

huge, pink, fluffy bath-towel and put on the boxer shorts Mr Cronk had lent him.

"So there you are, clean as a vicar," Mr Cronk shouted from across the water. "Come and meet my good lady."

Mrs Cronk.

She was reclining on one of those long, padded swing-seats suspended in a large frame. She must have been twenty years younger than Mr Cronk because she looked terrific in a black two-piece. Blonde, bronzed and superbly groomed, she was the biggest surprise yet.

Friendly, too. "Hi, Jason. Check those tattoos."

She didn't budge from the recliner, so he had to move in, crouch down and show her his biceps. She smelt expensive.

"Pure art. And on such an expansive canvas. Do you pump iron?"

"No, I break up cars for your old man."

She laughed. "So do I, but it doesn't give me muscle tone like that."

"You don't want it."

Mr Cronk said, more to himself than the others, "Many a true word." Then he turned to Jason. "Why don't you try the water?"

"Cheers. I will."

He wasted no time. He took a header, needing to get submerged fast, and not just because he was coming out in a sweat again. The water was deliciously cool. He was not a bad swimmer and he showed off a bit with his powerful crawl, doing a racing turn at the deep end.

After six lengths he stopped and stood up in the shallow end. The swing-chair was no longer occupied.

"She's getting changed," her husband said. "She's got to get to her flamenco class." Mr Cronk had changed too, into a T-shirt, shorts and sandals.

"Is she learning flamenco?"

"She teaches it, four nights a week."

Jason swam another four lengths, lazily, on his back, thinking about Mrs Cronk dancing the flamenco. After a bit, he turned over and swam on his front.

When he got out, there was a fresh towel ready. Mr Cronk handed it to him. Jason sat on the edge of the pool with the towel draped around his shoulders, dangling his feet in the pool.

Mr Cronk handed him a can of lager, ice-cold. He said, "You look so cool, I think I'll join you, Jason." He stepped out of his sandals and sat beside Jason. The light on the water shimmered over the coloured tiles, distorting the shapes.

"That chap you mentioned today. The, em, Fixer."

"Yeah?"

"You said he was reliable."

"Hundred per cent."

"Ten thousand pounds, the man paid, for his services?"

"Ten grand, yes."

"Tell me, Jason. How does the money work?"

"Come again, Mr Cronk?"

"Well, is he paid by results? Does he get the money after performing the, em . . . ?"

"I'm with you. No, there's got to be trust on both sides. Standard terms for that kind of job are half on agreement, half on completion. Five grand down, five at the death, so to speak."

After some reflection, Mr Cronk said, "It seems fair enough."

"Cash, of course. No point in cheques in a business like his."

"Or writing them, if you hire him," said Mr Cronk, churning the water with his feet, he was so amused by his own remark. "Do you know this fellow personally?"

"I've met him, yeah."

"Any chance I could meet him, just out of interest, so to speak?"

"No chance," said Jason.

"Oh."

"He doesn't meet no one on spec. Too risky."

"How did he ever meet the man you were telling me about?"

"It was set up by a third party. The bloke made it known he wanted to hire the Fixer. There was a meeting on neutral ground, the bloke and the Fixer. Five grand was handed over.

Disposing of Mrs Cronk

Nothing spoken. When the job was done, the other five grand had to be left in a case in a left luggage box. The key was handed to the third party, who gave it to the Fixer."

"Neat."

"That's the way it's done the world over, Mr Cronk." Jason stood up. "I'd better get changed and toddle off. I'm sure you've got things to do."

"I'll drive you back. No problem," said Mr Cronk.

Towards the end of the drive back to the flat Jason shared with Gary, Mr Cronk said, "I suppose you couldn't act as third party."

"In what way?" Jason tried to sound puzzled.

"As a contact with the Fixer. You said you met him."

"Just the once, a while ago." He paused. "I suppose I could sniff around, see if he's about."

"I'd make it worth your while – later."

"Five hundred?" said Jason.

"All right. When it's all over."

They drove on for a while in silence.

"This'll be all right. Drop me here."

Mr Cronk stopped the car. "Don't think too badly of me, Jason. I'm a deeply wounded man. Mine is nothing like the case you mentioned. Almost the reverse."

"I don't judge no one, Mr Cronk."

"You'll let me know?"

"Get a grip, Gary. He's the one wearing brown trousers, right?"

"Right."

"You look great. Wear the shades, and your rings. Walk tall. And don't forget to check the money."

"Where will you be, Jay?"

"Where I said – down the tube with the cases and the tickets. Piccadilly Line to Heathrow, the night flight to Athens and six weeks bumming around the Greek Islands. Any problem with that?"

"No problem, Jay."

"There's nothing he can do. I lose my job, and you get the golden handshake, eh, Gary?"

"Yes, sure."

"Try and look the part, then."

Mr Cronk emerged from a taxi and entered the ticket hall of the tube station at precisely 4 p.m. He was carrying a sportsbag containing five thousand pounds in twenty-pound notes. As instructed, he waited to the left of the news kiosk. He was trembling uncontrollably.

At 4.03, a tall young man in dark glasses and a black suit and bootlace tie walked right up to Mr Cronk and said, "Is it all there?"

Mr Cronk fumbled and almost dropped the bag as he handed it over to the Fixer.

The young man unzipped the bag and made a quick assessment of the contents.

Mr Cronk said, "When will you . . . ?"

"You'll get a phone call," the Fixer promised. He zipped the bag up again. Then he turned and walked quickly through the barrier and down the escalator.

Gary was all smiles on the platform. "Dead simple."

"Give us the bag," said Jason. He took it and looked inside. "Sorted."

The Heathrow train came in. They picked up the cases. On the journey, they opened one of the cases and stuffed the bag inside.

"It was a dream," said Gary, his confidence fully restored. "He was dead scared. You know what? If we played it right, we could roll him for the other five grand as well. Have a nice holiday, go back and screw him for the bloody lot. He wouldn't know it was a con till he got back and found his old lady still breathing."

Jason fixed him with those stone eyes and said, "You're a laugh a minute, Gary."

"Am I?"

"She's already dead."

"What?" Gary went white. "No! Jay, you never?"

"Couldn't let my old boss down, could I?" said Jason, enjoying this.

Disposing of Mrs Cronk

"For Christ's sake, mate, are you crazy?"

"Went for a swim with her this afternoon, didn't I? Pushed her face under the water and kept it there." He glanced at his watch. "He'll be finding her about now. He'll be saying, 'Jesus, that Fixer didn't waste time.' And when we get back to England, he'll pay up like a lamb."

Gary practically gibbered. "It was a scam, Jay, it was only meant to be a scam. We never agreed no violence."

Jason took pity. He'd had his fun, and other people in the train were starting to look at Gary. "I bet you still believe in the bloody tooth fairy and all. I never touched her."

Gary's breathing subsided. "Honest?"

"Honest. How could I? I was humping these cases to the station."

"Bastard."

"Get real, pal. We're on our way."

Their flight was due to take off at 23.10 from Terminal Four. They had plenty of time in hand. After checking in their cases and going through the passport control, they had a leisurely meal and a few drinks and started to get into the holiday mood.

"How long do you reckon it's going to take before old Cronk finds out he's been ripped off?" said Gary.

"Week. Longer," said Jason. "He might smell a rat when I don't come into work, but he'll think I'm ill, or something."

"And he can't do sweet f.a. about it. It's neat, Jay. Real neat."

"I'll drink to that."

Their flight was called. They walked to the departure lounge and showed their tickets and passports. One of the officials in suits said, "Would you come with me, gentlemen?"

"What for?" said Jason.

"This *is* your passport?"

"Yes."

"You are Jason Richardson and you, sir, are Gary Morton? You won't be boarding this flight. We're police officers with orders to arrest you."

After a scuffle, the pair were handcuffed and led away to the airport police office. They were cautioned and then questioned about their movements.

"You've got nothing on us," Jason said.

"We opened your luggage," the inspector said. "Almost five grand in twenties?"

"It's a long holiday," said Jason cleverly.

"Don't waste your breath, lad. We heard about you from Mr Cronk, getting yourself invited to his place and sussing it out for a robbery, knowing how scrap metal merchants have to handle large amounts of cash. That's naughty enough, but beating an innocent woman to death is evil."

Mrs Cronk dead?

Jason went cold. Suckered. He couldn't believe Mr Cronk had it in him.

Gary whimpered.

"Take their prints. See if they match up to the prints on the sledgehammer found at the scene. I'm confident they will. Armed robbery, murder and conspiracy to murder. Yes, it will be a long holiday, gentlemen."

THE SOUL OF DISCRETION

John Malcolm

What happens after a funeral often provides, as Agatha Christie amongst others has demonstrated, admirable material for a crime story. Whenever John Malcolm takes a break from his popular series of novels about the exploits of Tim Simpson, bank business consultant and amateur sleuth, the results are of much interest. This story has a wistful quality which suggests to me that, notwithstanding his achievements in the field to date, the best of Malcolm's crime writing is yet to come.

I was late getting to Reg Foster's funeral. A traffic jam on the London road would have been my excuse but the powerful Cobra seemed reluctant; it dawdled as we splashed over the wet grey roadways. The wipers flapped like tired wings on a fated bird. Reg was dead; crematorium ceremonies are depressing; suicide makes them worse. It was a relief to find, after I'd parked and slipped furtively into the back chairs of the curtained chapel, that they were already half-way through.

There'd be no hallowed ground for Reg.

The immediate family were grouped up front, bowed into a dark straggle of middle-aged and younger elements. Dotted here and there amongst the sparsely-polished birchwood chairs were one or two individuals like me and the occasional couple, one of them elderly. Unknown heads turned to observe my tardy arrival. Some would be relatives, some neighbours, some from business sources. I didn't see any from my time. There may have been more recent acquaintances but it wasn't much of a throng, not if you judge the sum of fifty-odd years by the crowd that waves you goodbye.

I sat down just as a black-and-white cassocked johnny stood up at a lectern and began to say something or another about Reginald and his unfortunate end in carefully-chosen phrases that betrayed far too much practice at that sort of thing. Not that I was unsympathetic; I admire the resolution it must take to officiate regularly at such events, quite apart from saying something relevant about an unknown character without causing offence. But it was certain that nothing of the late Reg's situation and the facts I knew would be reflected in this magpie stranger's bland, professional oration.

I closed my eyes to compose myself and put my mind back to the last time I'd seen Reg, something just over a month ago.

It was at a party given by some distant friends called Morrison who persuaded me to desert my normal territory on the grounds that they'd invited several old friends who were aching to see me after long absences. All lies; I should have known that as I entered the main room after effusive greetings from the hosts, blank faces would gape at me expectantly before going back to conversations too bright for mental absorption. No glad recognition shone back. Things were getting under way without even an acquaintance in sight. I remember standing in the doorway, hesitant at the thought of joining in.

I'm not much of a party man.

Then I saw Reg, standing at the back of the crowd, holding a drink and staring out of the French windows. His wife Elaine was holding court on the other side of the room, surrounded by smartly-dressed women like herself. Relieved, I threaded my way through the chatter without Reg seeing me and tapped a shoulder as I hove alongside the broad figure.

"Hello, Reg," I said, cheerfully. "How are you, you old dog?"

Reg Foster's face moved for a second or two before he replied, close and somehow magnified in the crowded space, so that pores and lines were prominent on his pale rubbery skin. There were dark pouches under his eyes.

"Good grief. What on earth are you doing here, Jimmy?"

His voice seemed disembodied. His gaze hardly focussed. As he spoke his head lifted to stare at something elsewhere, something not within the room. I realised that my old friend had been standing in isolation; the people close by meant nothing to him.

A distant laugh came from the women clustered round Elaine but Reg appeared not to notice.

I was looking at a stricken man.

Before I could say anything, Reg spoke again. "What?" he asked, craning his head to one side as though I'd said something a bit *sotto voce*, and his eyes actually saw me properly this time, in detail, so that I could tell he had come back from somewhere far away.

"Let's go outside," I said.

I took Reg's sleeve and pulled him gently towards the French windows, smiling apologetically at a maroon velveteen woman we had to nudge from behind to get by.

Outside it was slightly misty with a cold damp, not warm damp, so that the nerves in my back twitched in a pre-emptive shiver. On the terrace there were a couple of big garden urns in which the flowers were emerging reluctantly from thin withered greenery and grey sparse earth or compost, as though they felt it was still too soon to come out. It was quiet. I let go of Reg's sleeve and motioned towards the end of the flagstones, so that we could talk and watch the crowd inside from a spot where no-one could hear us.

"What's up, Reg?"

I used to think that I could read Reg like a book. When we were young it was even easier, but long marriage to Elaine had taught Reg minimal skills of concealment.

"Up?" Reg queried, putting on a sort of defence. "What do you mean, up?"

I shook my head sadly and smiled with one corner of my mouth like a raincoated wiseguy from an old Yankee film. Reg shook his head back in recognition and dropped his eyes.

"You never married again, Jimmy," he stated, staring at the York stone paving as though it was of archaeological interest or perhaps engraved with a worn but faintly-readable epitaph, "did you?"

"No," I said. "I didn't."

I hadn't seen him for quite a long time so it was a fair sort of preliminary statement even though we both knew the answer and that Reg was just stalling for time.

His rubbery face puckered in query. "Nothing – nothing like that on the go? Just now?"

"No," I said, easily. "Nothing like that. Not just now."

A definition of what "like that" means is infinitely flexible, depending on how you see "that". I wasn't in a mood for complicated explanations. Or masculine wit.

"You don't get lonely? After all this time?"

I took out a cigarette and, on the grounds that we were outside and no-one would object, lit it knowing Reg never smoked, puffed, and threw away a match while Reg watched absorbedly, waiting for an answer he wouldn't get.

"What's up, Reg? I can see that it's serious. Anything I can do to help?"

His eyes looked at the cigarette curiously for a moment, narrowed as though satisfied that in life some things and even some people do not change, moved to my glass, to his own, then away to stare at the garden.

"When," he asked, still looking away and speaking in tones that sounded thicker than normal, "do you think the very last time you'll have a willing woman will be? An enthusiastic one, I mean. You know, like it was when we were young. The last time? When? Will you know, for certain, that that was it? What will you do when you know, Jimmy?"

I didn't reply. I turned to look back into the house where Elaine was now regaling the little group of ladies with some story I couldn't hear. They all hung on her words. A husband hovered near them for a moment, smiled, then moved away towards the bar. Women had always liked Elaine. It was nothing physical;

she was a woman's woman in quite a recognizable, social sense. Her friends all spoke of her with admiration.

I turned back to look at Reg. "Who is she?" I asked.

"Was," Reg answered, a bit thicker now. "Was she, you mean. You've always been a perceptive bastard, Jimmy. Was. From today."

"Was? She's not dead or something, is she?"

His eyes flicked in anger for a moment, then went away again.

"Oh no. She's not dead. That's the worst part of it."

Even though I hadn't kept up much with Reg and Elaine as a couple, from past experience I would have bet good money that Reg had never strayed and that Elaine certainly wasn't interested in anything like that. Elaine would come down like a ton of bricks on a misdemeanour of that sort. Their marriage was in the old mould, I always reckoned, with Elaine pacing the way smartly along the straight and narrow and good old Reg puffing along behind.

Funny thing, life; I'd have lost the bet.

"It was on the motorway," Reg said, moving back a bit to turn towards me, half-aware of the babble inside the French windows. "Over a year ago. She'd broken down. On her own. The telephone was vandalised and I stopped to help. She was nervous of course, but she soon saw I was pretty safe, me. A widow. Forties. Husband went in a heart attack. The car had to go on a breakdown lorry."

I could have made a clever crack but it would have been cheap. I bit it back and I'm glad, now, that I did. This was serious.

"It didn't happen then." Reg watched the smoke curl off the end of my cigarette. "I went back to the garage the next day and there she was. Pleased to see me. Can't explain what happened, really. It turned out she'd been widowed for three years. I went home with her that day. She knew I was married. She was nervous. So was I. But there was something we both knew about each other straight away, you see. I don't know – I – oh yes I do."

He turned a bit more to look into the lighted interior, which seemed to have got fuller and louder. Elaine was obscured by new people moving in, although her voice could be heard, just briefly, through the babble.

I put out the cigarette. "What's happened?" I asked.

"She – Elizabeth, that's her name – says that she's got her confidence back. She never wanted to upset my marriage, you see. Said she didn't want to marry again all the time we – we met. It was perfect. Perfect. Exciting and stolen, yet safe. I can't leave Elaine, that's impossible. It was like heaven had granted me a blessing. We did things I've never—"

He stopped, embarrassed, and I was glad. I didn't want to hear about things Reg'd never. Most friendships can't deal with that.

"What's happened, Reg?" I asked again. "Today, that is."

"She says it's over. She'll never forget me. She's going to marry someone else. Make a new life. Devon. She says if she hadn't met me she'd just have declined steadily into widowhood. In a way, it's probably true; when I first met her she looked quite dowdy. Now she's smart and bright. Alert. Hell, Jimmy, when do you think the last time you'll have an eager woman will be? What will you do when you know?"

"Reg," I said, as gently as I could. "Reg, Reg, Reg. It's not all over yet, my boy."

"Not for you, maybe, Jimmy. But me, I'm facing the end. For me it'll be Elaine arranging this and Elaine arranging that and Elaine coming home from bridge at five o' clock ready for the long evening with no hope of anything at the end of it and me with no chance, going mad for what I've known. I'm over fifty. Look at me: I'm a businessman; a fat and boring businessman."

"You weren't to this Elizabeth."

Foster didn't hear, or if he did, he ignored it. "I can't stand tarts. I hate that sort of thing; sad old punters. That's horrible. I've seen the last happy day of my life and it's hit me at a party where I only have to look round to know I'll never get a real chance again. Never."

"Hush. Keep it down a bit, Reg. They'll hear you."

"Sorry. Sorry, Jimmy. You must think it's a bore. But thanks

The Soul of Discretion

for listening. I know you're the soul of discretion. You always have been."

"It's not a bore, Reg."

I put a hand on his arm, thinking of a book John Mortimer once wrote called *Clinging to the Wreckage* in which he tells the story of two men shipwrecked near a coast. The enterprising one strikes out for the shore and drowns in the currents on the way. The other clings to the wreckage until a helicopter comes to rescue him. The moral of the story is supposed to be that if you can't swim it's safer to cling to the wreckage than to strike out into the unknown.

Well, Reg had clung to his wreckage for a long time. And then he'd had a little swim with a mermaid to help comfort him until she'd gone away again.

That left him with his wreckage.

"Now," the pied sermoniser said, as a hum of machinery started up somewhere, "it is time for us all to say farewell to Reginald. Let us all—"

The coffin moved off slowly through a curtain. Reg hadn't done it straight away. Knowing Reg, I guessed he would have talked about something with Elaine first. Probably not telling about the other woman but the state he was in and what was bugging him.

The answer must have been no.

He ended it in his garage, with a hose pipe to the car exhaust. They say it's the calmest way to go. Just another quick wonder-statistic and on we all move, get the funeral over with, try not to think about it too much—

"Mr Weston?"

A dark-suited man was standing by my crematorium chair looking down at me. The voice was soft.

"Yes?"

"The family say you are welcome to join them at their home after the service."

"Oh, that's kind, but—"

"Mrs Foster – Elaine – is very touched that you were able to come. There are so very few of Reg's old friends present. She particularly asked me to persuade you."

159

I stared at him, trying not to be rude.

"Sorry. I'm Frank Sloman. From the office." He held out a hand. "We're all shattered at what's happened. I worked closely with Reg a year or two back."

I took the hand, let go of it, and nodded.

"Oh good. Elaine will be pleased. I think you know the way?"

"Yes, thank you," I said. "I know the way."

Outside, the rain had eased off but everyone seemed to hurry to their cars. Unmoving conifers and wide, shrubbed paths gave the place an impersonal, empty feeling. There were draughts.

Reg had gone.

"Are you going back to the reception?"

A biggish fair woman and a tall thin man had come up behind on the gravel. Her voice was brisk, suburban, rather self-consciously trying to be "normal" in what were rather daunting surroundings.

I nodded. "Yes."

"You're Jimmy Weston, aren't you?"

"Yes I am."

She held out a surprisingly slim and elegant hand. "I'm Sandy Creswell. This is my husband, Harry. We're almost next door neighbours to the Fosters. Reg and Harry played golf together. Reg often spoke of you."

I took the hand, shook it, then her husband's. "Oh?"

"Yes. He said you were at school together."

"We were."

The woman looked round briefly, as though guilty at being seen chatting in these circumstances, then smiled at me in a rather personal way. "See you back at the do, then."

"Yes."

She looked pleased as they moved off towards a bright saloon Jaguar and I strolled back to the Cobra. Reg never mentioned any Creswells either. When Reg and I used to meet, on rare occasions, we didn't talk of present life. It was nearly always about the past. Unhealthy if you like but necessary from time to infrequent time, like looking at old photographs that reassure you that it really happened, you did it, it's not just all made up. Or a dream.

160

The Soul of Discretion

Most of the time Reg and me were verbal photograph albums for each other.

Until that last party.

The Fosters' house was about four miles away, in a prosperous suburb. Reg was a hard worker, dependable and shrewd if self-effacing, the sort of man who gets to high executive level without threatening the top. Elaine would be covered by insurance policies; she might even be able to stay in the house after the mortgage was paid off and the luxury pension got into gear. I stopped about twenty yards short of the drive entrance, which was full of cars, so that I could make an unimpeded getaway after making my obeisances.

The house was surprisingly full considering the impression the crematorium had given, and people were starting to speak normally, with relief in their voices.

I went straight up to Elaine, who was standing in the hallway, kissed her cheek gently and murmured my sorrows. She was tastefully dressed in black and looked cool, slim and restrained. The widow keeping herself together with a courageous public face; it puckered at the sight of me.

"Jimmy. I can't tell you how much it means to us that you've come. Thank you, thank you so much. You know how much you meant to Reg. He loved it when you looked him up. The whole family thinks of you as part of us, if you know what I mean."

Reg had two sons and a daughter. I didn't know them well. I wasn't an example to them. Every solid, dependable citizen who leads the sort of temperate, predictable, responsible sort of life that Reg did has to have someone from their youth they can point to as a contrast. Someone who hasn't followed that path, hasn't played by the rules. Someone they can watch from their wreckage and say look, he's going to come a cropper on those rocks, or he'll drown over there, or that mermaid is a siren who'll drag him under. It's a sort of reassurance for them.

It occurred to me, then, that the reverse was true as well.

"Please go on in and help yourself to some cold lunch." Elaine seemed to be watching me very carefully. "It's pot luck, I'm afraid, but I'm – I've – not been up to – the children have been so splendid—"

"Elaine." One of her women friends had moved alongside. She gave me a significant glance as she put her arm around the widow's shoulders. "Come and sit down, there's a good girl. It's over at last. I'm sure Mr Weston will be well looked after."

"I'm sure I will." I nodded understandingly. "But if there's anything I can do, you will let me know, won't you? I mean it: anything at all. The children as well."

"Dear Jimmy."

Elaine engineered a suitably restrained but grateful smile as she allowed herself to be led away. The children were adults now. They didn't need contacts with her dead husband's slightly dubious old friends. I went into a panelled dining room and got myself a plate of cold ham and salad, refusing anything to drink. After a brief wander round I sat down in the lounge, where other people were coping with meals on their laps like any social occasion; well, a funeral is a social occasion, I suppose.

"Mind if we join you?"

It was the thin Creswell man and his big, fair wife. They were standing beside my chair indicating a low coffee table they wanted to put their plates on.

"Of course not. Please do. Harry, isn't it?"

"Yes, that's right."

"And Sandy?"

The big lady gave me an almost mischievous smile as she sat beside me with a flourish of her thin hands. "You've obviously got an awfully good memory. I'm hopeless at names."

"But you knew mine, at the crematorium."

"That's because I recognised you. You look just like Reg's description." She was looking at me steadily. "Tragic, isn't it?" She lowered her voice. "About Reg, I mean."

"Dreadful."

"No one can understand why on earth he did it."

"I'm sure they can't."

"I don't think it was cancer or anything. Elaine would have said. Although you never can tell. People are told they've got fatal diseases every day of the week. You never can tell how they'll take it. Reg just wasn't the type to give up, though. It seems so unlike him."

162

"It certainly does. I'd give a lot to know why."

I said the last sentence automatically, playing the role with an ease that surprised even myself, although now I thought a little more about it, perhaps the last good thing I could do for my old school friend would be to preserve him from those who knew him.

The Creswell woman was still observing me intently. "Elaine's dreadfully hit. It's awful. She's such a marvellous person. She says if she'd come home just a bit earlier from bridge instead of her normal time, she might have found him and prevented it. He was in the garage, you know. With the engine running."

"Yes, I gathered that."

"Horrible." Harry Creswell clearly felt it was time he interjected something to prevent his wife making all the conversational running but she appeared not to hear him.

"Instead of which," she murmured, "by six o' clock it was too late."

I stared at her, disconcerted. "I, er, I gathered that, too."

"He was only just over fifty."

"Yes, I know. He and I were at school together."

"Good heavens, of course you were. I'm hopeless about dates and numbers and things." She gave me a flirtatious look. "He looked much older than you."

"Reg was a hardworking man."

"They've told Elaine she's fully covered." Harry Creswell's voice was muted deferentially. "That Sloman fellow is from personnel. He's assured Elaine she'll be well looked after. I should think so, too. Reg gave them every bit of commitment he'd got."

"I'm very glad. So often nowadays companies try to avoid their responsibilities."

"Oh, Sloman's boss is no Maxwell. Not at all. He'd have been here, but duty called elsewhere. Middle East, or somewhere like that, I believe."

That didn't seem to need a response. Perhaps Reg's boss, like others of Reg's acquaintanceship, was put off by suicide enough not to attend. There might be a suggestion of work-induced stress, for example. It would be enough to let the company pension fund do their best for the widow.

I didn't say that, either. Suddenly I felt like the repository of too much knowledge, too many facts, that might somehow bubble to the surface and spill over in some detrimental way. I finished my plate of ham and salad, made my excuses to the Creswells and moved towards the front door.

I found Sloman, the personnel man, in front of me. His face was thin and curious.

"Mr Weston. Are you leaving already?"

He didn't move to one side. He stood directly facing me as though there was something that prevented him from moving.

"Yes." My voice sounded a bit short. "I'm afraid I must get on."

"Oh, that's a pity." Sloman's expression didn't change. "I'll tell Elaine."

"There's no need. I'm sure she would be better undisturbed."

"No, she particularly asked to speak to you before you left." His face moved closer. "Please wait here for a moment."

What the hell, I was about to ask, but then didn't, more from not wanting to make a scene at a wake than anything else, and anyway Sloman had vanished somewhere deep into the house, what the hell should I wait here for? But I was getting used to not saying anything that day and didn't want to break the mould.

Elaine came out from a back room somewhere and smiled faintly. She looked more in control of herself, as though she'd recovered from the ceremony at the crematorium.

"Thank you, Jimmy. Thank you very much for coming."

"Not at all, Elaine. He was one of my oldest friends."

"Of course. He used to love seeing you. To talk to you."

"Yes. We chewed over old times a great deal, I'm afraid."

I made the last remark almost defensively. Elaine Foster's expression wasn't right. Not right at all. She was looking at me detachedly, without pleasure. Not with hatred but without pleasure.

"Well, men have to have someone they can relax with, don't they?"

"Yes, I suppose they do. Just like women."

"And confide in."

The Soul of Discretion

"Er, well—"

"Reg did confide in you a lot, I think." Her voice sharpened a little. "When he saw you. I can't think of anyone else he trusted that way. There was that last party of the Morrisons, for example."

I paused before replying, which was a mistake. Elaine was one of the quickest to pick up a nuance.

"Not really, Elaine. We only talked over old times together. He hardly even spoke about your children, for example."

"Well, you're not exactly the children sort, are you, Jimmy?"

I blinked. Her voice had tightened further. Something was taking me out of my depth. "I suppose not." I managed a rueful smile. "Look, I'm afraid I must be off."

She nodded slowly. "You always were the soul of discretion, Jimmy. I'm glad you haven't changed."

"I'm sorry?" Knowledge, the knowledge someone was assuming I had, was suddenly getting too much. The sort of knowledge that screamed that Reg had said that Elaine always came home from bridge at five o' clock but the Creswell woman definitely said not until six.

A whole hour to be at home with Reg still in the garage, engine running, while Elaine Foster waited to make sure.

She held out her hand. "Good-bye then, Jimmy. Thanks again for coming."

It was a valediction. As I took the hand I knew she didn't mean to see me again, or encourage her children to.

"I know I can rely on you. The soul of discretion."

"Oh?"

Elaine smiled at me, a smile that seemed to be full of meanings I didn't want to take on board. "I'm sure you know what I'm talking about. I'm sure we can rely on you. As one of Reg's oldest friends. You wouldn't want to spoil a new beginning, would you? Even if it's only Devon. I know Reg wouldn't have wanted to, either. Not really. Not if he'd thought about it."

She let go of my hand, turned away and swished back down the hall to disappear through the rear door before I could answer. I went through the front door with two swift strides

165

and was halfway down the drive before I thought to turn back to look.

The garage doors were shut. They would be, if only out of tact. The garage was connected to the house by an intervening block that abutted the kitchen. All part of an integrated building. From the kitchen you would almost certainly be able to hear a car's engine running in the garage, especially if those doors were shut like they were now.

During the course of a whole hour you couldn't possibly miss the sound.

I walked carefully out into the roadway to make sure my car was still parked where I'd left it, ready and waiting to go. As I glanced back at the house again I thought I saw a pale face in the hall window, watching, but I might have been mistaken. There was no point in getting nervy, in jumping to conclusions.

I walked to the car, got in, lit a cigarette and started the engine in much the same way Reg must have, as the last thing he did. I would never know what Reg might have said to Elaine, that night, after the Morrisons' party. What he wanted to talk over, or maybe what he wanted her to do. Or said he might do if, say, Elaine didn't—.

I decided I never wanted to know. There was nothing to be gained from such knowledge. One of my oldest photograph albums had been snapped shut forever. Nothing could reopen it.

The rain had stopped; I didn't need the hood but I left it up and put the wipers on the intermittent switch for the journey back. I watched them flap wearily just once, clearing my vision as I sat at the wheel, thinking. Then I put the car in gear and drove quickly away.

DRIVING A HARD BARGAIN

A Kate Brannigan story

Val McDermid

The first private eye tales were short stories written for the pulp magazines. It seems to me, though, that most of the best work in this field has been done at novel length. Writers such as Chandler, Hammett, Grafton and Paretsky have benefited from having the extra elbow room afforded by the longer form. Yet with this story, Val McDermid reveals the possibilities of the short private eye story (and the idea of the perfect crime) for the modern writer. The secret of success lies in the sharpness of the writing – in characterisation, dialogue and plot, with the final paragraph echoing the first.

I'd find it a lot easier to believe in therapists if they acknowledged the existence of the Inner Spiv as well as the Inner Child, Parent, Teacher and Washing Machine Mechanic. We've all got one. No matter how hard we try to be stylish and sophisticated, our Inner Spiv will sabotage us every time. It's the driving force that dictates Prince Charles' cuff-links, Hugh Grant's sexual hot button and Mary Archer's taste in men.

I share my weakness with Princess Diana. No, I'm not talking bleating, indiscreet men. I'm talking motors. But it's not the big Mercs and the turbo-charged Bentleys that speak to the spiv in me. It's flashy cabriolets, the roar of twin carbs in the still spring evening, sleek feline coupés that make teenage boys on street corners drool. Tragically these days, like sex for men with XXXX-large beer guts, it's all in the mind. The one drawback to my chosen career as Kate Brannigan, private eye, is that when it comes to cruising the mean streets of Manchester, it's anonymity that cuts it, not flamboyance.

A girl can still dream, though. So when Gerry Banks told me he'd lost his BMW Z3 roadster, one of only half a dozen currently in the country, an advance release that had cost him a small fortune to come by and which turned every head when he drove down the street, I understood why he spoke as if he was talking about a particularly close and beloved family member. If I'd been lucky enough to own one of those little beauties, I'd have probably replaced the bedroom wall with an up-and-over door so I could sleep with it. And if some rat had kidnapped my baby and held it to ransom, I'd have hired every investigator in the kingdom if it meant bringing my darling home to me.

Banks had revealed his pain behind the closed door of his office, a functional box on the upper floor of the custom-built factory where his company made state of the art electronic components for washing machines and dishwashers. The best you could call the view would be "uninspiring". But if, like Gerry Banks, all you could see was a hole in the car park where a scarlet roadster ought to be, it must have been heartbreaking.

"I take it that's the scene of the crime," I said, joining him by the window.

He pointed to the empty parking space nearest the door, the series of smooth curves that made up his features rearranging themselves into corrugated lines. "Bastard," was all he said.

I waited for a couple of minutes, the way you do when someone's paying their respects to the dead. When I did speak, my voice was gentle. "I'm going to need full details."

"Fine," he sighed, turning away and throwing himself miserably into his black leather executive chair. I was left with the bog-standard visitor's number in charcoal tweed and tubular metal. Just in case I didn't know who was the boss here.

Driving a Hard Bargain

"Take me through it from the beginning," I urged when he showed no sign of communicating further.

"He turned up on Tuesday morning at nine. He said his name was John Wilkins and he runs an executive valet service for cars. He gave me a business card and a glossy brochure. It names half a dozen top Manchester businessmen, quotes them and everything, all of them saying what a great job this Valet While-U-Work does." His voice was the self-justifying whine of a man desperate not to be seen as the five-star dickhead he'd been. He pushed a folded A4 sheet towards me, a business card lying on top of it. I gave them the brief glance that was all they deserved. Nothing that couldn't come out of any neighbourhood print-shop.

"So you agreed to let him valet your car?"

He nodded. "I gave him the keys and he promised to have it back by close of business. But he didn't." He clenched his jaw, bunching the muscles under his ear.

"And that's when you got the fax?"

He looked away, ostensibly searching for the piece of paper I knew was right under his hand. "Here," he said.

I picked it up. There was no identifying sender's fax number at the top of the sheet. "We've got your car. By this time Friday, you'll have £10,000. Fair exchange is no robbery. Yours faithfully, Rob It While-U-Work," I read. A villain with a sense of humour. "The price seems a bit steep," I said. "I thought the car only cost about twenty grand new."

"If you can get one. They're not officially released till next January, and there's already a two-year waiting list. Money can't buy a replacement. I'm not interested in common rubbish. You know where I live? Not in some poxy executive development. A sixteenth century converted chapel. There's not another one like it in the world. Anywhere. I want my car back, you understand. Without a scratch on it," Banks said, the ghost of his management skills starting to emerge from the shadows of his grief. "I'll have the money here tomorrow afternoon, and I want you to take care of the handover. The cash for the car. Can you handle that?"

I'm so used to middle-aged businessmen taking one look at my twenty-nine year old five feet and three inches and treating me like the tea-girl that it barely registers on the Brannigan scale of indignation any more. "I can handle it," I said mildly. "But wouldn't you rather get the car back *and* hang on to the cash?"

His eyebrows, half moon arcs like Paul McCartney's, concertina-ed into a frown. "You think you could do that? Without putting the car at risk?"

I gave him the stare I'd copied from Pacino. "I can try."

Like journalists, private eyes are only as good as their sources. Unfortunately our best ones tend to be people your mother would bar from the doorstep, never mind the house. Like my mechanic. Handbrake's no ordinary grease monkey. He learned his trade tuning up the wheels for a series of perfect getaways after his mates had relieved some financial institution of a wad they hadn't previously realised was surplus to requirements. He only got caught the once. That had been enough.

When he got out, he'd set himself up in a backstreet garage and gone straight. Ish. But he still knew who was who among the players on the wrong side of the fence. And as well as keeping my car nondescript on the outside and faster than a speeding bullet on the inside, he tipped me the odd wink on items he thought I might be interested in. It sat easier with his conscience than talking to Officer Dibble. He answered the phone just as I was about to give up. "Yeah?" Not a man to waste time or money on inessentials like chat. Or a receptionist.

"Handbrake, Brannigan." The conversational style was catching. "I'm working for a punter who's had his BMW Z3 ripped for a ransom. The guy called himself John Wilkins. Valet While-U-Work. Any ideas?"

"Dunno the name, but there's a couple of teams have tried it on," he told me. "A Z3, you said? I didn't think there were any over here yet."

"There's only a handful, according to the punter."

"Right. Rarity value, that's what makes it worth ransoming. Anything else, forget it – cheaper to let the car walk, cop for the insurance. I'll ask around, talk to the usual suspects, see what the word is."

Driving a Hard Bargain

I started the engine and slipped the car into gear at about the same time my brain did the same thing. A couple of minutes later, I was grinning at Gerry Banks' receptionist for the second time that morning. "Me again," I chirped. Nothing like stating the obvious to make the victim of your interrogation feel superior.

"Mr Banks has gone into a meeting with a client," she said in the bored sing-song you need to master before they let you qualify as a receptionist.

"Actually, it was you I wanted a word with." Ingratiating smile.

She looked startled. I'd obviously gone for a concept she was unfamiliar with. "Why?"

"I'm the investigator Mr Banks has hired to try and get his car back," I said. "I just wanted to ask you a couple of questions."

She shrugged.

"When the car valet bloke arrived, did he ask who the Z3 belonged to?"

She shook her head. "He said, could he have five minutes with Mr Banks concerning the on-going maintenance of his roadster. I buzzed Mr Banks, then sent him through."

"Those were his actual words? He said roadster?"

"That's right. Like Mr Banks always calls it."

I'd been afraid that's what she would say.

I was being ushered into the presence of my financial advisor when Handbrake rang me back. Not to talk about my pension plan, but to pick his brains. Whoever labelled women gossips never met Josh Gilbert, the man who knows the inside story on every player in the financial world up north. He waved me to one of the comfortable grey leather armchairs in his office while I wrestled the phone out of my bag and to my ear. "Handbrake," he said. "You got a problem I can't solve. Whoever's got your punter's motor, either they're not from around here, or they're new talent. So new nobody knows who they are."

"I had a funny feeling you were going to tell me that," I said. "I owe you one."

"I'll add it to your next service."

I hung up. This was beginning to look more and more like something very personal. I frowned and Josh shook his head in mock sorrow. "You never manage just one thing at a time, do you, Kate?"

"Woman's work, never done."

"Drink?"

"I'm not stopping. This is just a quick smash and grab raid. Gerry Banks, Compuponents. Who's got it in for him?"

The only thing in common between Gerry Banks' home and the flat whose bell I was leaning on was that they'd both been converted. Much as I hate gargoyles and draughts, I'd rather live in Banks' bijou residence than in this scruffy Edwardian rat-trap in the hinterland between the curry restaurants of Rusholme and the hookers of Whalley Range.

Eventually, the door opened on a woman in jeans faded to the colour of her eyes, a baggy chenille jumper and her early thirties. Dark blonde hair was loosely pulled back in a pony tail. She had the kind of face that makes men pause with their pints halfway to their lips. "Yeah?" she asked.

"Tania Banks?"

Her head tilted to one side and two little lines appeared between her perfectly groomed eyebrows. "Who wants to know?"

I held a business card at eye level. "I've come about the car."

The animation leaked out of her face like air from a punctured tyre. "I haven't got a car," she said, her voice grating and cold.

"Neither has your husband."

A muscle at the corner of her mouth twitched. "I've got nothing to say."

I shrugged. "Please yourself. I thought we could leave the police out of it, but if you want to play it the other way . . ."

"You don't frighten me," she lied.

"Maybe not, but I'm sure your husband knows people who would."

Her shoulders sagged, her mouth slackened in defeat. "You better come in."

172

Driving a Hard Bargain

The bedsit was colder and damper than the street outside in spite of the gas fire hissing at full blast. She perched on the bed, leaving the chair to me. "You left him three months ago," I said.

"I got tired of everybody feeling sorry for me. I got tired of him only ever coming home because the next Mrs Banks was out of town on a modelling assignment," she sighed, lighting a cheap supermarket cigarette.

"And you wanted a life. That's why you've been doing the part-time law degree," I said.

Her eyebrows flickered. "I finished the degree. I've just started the one-year course you need to be a solicitor."

"You don't get a grant." Some of my best friends are lawyers; I know about these things. "The fees are somewhere around four and a half grand. Plus you've got to have something to live on. Which you expected to get from the divorce settlement. Only, there's a problem, isn't there?"

"You're well informed," she said.

"It's my job. He's clever with money, your husband. On paper, he's potless. It's the offshore holding company that owns the car, the house, everything. He takes a salary of a few hundred a month. And the company pays for everything else. And it's all perfectly legal. On paper, he can't afford to pay you a shilling. So you decided to extract your divorce settlement by a slightly unorthodox route."

She looked away, studying the hand that held the cigarette. "Ten grand's a fraction of what I'm entitled to," she said softly. The admission of guilt didn't produce the usual adrenaline rush. She sighed again. "You have no idea the crap I've put up with over the years."

I submitted my account to Gerry Banks without a qualm. I'd done the job he asked me to do, and as far as I was concerned, he should be grateful. He'd asked me to handle the exchange, to make sure his car came back to him in one piece. It had been me who'd made the foolish offer to get the Z3 back without handing over the cash. And everybody knows that we women aren't up to the demanding job of being private eyes,

173

Val McDermid

don't they? Hardly surprising I wasn't able to live up to my promises.

Besides, we'll have forgotten each other inside six months. But I'll never forget the wind in my hair the night Tania Banks and my Inner Spiv cruised the M6 till dawn with the top down.

MOVING ON

Susan Moody

This variation on the perfect crime theme is well worth reading (at least) twice. Once to relish the fast-moving story for its own sake and a second time to appreciate the technical skill with which it is composed. The wit of Susan Moody's novels and stories has been much praised, but the cleverness with which she crafts her fiction is perhaps less often recognised. Here, she takes the risk of shifting the viewpoint of the story continually. In the space of a few pages, we have three sections narrated by Martin and three by Gerard, together with a lengthy newspaper report and a book review. In the hands of a less skilled practitioner, the effect would have been jerky and disjointed, but Moody manages to make it look easy, providing a reminder that although she is not one of our most prolific short story writers, she is one of the best.

i. Martin:

I see we're moving on. All three of us. Gerry and Susanna, who live in the big house opposite mine. And, as inevitably as Ivory follows Merchant, or Lybrand follows Coopers, me.

They put the "For Sale" sign up yesterday. I wonder where we'll go this time. I wouldn't mind being nearer London,

I must say. Or even *in* London. Kensington, maybe, or Notting Hill Gate. Holland Park. Somewhere in there. It's not as if the bastard can't afford it, not with the amount he must be making from those crappy books of his. Perhaps I should suggest it to him. Walk right up the path and knock on the door. Say: "Look here, Gerry, old man. How about the metropolis this time, hm? How about bloody London this time?"

And I know what he'd answer. He'd raise those trademark eyebrows of his. He'd curl that famous well-shaped lip. He'd say: "Have you taken a look at yourself recently, Marty? Do you know what a pathetic figure you've become?"

If he did, I could say yes, I do. I could say that I'm every bit as disgusted with the way I am these days as he is. With the crumpled look which seems to have settled over me. With the stink of fags and stale booze and unwashed armpits that I carry about with me.

I could add that I blame him for it, that it's all his fault. But what point would there be? I don't want to give him the satisfaction. Anyway, he knows.

You could argue that I should have got over it by now. That my behaviour is immature and I'm only using Anna's death as an excuse to waste my own life. Maybe you'd be right. Sixteen years ago and I still haven't come to terms with it. Still haven't moved on from where I was then. Loving not wisely but too well is always a mistake. It blinkers you. Holds you back.

You may be wondering what I meant by that opening sentence: *We're moving on . . .* It's quite simple, really. When they sell up, I sell up. When they move on, I move on. Like Rachel and Naomi, in the Bible. *Whither thou goest, I will go; and where thou lodgest, I will lodge.* If you didn't know the reason for it, you might find it quite touching. Boyhood chums and all that. Still friends after all these years.

Still enemies, after all these years would be nearer the mark.

We didn't start out like that. Not at all. When we first met at university, we fell into a friendship of the warmest kind. I'm not talking sex here, of course. I'm not talking gays or poofters or queers or whatever you want to call it, though I've got absolutely nothing against homosexuality, male *or* female. I'm talking friendship. Maybe even love. *Agape*, though, not *eros*. We were both freshers, both on the same staircase, both reading Eng. Lit. Both grammar school oiks. We fizzed with enthusiasm for poetry, for cultural thought and, yes, for the idea of literature at its highest level. We spent hours together talking, discussing, arguing about the merits of words over music or painting, about the difficulty of manipulating language into the expression of emotion. We both wanted to be writers in those days. Authors. Whatever the difference is.

In the course of that first year, he came to my home and met my family. I went to his. During term-time, we did everything together. Went out with girls (often the same ones, though consecutively rather than simultaneously), drank, worked, walked, talked. About the only activity we didn't share was screwing. No, we didn't do that but we certainly talked about it afterwards. Extensively. Compared notes. Awarded points.

That went on for nearly two years. Until the second long vacation, in fact. Then he got a summer job with one of those market research companies, and I was taken on for six weeks as a general dogsbody by one of the national dailies. Old boy network, not merit. My father knew somebody who knew somebody. It still worked like that, back then. We wanted to find a place to share, Gerry and I, but our funds didn't run to that. But at least we were both in London, so we were able to meet up most days.

It was in July that I met Anna. July 29th, to be exact.

ii. Gerard:

"I don't want to move again," Susanna said.

"We have to," I said.

"I just can't face it, Gerry. Not again."

"I can't write," I said. "I haven't written a decent word since he tracked us down."

"This is the best house we've had," she said. She squared her shoulders and stuck out her jaw and as usual, I experienced a surge of desire. We were sitting in bed reading the Sunday papers and the shoulder-squaring bit made her small breasts more prominent. Her nipples pushed against the dove grey satin of the nightdress she wore and made me want to fling aside the coloured supplements and the book review pages and yet again, as so many times over the years, make love to her.

Usually she was as eager as I was, but I knew that this morning it would be wiser to forgo the pleasures of the flesh, however mutual they might be. The men from the estate agent had arrived yesterday afternoon to erect the "For Sale" board outside our house and Susanna had been restive ever since.

"The best house," she repeated. "Gerry, I'm happy here. Truly happy. I really don't want to move."

"Even with that maniac living down the lane?"

"Even with that."

"You know why he does it, don't you?"

"I know what you've told me."

"He thinks I was having an affair with his bloody wife."

"But you weren't."

"You *know* I wasn't. I'm not even sure I liked her, let alone wanted to jump into bed with her. But will he believe that? Will he hell."

"Can't you just ignore him?"

"Of course I can't. It's absolutely impossible. And while he's around, I can't write. Which means, my precious sweetheart, that I can't earn a living."

"Can't you bribe him to go away?"

"I tried that once. He just laughed in my face. The trouble is, he earns a fair old whack himself. Or used to, before he started drinking so much. And when his parents died they left him quite a bit, too."

"Seven moves in ten years. I had enough of that with Daddy." Susanna's father was a military man.

"I know, darling, but what else can we do?"

"The garden," wailed Susanna. "And the friends I've made. The people here are so warm and friendly." Tears started to fall down her cheeks. "Maria," she snuffled. "I haven't had a friend as close as Maria since I left school."

"Darling." I took her little hand in mine. "I promise you

we'll find another house, just as nice as this. And other friends."

"How?" she demanded. She knuckled her eyes, looking as if she were about eight years old, instead of twenty more than that. "Wherever we go, he'll find us. He always has before. Every time I start to settle in, we're off again."

"I've been thinking about that," I said. "We could change our names, for a start."

"But you can't begin from scratch, Gerry. People wait for the new Gerard O'Connell the way they wait for the new Robert Ludlum or – or Danielle Steel." Even in her distress, my wife wasn't going to place me up there with the greats, with the Amises or the Rushdies. I didn't care. Her assessment of my talent just about matched my own and that wasn't particularly high. I made a hell of a lot of money and frankly, I wasn't too bothered about what the critics thought. You could say that I'd sold out, or you could say that I had moved on from my early unattainable goals, had come to terms with what I was, that I was an honest, even a happy, man, in that I made the very best use of what gifts I had.

Of course, in our university days, I had higher aspirations. Literature, no less. I was going to write the Great British Novel, the Great Global Novel. I was going to take the world by storm. And not just once, but many times as the years went by and I matured into Grand Old Manhood, as I drew round my more-than-worthy shoulders the mantle of literary genius.

Of course it didn't work out like that. I spent a year on the Great Novel, only to discover that in me, the seam of literary gold ran thin indeed. I mined it assiduously, buffed and polished it, spun it into fantastical filigree. Metaphor and allegory were my tools, myth and dream the scaffolding on which I erected my plot. Flimsy, you'll agree. Insubstantial. Far too slight to carry the burden of my pretensions. Nobody, in short, would touch it.

I found myself a series of part-time, dead-end jobs, the sort of thing which kept body and soul together but little more. In my spare time, I wrote another novel, and another. The publishers remained distinctly unenthusiastic and I grew more and more depressed. We'd have starved if Susanna had not found a job as a PA to some high-powered executive in the oil business.

Then one cold winter, just before Christmas, my darling wife came home from work and said she'd been given a bonus. Why didn't we, she asked, splash out, spoil ourselves? Forget the bills, and blow it all on a package holiday to somewhere warm? So that's what we decided to do. Of course, after the first euphoria, common-sense prevailed. Package holidays cost an arm and a leg and we only had a small bonus to spend. We listed everyone we knew who lived abroad and might be prepared to let us foist ourselves upon them for a fortnight, and finally came up with South Africa, where Susanna had cousins she hadn't seen for years. That's where we went.

The cousins – a couple from Surrey with two young children – farmed acres of dusty red soil under wide blue skies. They lived among people whose skins were the colour of aubergines and whose expectations dared not rise above the next meal for their children. They lived inside a heavily-walled and guarded compound, with a couple of fierce dogs prowling the perimeters of the grounds. There were cars, horses, tennis courts. There was a blue swimming pool and gardens kept green by constant watering. Conspicuous consumption. Conspicuous indifference.

While we were there, unrest bloomed in the cities. News came of bombs thrown, of troubles in Soweto, of houses burned and young men shot. It disturbed Susanna and me. The cousins said they had learned to live with it and we didn't like to ask at what price.

One afternoon, Susanna and I travelled by jeep to visit friends of friends of Susanna's parents. The house we visited was very similar to the one where the cousins lived and I thought then how strange it was that people could exist without worry in a situation of such contrast, such polarisation. We stayed the night, enjoying a barbecue out on the wide patio beneath stars far more significant than those we knew at home, served by silent young men with blank faces and expressive eyes.

The next day we drove back to the cousins' house. We would be leaving in two days time. We agreed that we had enjoyed this glimpse of an alien way of life but we would

not be sorry to return to our own much humbler existence.
Susanna said:

"Do you suppose it was it like this in India, during the
Raj?"

"No," I said. "In India, the two separate cultures existed side
by side. There was a lot of unfairness about the British rule, I'm
sure, but they did attempt to be benevolent. There was none of
this deliberate repression, this denial of the rights of others."

"I hate it," Susanna said, with a shiver. "There's something so
sinister about it. I'll never come back, at least, not while things
are the way they are."

But while I never came to terms with South Africa – as it
used to be under apartheid, I mean – I can't feel truly negative
about the place. If I sound utterly callous about this, I certainly
don't mean to, but it was entirely thanks to our visit that our
fortunes changed.

Thanks to the visit, and, of course, to old Marty. I might still
be working at some boring job during the day and trying, in my
spare time, to fashion the crystalline prose of which I knew I was
capable into something that a publisher would want to print, if
he hadn't invited me to his birthday party.

But he did. And it was there that I met a young woman who
was a commissioning editor with some publishing house. It was
there that, in fact, I met his Anna.

iii. Martin:

July 29th. The day I fell in love for the first – and it appears,
the last – time. Totally, irrevocably, head over heels. All that
crap. Anna was the light of my life, the icing on my cake,
the song in my heart, the fairy on my Christmas tree. All *that*
crap. I'd have crossed Saharas to see her, swum Hellesponts to
reach her. I sighed for her. I'd have died for her. I loved her.
The miracle of it was, that she loved me back.

She was a year older than I was. Just finished a degree at
Bristol. Filling in time before taking up the job she'd got in
one of the major publishing houses. Nothing grand. Secretarial

work. But it would lead on to better things, she said. It always does, she said. Publishing is dominated by women. I'm going to be one of them, she said.

And, in due course, she was.

When we went back for our final year, Gerry and I, things had altered between us. He'd met Susanna somewhere during the summer and was much occupied with her. I'd got Anna. He told me all about Susanna. I told him little or nothing about Anna. At that stage, she was too precious to be shared. Even with Gerry. Susanna visited him often, but I always went back to London to see Anna. She was preoccupied with her job, with learning the ropes, with working out how to get ahead. I was content just to be in her orbit. She had little time to spare and I was grateful when she spared it with me.

By the end of the summer term, Gerry and Susanna were engaged. As a wedding present, his parents bought them a flat in St John's Wood. An aunt or something gave him a large sum of money, and he told me he was going to take a year off to write his novel. I was happy for him. I thought that some day soon I'd introduce Anna to the two of them.

Somehow, I never did. There wasn't time. I got a job on my local newspaper. I'd stopped worrying about being a novelist. Pragmatic, that's me. I just didn't have what it takes. Dedication. Doggedness. Self confidence. I realised I wasn't a marathon man. More of a fifty yard dash man. The short rather than the long haul. Journalism suited me. I had plenty of the ratlike cunning that is a prerequisite of the job. I moved on. Up to Manchester, then down again to London. A stint on the foreign desk in Japan, another in Germany. Back to London. I got lucky. Wrote a piece or two which caught the attention of those who matter. Wrote theatre reviews for a prestigious magazine, then edited the book pages of a Sunday. Got asked to do the restaurant critiques. Became a columnist on one of the dailies. Appeared regularly on a bookish game show on Radio 4. Became, eventually, famous. Not for very much, I admit. Except drinking. Got kicked out of the Groucho once. Picked a fight with Peter Ackroyd. Made acerbic comments on TV about the finalists for the Booker Prize. Threw up at some literary award luncheon. The *enfant terrible* of the chattering classes.

Anna and I set up together. Bought a house in Hampstead. The place smelled of dry rot and mice, but I didn't care, as long as she was there with me. And she was. She loved me. In bed, or out of it. Adored me. As I adored her. Looking back, I can see that it's not good. A love like that spoils you for anyone else. She was my hostage to fortune.

We gave a party. A celebration. Anna's birthday. A book she'd commissioned had reached the Top Ten in the *Sunday Times* Best Seller List. My own collection of pieces was doing well on the non-fiction lists. I invited Gerry and Susanna, who were recently back from a trip to South Africa. He still hadn't managed to get published. Anna had looked at his books but said that though they had good bits in them, the whole was distinctly less than the sum of the parts. That he was a gnat straining at a fly. Something like that. I can't remember exactly how she put it but it summed poor Gerry up.

I noticed them at the party, talking together in a corner, Gerry and Anna. They were still there, looking serious, half an hour later. When they'd gone, when we were in bed, Anna said: "I think we could have a best seller on our hands."

"Who?" I said.

"Your mate. Your chum. Gerard O'Connell."

"Gerry? A best *seller*? He's been trying for years to get published. Can't even get onto the slush pile."

"He just might," Anna said, "turn out to be the new Wilbur Smith."

"What's wrong with the old one?"

She fitted herself against me, her long limbs cool. "He'll need editing, of course. He's got literary pretensions, but we'll soon sort him out."

And she was right. The first Gerard O'Connell, assisted by judicious and plentiful publicity, got into the Best Seller list. So did the second, and the third. And all the ones after that.

At first I didn't mind the time he spent with Anna. Just part of the job. They went down each year to the cottage in Wales which Gerry bought with the proceeds from the fourth or fifth book. Editing. Ten days, two weeks. It didn't occur to me that anything was going on. I mean, he had Susanna. She was devoted. He was uxorious. The happy couple. Call me naive, but it never bloody well crossed my mind.

iv. Gerard:

I told her, this Anna, whom Martin had not introduced to us before, what had happened in South Africa. How we'd come back to find the gate of the compound hanging open. How we'd realised there was something wrong when the dogs didn't come running from the house at the sound of our car. How we'd pushed open the front door and seen – well, *I'd* seen. I'd managed to push Susanna away before she could step inside the house, ordered her to stay in the car. The shock . . . just telling Anna about it brought everything back, all the horror of it. Limbs. Severed limbs. A child's head. Three fingers lying on a table. A tongue. Blood everywhere. Absolutely everywhere. I found bits of them scattered all through the house. Just bits. The girls, Susanna's cousin and the little girl, had been raped in the grossest kind of way and then hacked to pieces. The other two, the boy and his father, had been treated even worse. All I could think of was that if we'd been there, Susanna and I would have suffered the same fate.

I wouldn't let her into the house. We got away as fast as we could, to the police station, to the consulate. Susanna drove. I was incapable of holding the wheel. Shivering and weeping, and occasionally getting her to stop while I spewed up my guts at the side of the road. Oh, God. It was impossible to describe the horror of that house.

Until, that is, I met Anna. She persuaded me to write it down, to turn it into a story. She said that at worst, it would be therapy for me, at best, it might even be a publishable book.

She was right. By the time I'd finished writing it, I was already thinking of a plot for the second book. There was an incident in my childhood, on a visit to an uncle in New Zealand . . . The books went on from there. The new Gerard O'Connell became as much a fixture in the publishing calendar as the annual Dick Francis. Anna helped me. I freely admit that I wouldn't have got off the ground if it hadn't been for her. It was a strictly professional relationship, whatever Martin chose to believe. I'm not attracted by those big women with long legs and manes of sweeping black hair. They frighten me, actually. I'm always afraid that one day they'll open their wide gashes of mouths and swallow me whole. Susanna is a little thing who needs my protection and therefore makes me feel like a man. She doesn't ask for independence, or even equality. She is as happy to let me take the decisions for us both as I am to make them.

Anyway . . . it became a regular routine. I'd write the new book in first draft. Go through and produce a second draft, send it off to Anna for consideration, then hole up with the computer in our Welsh cottage to come up with a third draft. After which, Anna would join me down in Wales and we'd go through the book again, line by line, until it was as good as I – as *we* – could make it.

We were rich, Susanna and I. I loved all the trappings that went with the money, all the fame and adulation, the invitations, the appearances on TV, the requests for my opinion on almost any subject under the sun. I never heaved a sigh for the great literary novels I might have written. I had found my proper level and I rejoiced in it. I felt no need to justify myself, not in any way.

One year, the book was to be about a man living quietly in the house where he was born, which had been handed down through the generations. A few hundred acres, country pursuits, sense of duty, wife and kids, no surprises. And then, pow! into his life comes a dangerous stranger, demanding, insisting, threatening everything that our hero holds dear. If he is to regain his peace of mind, he has no choice but to deal with the matter. Gun running came into it. Brazilian gold. Beautiful temptresses. Even drugs, though I try to keep off the subject since market research has shown that my readers don't want to know about them except in the most general and sanitised form. Gun running . . . I went down to Wales to write the final chapters, taking with me, as part of my research, the Purdey my father had given me for my twenty-first birthday, and the Heckler & Koch P7K3 I borrowed from Martin which he had acquired in (according to him) rather strange circumstances while he was in Germany

The book went like a dream. I wrote ferociously, getting up early every day, working well into every night, existing on strong coffee and frozen meals. Every lunchtime, I went out for an hour with the guns, taking pot shots at crows and rabbits, experiencing for myself the pull and kick, noting the eye-hand coordination needed, the smell of the thing, the weight, the determination needed to aim at a target, to blow away a piece of vermin, be it animal or human. It was what gave my books that personal yet professional touch, according to Anna.

When I was ready, she came down to Wales to work on the typescript. As with Marty, all those years ago, we worked, we walked, we worked again. In the evening, we sat over a bottle or two of wine and talked, as always. I of my Susanna, she of her ambitions and of Martin. This time there was a new theme to her conversation: biological clocks, the running out of.

"I'm nearly thirty five," she said.

"Aren't we all?" I joked.

"Children," she said. "Until now, my career has been everything to me. I never thought I'd feel the urge to be a mother, but suddenly, I do."

"What will Marty think?" I asked.

"I'm afraid he won't like the idea. I'm afraid he won't want to share me. We love each other," she said simply, "we're everything to each other. We've always lived in each other's pockets, perhaps almost too much and I don't know how our relationship will stand the strain of enlarging the magic circle."

"It'll survive," I said.

"I'm sure it will. It would have to. I couldn't live without Martin." She picked up the H&K which was lying on the windowsill. "He's got a gun just like this."

"It's his, actually."

"Oh." Her mouth – that engulfing slash of a mouth – drooped. "Gerry, I'm so torn."

"Poor love," I said sympathetically.

"I mean, I really want a baby. Really *really*." Maybe she was a little pissed, maybe just being sincere. "But if anything happened to destroy the relationship between Marty and me, I might just have to kill myself." Before I could stop her, before I could do a damn thing about it, she had pointed the gun – laughing – at the side of her head and pulled the trigger.

Everyone knows you should never do that.

My fault. It was all my fault. I'm not usually so careless. Like anyone who's ever had anything to do with guns, I know how vital it is to remove the cartridges. Normally, I always do. This time . . . I could only plead pressure of work. I hadn't touched the damn thing for several days, since before Anna came down. And now – well, it was like South Africa all over again. She was dead long before she hit the floor.

v. Martin:

I might have bought it. Probably would have, if the next Gerard O'Connell hadn't featured a love affair between a man and his best friend's wife. Ostensibly, it was the usual bollocks about a bloke getting into and out of trouble in any political trouble-spot you cared to name. But this time, it was really a sex manual for retards. Lust in Leningrad. Sex and saunas in Sarajevo. Passion under the palm trees. An exposé, if you please,of his liaison with my wife. At the end of the book, she turns on him, spurns him, tells him she's moving on, that she loves her husband and it's all over. He picks up a gun – his best friend's gun, at that – and shoots her. "If I can't have you, no one else will," he grates. Gerry's heroes are good at grating.

I couldn't believe the brass neck of the man. Perhaps the results of the inquest, which, while noting his carelessness, exonerated him of any blame, made him feel that he was God. That he could get away with anything. It was clear that he'd seduced Anna, and when she tried to get away from him, his overweening vanity wouldn't allow it, and he'd shot her. I told the coroner this but he dismissed it. I wrote letters but nobody would take any notice. I spread the story among my pals in the newspaper world but they didn't want to know. Accused me of

Susan Moody

paranoia. I went to see Susanna, told her of my suspicions. She just laughed. Said I was jealous. Jealous? Of *Gerry*?

It was the perfect crime. He'd got away with it. Or he thought he had. That's when I decided to do something about it. Follow him. Haunt him. He'd know that I knew. He'd never get rid of me, until death did us part. Just as it had parted Anna and me. So I went where he went. Where he lodged, I lodged as well. Always there, down the road, round the corner, across the lane. A reminder that there's no such thing as a free fuck. Especially not with someone else's wife. I'm not even discussing the emptiness I feel. The despair. The hole she has left in my life. The hole I fill with alcohol. The bottomless pit.

Yes. I have become disgusting. Red faced. Coarse featured. My hands shake most of the time. My clothes are not clean. I don't know when I last had a bath. I'm not proud of it. I smoke too much – first thing I do when I wake is to light up. Drink too much – most of the time I sit among the whisky bottles and think about Anna. About the fairy on my Chernobylled Christmas tree. About the icing on my poisoned cake, the dirge in my heart. When I don't think about her, I think about him.

And when I'm not thinking, I'm packing up my increasingly meagre possessions, ready to follow where they lead, ready to go where they go. Moving on.

vi. Gerard:

All right. It was insensitive of me. Damned insensitive. Even Susanna said so and she doesn't often criticise me. But Anna herself had taught me all about what she called the Fuck Mother factor. That is, the answer to the timid author's question: *But if I write that, what will Mother say?* A best-selling author, she told me, has no room for sensitivity. He is shameless, he uses the material to hand and never mind who objects. So I fucked Mother. Used Anna's accident. I know she'd have wanted me to. I dressed it up with an affair, added some steamy sex scenes in various places, had the man kill her when she spurns him, and then get away with it. He suffers, of course. He tries to expiate the crime and in the end dies nobly, sacrificing himself to save someone else. The critics thought it was the best book I'd done.

It honestly didn't occur to me for a single minute that old Martin would take it as some kind of confession. Anna and I had a professional relationship, nothing more. She wasn't my type. We could have shared a bed naked, and I doubt if I'd have raised a stand. She simply didn't turn me on. Martin can't believe that. Cock-ridden himself, he believes everyone else must have been too. He thinks I killed her for spurning my advances. I've tried to explain but he won't believe me.

The persecution started about ten years ago. Susanna and I decided to move, just because I couldn't bear the guilt of what had happened and wanted to get out of the house. When Marty turned up living practically next door, I thought at first that it was a bizarre coincidence. I found it impossible to write with him so close. Naturally I felt guilty enough about what had happened without him there all the time as well, a living breathing reproach. We sold up again before the place had even been redecorated and moved elsewhere. So did he. The third time, I realised it was deliberate. I've tried to choose places he'll hate; I've tried swearing the agents, the solicitors, my publishers to secrecy; I've even bought a new house without selling the old. It's no good; he always manages to track us down.

I've tried to persuade Susanna to move to Hollywood: it wouldn't be difficult, with the first three books under option to one of the major studios and principal photography already started on the first. Keanu Reeves, Sandra Bullock and Gene Hackman – it should be good. But Susanna doesn't want to leave England, or her family. The trappings of fame and fortune don't mean a lot to her, frankly. Our houses are always fairly modest, and so are our cars, though we splash out on holidays and own a place in Italy. I've told her that if we moved on, went upmarket, we'd be able to shake Marty off just because he couldn't afford the kind of place that we can, but she says that after what we saw in South Africa, she'd feel uncomfortable in anything too grand. As a matter of fact, so would I.

Now, with the 'For Sale' sign up once more, with the

wellsprings of creation dried up yet again, as I think of that
poor sad bastard just down the lane, the quiet reproach on his
face, the hatred I sense in his heart, I realise that something
must be done. I've thought about it for a while. I've plotted it
as though it were a book.

Given the condition he's sunk to, given the vices he increasingly
gives in to, the fags, the booze, I don't think that it will be too terribly
difficult. I know him too well. Starts the day on a fag, ends it at the
wrong end of a whisky bottle. I can see exactly how to do it. I can't
think why I didn't do it before.

The Southbury & District Chronicle

At the inquest today on Martin Blowers, 44, a
journalist, of Linstead Lane, the Coroner paid particular
attention to the deceased's lifestyle as having a
significant bearing on his death. Peter Atkinson,
landlord of the Three Feathers in the High Street,
stated that Blowers was a regular customer and on the
night in question, had consumed at least six pints of
bitter followed by several double brandies. Asked if, in
his opinion, the deceased was drunk, Atkinson said that
he would not necessarily have said drunk but certainly
well lit up. Since he knew that Mr Blowers, who lived
about half a mile from the pub, would not be driving
home, he had not considered it necessary to limit the
amount served to him. In answer to a question from
the Coroner, he agreed that with hindsight, it might
have been wiser to refuse to serve him.

Mrs Maggie Clifford stated that she had worked as
a domestic for Mr Blowers for the past eight months,
ever since he had bought the house in Linstead Lane.
She said that in her opinion, he was an accident
waiting to happen. Asked by the Coroner to explain this
remark, she said that for instance, she had come in
one morning to find water coming through the ceiling
and on going upstairs, had found the bath taps full on
and Mr Blowers slumped asleep on the landing outside

the bathroom. Just a week earlier, he had put a pan of
water to boil on the gas stove and then forgotten about
it. If a neighbour hadn't noticed the smoke and called
the fire brigade, anything might have happened. She
said that the deceased often forgot to lock the doors
of his house at night, despite the fact that in recent
weeks, he had been burgled twice. She added that the
way he left lighted cigarettes lying around, it was a
miracle that he hadn't either burned down the house or
blown himself to bits long before this.

Mr Gerard O'Connell, the well-known thriller writer and
a neighbour of Mr Blowers, stated that he had known
the deceased since their undergraduate days, and that
in the past three or four years, Mr Blowers' physical
condition had deteriorated markedly. Asked to what he
attributed this deterioriation, Mr O'Connell said that in
his opinion, following the death of his wife, Mr Blowers
had developed a serious drink problem.
    Coroner: In other words, he was an alcoholic?
    O'Connell: I don't think that would be overstating the
case.
    Asked if he had noticed any other indications of
impaired faculties, Mr O'Connell mentioned his friend's
recent inability to meet deadlines at work, and an
increasing degree of memory impairment. He agreed
with Mrs Clifford that Mr Blowers often failed to
secure his house at night, and said that it was he who
had, on a recent occasion, seen smoke pouring from
the kitchen windows and had called the fire services
before entering the house to find Mr Blowers asleep on
the sofa in the living room. He added that it had been
extremely difficult to rouse him.
    Coroner: In your opinion, was he suffering, on that
occasion, from the effects of alcohol?
    O'Connell: In my opinion, for what it is worth, yes,
he was.

Susan Moody

Evidence was given by the chief fire officer who stated that on the night in question, the gas fire in the living room had been turned full on but not lit. Given Mr Blowers' habit of smoking as soon as he woke up, before getting out of bed, he gave it as his opinion that by the time Mr Blowers had struck the match for his first cigarette of the day, the whole house would have been full of gas fumes.

Verdict: accidental death, aggravated by the problems of a reliance on alcohol.

From the *Sunday Times*:

Perfect Crime
by Gerard O'Connell

Steven Laidlaw

Another thumping good read, the new Gerard O'Connell is very much the mix as before, with plenty of action in various exotic locales, the statutory gorgeous bimbo, evil villains, and right, in the end, overcoming might. In this one, our hero – all jutting jaw and steely eyes – seeks to revenge the death of his best friend in what seems to be a domestic gas explosion. Best friend is a burned-out wreck who is slowly drinking and smoking himself into an early grave. Although the police consider it an accident, our hero is convinced that the forces of evil – in this case, the Yakuza, whom his dead friend investigated during his days as a journalist in Tokyo – are responsible, having sneaked into the house while the best friend was sleeping off his most recent binge, turned on the gas fire and somehow forgotten to light it. There are plenty of the sort of thrills and spills which only O'Connell can provide, with much convincing technical detail, elegant sex, graphic fisticuffs and the hero conquering all. But there is more to it than this. In his most recent books, O'Connell has definitely moved on from producing mere hokum; there is a dark and satisfying edge to his recent work which transcends the genre in which he has chosen to make his mark and offers

192

Moving On

glimpses of a real – I might even suggest a great – novelist trying very hard to fight his way out from under.

(Steven Laidlaw's new thriller, *Root of Evil*, will be published by Hodder & Stoughton in September £15.99)

HERBERT IN MOTION

Ian Rankin

"Sometimes you struggle with a short story for days or weeks," says Ian Rankin. "And then there are times when everything seems to go right. Like Herbert In Motion." *He wrote the story in a single day, although I doubt whether readers would ever guess it. The pace is just right: swift, but with no hint of breathlessness. Of all the crime writers to have emerged in the past decade, I would rate Rankin, along with the under-estimated Chaz Brenchley, as perhaps the most talented exponent of the short story. Rankin enjoyed writing* Herbert In Motion *and says simply, "I wish it was like this all the time." Rankin is often bracketed with the tough "realistic" school of younger British crime writers, but the real reason why he is, I believe, destined to become a major force in the genre is that his strengths are the conventional yet all-important ones: imagination, insight and a determination to keep the reader entertained.*

My choices that day were twofold: kill myself before or *after* the Prime Minister's cocktail party? And if after, should I wear my Armani to the party, or the more sober YSL with the chalk stripe?

The invitation was gilt-edged, too big for the inside pocket of my workaday suit. Drinks and canapes, six pm till seven. A minion had telephoned to confirm my attendance, and to brief me on protocol. That had been two days ago. He'd explained that among the guests would be an American visiting London, a certain Joseph Hefferwhite. While not quite spelling it out – they never do, do they? – the minion was explaining why I'd been invited, and what my role on the night might be.

"Joe Hefferwhite," I managed to say, clutching the receiver like it was so much straw.

"I believe you share an interest in modern art," the minion continued.

"We share an interest."

He misunderstood my tone and laughed. "Sorry, 'share an interest' was a bit weak, wasn't it? My apologies."

He was apologising because art is no mere interest of mine. Art was – is – my whole life. During the rest of our short and one-sided conversation, I stared ahead as though at some startling new design, trying to understand and explain, to make it all right with myself, attempting to wring out each nuance and stroke, each variant and chosen shape or length of line. And in the end there was . . . nothing. No substance, no revelation; just the bland reality of my situation and the simple framing device of suicide.

And the damnation was, it had been the perfect crime.

A dinner party ten years before. It was in Chelsea, deep in the heart of Margaret Thatcher's vision of England. There were dissenters at the table – only a couple, and they could afford their little grumble: it wasn't going to make Margaret Hilda disappear, and their own trappings were safe: the warehouse conversion in Docklands, the BMW, the Cristal champagne and black truffles.

Trappings: the word seems so much more resonant now.

So there we were. The wine had relaxed us, we were all smiling with inner and self-satisfied contentment (and wasn't that the dream, after all?), and I felt just as at home as any of them. I knew I was there as the Delegate of Culture. Among the merchant bankers and media figures, political jobsworths and "somethings" (and dear God, there was an estate agent there too, if memory serves – *that* fad didn't last long), I was there to reassure them that they were composed of something more lasting and nourishing than mere money, that they had some meaning in the wider scheme. I was there as the curator to their sensibilities.

In truth, I was and am a Senior Curator at the Tate Gallery, with special interest in twentieth-century North American art (by which I mean paintings: I'm no great enthusiast of modern sculpture, yet less of more radical sideshows – performance art, video art, all that). The guests at the table that evening made the usual noises about artists whose names they couldn't recall but who did "green things" or "you know, that horse and the shadow and everything". One foolhardy soul (was it the estate agent?) digressed on his fondness for certain wildlife paintings, and trumpeted the news that his wife had once bought a print from Christie's Contemporary Art.

When another guest begged me to allow that my job was "on the cushy side", I placed knife and fork slowly on plate and did my spiel. I had it down to a fine art – allow me the pun, please – and talked fluently about the difficulties my position posed, about the appraisal of trends and talents, the search for major new works and their acquisition.

"Imagine," I said, "that you are about to spend half a million pounds on a painting. In so doing, you will elevate the status of the artist, turn him or her into a rich and sought-after talent. They may disappoint you thereafter and fail to paint anything else of interest, in which case the resale value of the work will be negligible, and your own reputation will have been tarnished – perhaps even more than tarnished. Every day, every time you are asked for your opinion, your reputation is on the line. Meanwhile, you must propose exhibitions, must plan them – which often means transporting works from all around the world – and must spend your budget wisely."

"You mean like, do I buy four paintings at half a mil each, or push the pedal to the floor with one big buy at two mil?"

I allowed my questioner a smile. "In crude economic terms, yes."

"Do you get to take pictures home?" our hostess asked.

"Some works – a few – are loaned out," I conceded. "But not to staff."

"Then to whom?"

"People in prominence, benefactors, that sort of person."

"All that money," the Docklands woman said, shaking her head, "for a bit of paint and canvas. It almost seems like a crime when there are homeless on the streets."

"Disgraceful," someone else said. "Can't walk along the Embankment without stumbling over them."

At which point our hostess stumbled into the silence to reveal that she had a surprise. "We'll take coffee and brandy in the Morning Room, during which you'll be invited to take part in a murder."

She didn't mean it, of course, though more than one pair of eyes strayed to the Docklanders, more in hope than expectation. What she meant was that we'd be participating in a parlour game. There had been a murder (her unsmiling husband the cajoled corpse, miraculously revivified whenever another snifter of brandy was offered), and we were to look for clues in the room. We duly searched, somewhat in the manner of children who wish to please their elders. With half a dozen clues gathered, the Docklands woman surprised us all by deducing that our hostess had committed the crime – as indeed she had.

We collapsed thankfully onto the sofas and had our glasses refilled, after which the conversation came around to crime – real and imagined. It was now that the host became animated for the first time that night. He was a collector of whodunnits and fancied himself an expert.

"The perfect crime," he told us, "as everyone knows, is one where no crime has been committed."

"But then there *is* no crime," his wife declared.

"Precisely," he said. "No crime . . . and yet a crime. If the body's never found, damned hard to convict anyone. Or if something's stolen, but never noticed. See what I'm getting at?"

I did, of course, and perhaps you do, too.

The Tate, like every other gallery I can think of, has considerably less wall-space than it has works in its collection. These days, we do not like to cram our paintings together (though when well done, the effect can be breathtaking). One large canvas may have a whole wall to itself, and praise be that Bacon's triptychs did not start a revolution, or there'd be precious little work on display in our galleries of modern art. For every display of gigantism, it is blessed relief, is it not?, to turn to a miniaturist. Not that there are many miniatures in the Tate's storerooms. I was there with an acquaintance of mine, the dealer Gregory Jance.

Jance worked out of Zurich for years, for no other reason, according to interviews, than that "they couldn't touch me there". There had always been rumours about Jance, rumours which started to make sense when you tried to balance his few premier league sales (and therefore commissions) against his lavish lifestyle. These days, he had homes in Belgravia, Manhattan's Upper East Side, and Moscow, as well as a sprawling compound on the outskirts of Zurich. The Moscow home seemed curious until one recalled stories of ikons smuggled out of the old Soviet Union and of art treasures taken from the Nazis, treasures which had ended up in the hands of Politburo chiefs desperate for such things as hard dollars and new passports.

Yes, if even half the tales were true, then Gregory Jance had sailed pretty close to the wind. I was counting on it.

"What a waste," he said, as I gave him a short tour of the storerooms. The place was cool and hushed, except for the occasional click of the machines which monitored air temperature, light, and humidity. On the walls of the Tate proper, paintings such as those we passed now would be pored over, passed by with reverence. Here, they were stacked one against the other, mostly shrouded in white sheeting like corpses or Hamlet's ghost in some shoddy student production. Identifier tags hung from the sheets like so many items in a lost property office.

"Such a waste," Jance sighed, with just a touch of melo-drama. His dress sense did not lack drama either: crumpled cream linen suit, white brogues, screaming red shirt and white silk cravat. He shuffled along like an old man, running the rim of his panama hat through his fingers. It was a nice performance, but if I knew my man, then beneath it he was like bronze.

Our meeting – *en principe* – was to discuss his latest crop of "world-renowned artists". Like most other gallery owners – those who act as agents for certain artists – Jance was keen to sell to the Tate, or to any other "national" gallery. He wanted the price hike that came with it, along with the kudos. But mostly the price hike.

He had polaroids and slides with him. In my office, I placed the slides on a lightbox and took my magnifier to them. A pitiful array of semi-talent dulled my eyes and my senses. Huge graffiti-style whorls which had been "in" the previous summer in New York (mainly, in my view, because the practitioners tended to die young). Some neo-cubist stuff by a Swiss artist whose previous work was familiar to me. He had been growing in stature, but this present direction seemed to me an alley with a brick wall at the end, and I told Jance as much. At least he had a nice sense of colour and juxtaposition. But there was worse to come: combine paintings which Rauschenberg could have constructed in kindergarden; some not very clever geometric paintings, too clearly based on Stella's "Protractor" series; and "found" sculptures which looked like Nam June Paik on a very bad day.

Throughout, Jance was giving me his pitch, though without much enthusiasm. Where did he collect these people? (The unkind said he sought out the least popular exhibits at art school graduation shows.) More to the point, where did he sell them? I hadn't heard of him making any impact at all as an agent. What money he made, he seemed to make by other means.

Finally, he lifted a handful of polaroids from his pocket. "My latest find," he confided. "Scottish. Great future."

I looked through them. "How old?"

He shrugged. "Twenty-six, twenty-seven."

I deducted five or six years and handed the photos back. "Gregory," I said, "she's still at college. These are derivative – evidence she's learning from those who have gone before – and stylised, such as students often produce. She has talent, and

I like the humour, even if that too is borrowed from other Scottish artists."

He seemed to be looking in vain for the humour in the photos.

"Bruce McLean," I said helpfully, "Paolozzi, John Bellany's fish. Look closely and you'll see." I paused. "Bring her back in five or ten years, *if* she's kept hard at it, *if* she's matured, and *if* she has that nose for the difference between genius and sham . . ."

He pocketed the photos and gathered up his slides, his eyes glinting as though there might be some moisture there.

"You're a hard man," he told me.

"But a fair one, I hope. And to prove it, let me buy you a drink."

I didn't put my proposition to him quite then, of course, not over coffee and sticky cakes in the Tate cafeteria. We met a few weeks later – casually as it were. We dined at a small place in a part of town neither of us frequented. I asked him about his young coterie of artists. They seemed, I said, quite skilled in impersonation.

"Impersonation?"

"They have studied the greats," I explained, "and can reproduce them with a fair degree of skill."

"Reproduce them," he echoed quietly.

"Reproduce them," I said. "I mean, the influences are there." I paused. "I'm not saying they *copy*."

"No, not that." Jance looked up from his untouched food. "Are you coming to some point?"

I smiled. "A lot of paintings in the storerooms, Gregory. They so seldom see the light of day."

"Yes, pity that. Such a waste."

"When people could be savouring them."

He nodded, poured some wine for both of us. "I think I begin to see," he said. "I think I begin to see."

That was the start of our little enterprise. You know what it was, of course. You have a keen mind. You are shrewd and discerning. Perhaps you pride yourself on these things, on always being one step ahead, on knowing things before those around you have perceived them. Perhaps you, too, think yourself capable of the perfect crime, a crime where there is no crime.

There was no crime, because nothing was missing from the quarterly inventory. First, I would photograph the work. Indeed, on a couple of occasions, I even took one of Jance's young artists down to the storerooms and showed her the painting she'd be copying. She'd been chosen because she had studied the minimalists, and this was to be a minimalist commission.

Minimalism, interestingly, proved the most difficult style to reproduce faithfully. In a busy picture, there's so much to look at that one can miss a wrong shade or the fingers of a hand which have failed to curl to the right degree. But with a couple of black lines and some pink waves . . . well, fakes were easier to spot. So it was that Jance's artist saw the work she was to replicate face to face. Then we did the measurements, took the polaroids, and she drew some preliminary sketches. Jance was in charge of finding the right quality of canvas, the correct frame. My job was to remove the real canvas, smuggle it from the gallery, and replace it with the copy, reframing the finished work afterwards.

We were judicious, Jance and I. We chose our works with care. One or two a year – we never got greedy. The choice would depend on a combination of factors. We didn't want artists who were *too* well known, but we wanted them dead if possible. (I had a fear of an artist coming to inspect his work at the Tate and finding a copy instead.) There had to be a buyer – a private collector, who would *keep* the work private. We couldn't have a painting being loaned to some collection or exhibition when it was supposed to be safely tucked away in the vaults of the Tate. Thankfully, as I'd expected, Jance seemed to know his market. We never had any problems on that score. But there was another factor. Every now and then, there would be requests from exhibitions for the loan of a painting – one we'd copied. But as the curator, I would find reasons why the work in question had to remain at the Tate, and might offer, by way of consolation, some other work instead.

Then there was the matter of rotation. Now and again – as had to be the case, or suspicion might grow – one of the copies would have to grace the walls of the gallery proper. Those were worrying times, and I was careful to position the works in the least flattering, most shadowy locations, usually with a much more interesting picture nearby, to lure the spectator away. I would watch the browsers. Once or twice, an art student would come along and sketch the copied work. No one ever showed a moment's doubt, and my confidence grew.

But then . . . then . . .

We had loaned works out before, of course – I'd told the dinner party as much. This or that cabinet minister might want something for the office, something to impress visitors. There would be discussions about a suitable work. It was the same with particular benefactors. They could be loaned a painting for weeks or even months. But I was always careful to steer prospective borrowers away from the twenty or so copies. It wasn't as though there was any lack of choice! For each copy, there were fifty other paintings they could have. The odds, as Jance had assured me more than once, were distinctly in our favour.

Until the day the Prime Minister came to call.

This is a man who knows as much about art as I do home brewing. There is almost a glee about his studious ignorance – and not merely of art. But he was walking around the Tate, for all the world like a dowager around a department store, and not seeing what he wanted.

"Voore," he said at last. I thought I'd misheard him. "Ronny Voore. I thought you had a couple."

My eyes took in his entourage, not one of whom would know a Ronny Voore if it blackballed them at the Garrick. But my superior was there, nodding slightly, so I nodded with him.

"They're not out at the moment," I told the PM.

"You mean they're in?" He smiled, provoking a few fawning laughs.

"In storage," I explained, trying out my own smile.

"I'd like one for Number 10."

I tried to form some argument – they were being cleaned, restored, loaned to Philadelphia – but my superior was nodding again. And after all, what did the PM know about art? Besides, only one of our Voores was a fake.

"Certainly, Prime Minister. I'll arrange for it to be sent over."

"Which one?"

I licked my lips. "Did you have one in mind?"

He considered, lips puckered. "Maybe I should just have a little look . . ."

Normally, there were no visitors to the storerooms. But that morning, there were a dozen of us posed in front of the two Ronny Voores, *Shrew Reclining* and *Herbert in Motion*. Voores was very good with titles. I'll swear, if you look at them long enough, you really can see – beyond the gobbets of oil, the pasted-on photographs and cinema stubs, the splash of emulsion and explosion of colour – the figures of a large murine creature and a man running.

The Prime Minister gazed at them in something short of thrall. "Is it 'shrew' as in Shakespeare?"

"No, sir, I think it's the rodent."

He thought about this. "Vibrant colours," he decided.

"Extraordinary," my superior agreed.

"One can't help feeling the influence of Pop Art," one of the minions drawled. I managed not to choke: it was like saying one could see in Beryl Cook the influence of Picasso.

The PM turned to the senior minion. "I don't know, Charles. What do you think?"

"The shrew, I think."

My heart leapt. The Prime Minister nodded, then pointed to *Herbert in Motion*. "That one, I think."

Charles looked put out, while those around him tried to hide smiles. It was a calculated put-down, a piece of politics on the PM's part. Politics had decided.

A fake Ronny Voore would grace the walls of Number 10 Downing Street.

I supervised the packing and transportation. It was a busy week for me: I was negotiating the loan of several Rothkos for an exhibition of early works. Faxes and insurance appraisals were flying. American institutions were *very* touchy about lending stuff. I'd had to promise a Braque to one museum – and for three months at that – in exchange for one of Rothko's less inspired creations. Anyway, despite headaches, when the Voore went to its new home, I went with it.

I'd discussed the loan with Jance. He'd told me to switch the copy for some other painting, persisting that "no one would know."

"He'll know," I'd said. "He wanted a Voore. He knew what he wanted."

"But why?"

Good question, and I'd yet to find the answer. I'd hoped for a first floor landing, or some nook or cranny out of the general view, but the staff seemed to know exactly where the painting was to hang – something else had been removed so that it could take pride of place in the dining-room. (Or one of the dining rooms, I couldn't be sure how many there were. I'd thought I'd be entering a house, but Number 10 was a warren, a veritable Tardis, with more passageways and offices than I could count.)

I was asked if I wanted a tour of the premises, so as to view the other works of art, but by that time my head really did ache, and I decided to walk back to the Tate, making it as far as Millbank before I had to rest beside the river, staring down at its sludgy flow. The question had yet to be answered: why did the PM want a Ronny Voore? Who in their right mind wanted a Ronny Voore these days?

The answer, of course, came with the telephone call.

Joe Hefferwhite was an important man. He had been a senator at one time. He was now regarded as a "senior statesman", and the American president sent him on the occasional high-profile, high-publicity spot of troubleshooting and conscience-salving. At one point in his life, he'd been mooted for president himself, but of course his personal history had counted against him. In younger days, Hefferwhite had been a bohemian. He'd spent time in Paris, trying to be a poet. He'd walked a railway line with Jack Kerouac and Neal Cassady. Then he'd come into enough money to buy his way into politics, and had prospered there.

I knew a bit about him from some background reading I'd

204

done in the recent past. Not that I'd been interested in Joseph Hefferwhite . . . but I'd been *very* interested in Ronny Voore. The two men had met at Stanford initially, then later on had met again in Paris. They'd kept in touch thereafter, drifting apart only after "Heff" had decided on a political career. There had been arguments about the hippie culture, dropping out, Vietnam, radical chic – the usual '60s US issues. Then in 1974 Ronny Voore had lain down on a fresh white canvas, stuck a gun in his mouth, and gifted the world his final work. His reputation, which had vacillated in life, had been given a boost by the manner of his suicide. I wondered if I could make the same dramatic exit. But no, I was not the dramatic type. I foresaw sleeping pills and a bottle of decent brandy.

After the party.

I was wearing my green Armani, hoping it would disguise the condemned look in my eyes. Joe Hefferwhite had *known* Voore, had seen his style and working practice at first hand. That was why the PM had wanted a Voore: to impress the American. Or perhaps to honour his presence in some way. A political move, as far from aesthetics as one could wander. The situation was not without irony: a man with no artistic sensibility, a man who couldn't tell his Warhol from his Whistler . . . this man was to be my downfall.

I hadn't dared tell Jance. Let him find out for himself afterwards, once I'd made my exit. I'd left a letter on my desk. It was sealed, marked personal, and addressed to my superior. I didn't owe Gregory Jance anything, but hadn't mentioned him in the letter. I hadn't even listed the copied works – let them set other experts on them. It would be interesting to see if any *other* fakes had found their way into the permanent collection.

Only of course I wouldn't be around for that.

Number 10 sparkled. Every surface was gleaming, and the place seemed nicely undersized for the scale of the event. The PM moved amongst his guests, dispensing a word here and there, guided by the man he'd called Charles. Charles would whisper a brief to the PM as they approached a group, so the PM would know who was who and how to treat them. I was way down the list apparently, standing on my own (though a minion had

205

attempted to engage me in conversation: it seemed a rule that no guest was to be allowed solitude), pretending to examine a work by someone eighteenth century and Flemish – not my sort of thing at all.

The PM shook my hand. "I've someone I'd like you to meet," he said, looking back over his shoulder to where Joe Hefferwhite was standing, rocking back on his heels as he told some apparently hilarious story to two grinning civil servants who had doubtless been given their doting orders.

"Joseph Hefferwhite," the PM said.

As if I didn't know; as if I hadn't been avoiding the man for the past twenty-eight minutes. I knew I couldn't leave – would be reminded of that should I try – until the PM had said hello. This was all that had kept me from leaving. But now I was determined to escape. The PM, however, had other plans. He waved to Joe Hefferwhite like they were old friends, and Hefferwhite broke short his story – not noticing the relief on his listeners' faces – and swaggered towards us. The PM was leading me by the shoulder – gently, though it seemed to me that his grip burned – over towards where the Voore hung. A table separated us from it, but it was an occasional table, and we weren't too far from the canvas. Serving staff moved around with salvers of canapés and bottles of fizz, and I took a refill as Hefferwhite approached.

"Joe, this is our man from the Tate."

"Pleased to meet you," Hefferwhite said, pumping my free hand. He winked at the PM. "Don't think I hadn't noticed the painting. It's a nice touch."

"We have to make our guests feel welcome. The Tate has another Voore, you know."

"Is that so?"

Charles was whispering in the PM's ear. "Sorry, have to go," the PM said. "I'll leave you two to it then." And with a smile he was gone, drifting towards his next encounter.

Joe Hefferwhite smiled at me. He was in his seventies, but extraordinarily well-preserved, with thick dark hair that could have been a weave or a transplant. I wondered if anyone had ever mentioned to him his resemblance to Blake Carrington . . .

He leaned towards me. "This place bugged?"

I blinked, decided I'd heard him correctly, and said I wouldn't know.

"Well, hell, doesn't matter to me if it is. Listen," he nodded towards the painting, "that is some kind of sick joke, don't you think?"

I swallowed. "I'm not sure I follow."

Hefferwhite took my arm and led me around the table, so we were directly in front of the painting. "Ronny was my friend. He blew his brains out. Your Prime Minister thinks I want to be *reminded* of that? I think this is supposed to tell me something."

"What?"

"I'm not sure. It'll take some thinking. You British are devious bastards."

"I feel I should object to that."

Hefferwhite ignored me. "Ronny painted the first version of *Herbert* in Paris, '49 or '50." He frowned. "Must've been '50. Know who Herbert was?" He was studying the painting now. At first, his eyes flicked over it. Then he stared a little harder, picking out that section and this, concentrating.

"Who?" The champagne flute shook in my hand. Death, I thought, would come as some relief. And not a moment too soon.

"Some guy we shared rooms with, never knew his second name. He said second names were shackles. Not like Malcolm X and all that, Herbert was white, nicely brought-up. Wanted to study Sartre, wanted to write plays and films and I don't know what. Jesus, I've often wondered what happened to him. I know Ronny did, too." He sniffed, lifted a canape from a passing tray and shoved it into his mouth. "Anyway," he said through the crumbs, "Herbert – he didn't like us calling him Herb – he used to go out running. Healthy body, healthy mind, that was his creed. He'd go out before dawn, usually just as we were going to bed. Always wanted us to go with him, said we'd see the world differently after a run." He smiled at the memory, looked at the painting again. "That's him running along the Seine, only the river's filled with philosophers and their books, all drowning."

He kept looking at the painting, and I could feel the memories

207

welling in him. I let him look. I wanted him to look. It was more his painting than anyone's. I could see that now. I knew I should say something . . . like, "that's very interesting", or "that explains so much". But I didn't. I stared at the painting, too, and it was as though we were alone in that crowded, noisy room. We might have been on a desert island, or in a time machine. I saw Herbert running, saw his hunger. I saw his passion for questions and the seeking out of answers. I saw why philosophers always failed, and why they went on trying despite the fact. I saw the whole bloody story. And the colours: they were elemental, but they were of the city, too. They *were* Paris, not long after the war, the recuperating city. Blood and sweat and the simple, feral need to go on living.

To go on living.

My eyes were filling with water. I was about to say something crass, something like "thank you", but Hefferwhite beat me to it, leaned towards me so his voice could drop to a whisper.

"It's a hell of a fake."

And with that, and a pat on my shoulder, he drifted back into the party.

"I could have died," I told Jance. It was straight afterwards. I was still wearing the Armani, pacing the floor of my flat. It's not much – third floor, two bedrooms, Maida Vale – but I was happy to see it. I could hardly get the tears out of my eyes. The telephone was in my hand . . . I just had to tell *some*body, and who could I tell but Jance?

"Well," he said, "you've never asked about the clients."

"I didn't want to know."

"Maybe I should have told you anyway. It would save this happening again."

"Jance, I swear to God, I nearly died."

Jance chuckled, not really understanding. He was in Zurich, sounded further away still. "I knew Joe already had a couple of Voores," he said. "He's got some other stuff too – but he doesn't broadcast the fact. That's why he was perfect for *Herbert in Motion*."

"But he was talking about not wanting to be reminded of the suicide."

"He was talking about *why* the painting was there."

"He thought it must be a message."

Jance sighed. "Politics. Who understands politics?"

I sighed. "I can't do this any more."

"Don't blame you. I never understood why you started in the first place."

"Let's say I lost faith."

"Me, I never had much to start with. Listen, you haven't told anyone else?"

"Who would I tell?" My mouth dropped open. "But I left a note."

"A note?"

"In my office."

"Might I suggest you go retrieve it?"

Beginning to tremble all over again, I went out in search of a taxi.

The night security people knew who I was, and let me into the building. I'd worked there before at night – it was the only time I could strip and replace the canvases.

"Busy tonight, eh?" the guard said.

"I'm sorry?"

"Busy tonight," he repeated. "Your boss is already in."

"When did he arrive?"

"Not five minutes ago. He was running."

"Running?"

"Said he needed a pee."

I ran too, ran as fast as I could through the galleries and towards the offices, the paintings a blur either side of me. There was a light in my superior's office, and the door was ajar. But the room itself was empty. I walked to the desk and saw my note there. It was still in its sealed envelope. I picked it up and stuffed it into my jacket, just as my superior came into the room.

"Oh, good man," he said, rubbing his hands to dry them. "You got the message."

Ian Rankin

"Yes," I said, trying to still my breathing. Message: I hadn't checked my machine.

"Thought if we did a couple of evenings it would sort out the Rothko."

"Absolutely."

"No need to be so formal though."

I stared at him.

"The suit," he said.

"Drinks at Number 10," I explained.

"How did it go?"

"Fine."

"PM happy with his Voore?"

"Oh yes."

"You know he only wanted it to impress some American? One of his aides told me."

"Joseph Hefferwhite," I said.

"And was he impressed?"

"I think so."

"Well, it keeps us sweet with the PM, and we all know who holds the purse-strings." My superior made himself comfortable in his chair and looked at his desk. "Where's that envelope?"

"What?"

"There was an envelope here." He looked down at the floor.

I swallowed, dry mouthed. "I've got it," I said. He looked startled, but I managed a smile. "It was from me, proposing we spend an evening or two on Rothko."

My superior beamed. "Great minds, eh?"

"Absolutely."

"Sit down then, let's get started." I pulled over a chair. "Can I let you into a secret? I detest Rothko."

I smiled again. "I'm not too keen myself."

"Sometimes I think a student could do his stuff just as well, maybe even better."

"But then it wouldn't be *his*, would it?"

"Ah, there's the rub."

But I thought of the Voore fake, and Joe Hefferwhite's story, and my own reactions to the painting – to what was, when all's said and done, a copy – and I began to wonder . . .

210

THE COST OF LIVING

Andrew Taylor

The amoral but appealing William Dougal first appeared in Caroline Minuscule, *which earned for Andrew Taylor the CWA John Creasey Memorial Award for the best first crime novel of its year. Since then, Dougal has become established as a quirky and distinctive series character and a particular virtue of the books is that Taylor never allows them to become formulaic. Until now Dougal has never featured in a short story and I am delighted that* Perfectly Criminal *has provided Taylor with the opportunity to rectify that omission at long last.* The Cost Of Living *has all the strengths of the Dougal novels: a neat yet unusual story-line, convincing characterisation and that poignancy which is so characteristic of Taylor's writing.*

Everything takes twice as long when you're in a hurry. Add panic to haste and time becomes more elastic still, a noose around eternity.

In the end William Dougal despaired of finding a gap in the traffic. He pushed the Honda into the endless stream of cars travelling south down Kew Road. A Mercedes braked sharply, its horn blaring like an angry trumpet.

Thank God the traffic was moving. It was mid morning so the worst of the Monday rush hour was over. The long high wall of Kew Gardens slipped by on the right. A few minutes later, the cars ahead slowed for the Richmond roundabout. *Can't you bloody hurry?*

The world through the windscreen belonged elsewhere: shops on either side of the street; smears of dirty snow on gutters and roofs; pedestrians and cyclists weaving through the traffic; parked cars and a delivery van partly blocking the road. Dougal glanced at the phone and wondered yet again whether he should call the police.

If only this hadn't been his day off. If only he had got up earlier. If only he had stayed in London last weekend. He shivered violently. The car hadn't warmed up yet.

This is my fault. I should have phoned Alan on Saturday.

At last he was on the Twickenham Road. The traffic was beginning to move faster, slipping past the railway on the left and the recreation ground on the right. The Honda rolled over Twickenham Bridge, over the dull, seagull-haunted waters of the Thames.

The Twickenham Road hit a series of roundabouts and at length became the Chertsey Road instead. It was dual carriageway here. Dougal moved into the outside lane and pushed the car well over the speed limit. There was the possibility – probability? – that he was too late, far too late. Better not to think of that.

And then the question of blame. It was all very well saying that a private investigator was merely an agent acting within certain ethical constraints on behalf of a client. It wasn't Dougal's fault that Alan hadn't liked the information Dougal had brought him. Truth wasn't always desirable: facts could be awkward, clumsy things with sharp corners; small wonder, then, that many people preferred the rounded edges and streamlined shapes of convenient fictions. Not Alan, though.

It wasn't Dougal's fault, either, that he liked Alan. It happened that way sometimes, and with the most unlikely people: a spark of shared humanity leapt from one to the other, connecting if only for an instant what age and background usually divided.

There were roadworks near the junction with Hounslow Road, complete with temporary traffic lights and long queues. Dougal hammered the steering wheel in frustration. Once more he glanced at the phone. As he reached out his left hand for it, the lights changed and the cars ahead of him began to inch forwards. No point in calling the police – with any luck he'd be there before them.

Besides, what if this were a false alarm? Alan would never forgive him for making a fuss. Alan hated looking ridiculous. That was part of the problem. That was why he'd hired Dougal in the first place.

By now the traffic was moving with some speed. The start of the M3 loomed up ahead. At Sunbury Cross roundabout, however, Dougal swung right and accelerated hard into the Staines Road. Half a mile later he made the sharp left-hand turn into Roth Road.

Roth had neither beginning nor end. Once upon a time it had been a village. Few traces were left. Sandwiched between reservoirs and the motorway, Roth was a state of mind as much as a place: a miniature suburb within a suburb, clinging to the tenuous remnants of its old identity. Alan lived in one of the older houses beyond the church.

Dougal drove over the bridge that crossed the river, a tiny tributary of the Thames. Alan's house was set back from the road and sheltered from the eyes of strangers by a privet hedge in need of trimming. Dougal turned into the drive. The house, which stood sideways to the road, was late-Victorian with more recent extensions sprouting in several directions. Alan had bought the place just after his retirement and spent thousands doing it up. He had installed three bathrooms, each with a bidet. ("Don't use them, mind, but Susie likes them.") There were double-glazed windows and solar heating panels. He had built a garage block, the newest of the extensions, with room for two large cars and a workshop at the side.

"It's funny," he had said to Dougal on Friday evening, when Dougal told him the news. "I did a lot of carpentry before I retired. Any brains I got are in my hands. Used to make beds, chests of drawers even. And when I retired, I thought I'd have all the time in the world for it. But it didn't work out that way." He poured himself some more brandy, slopping a few drops on a table he had made himself. "Nothing ever turns out how you think it's going to, does it? There's always a price to pay." He stared at Dougal over the rim of his glass. "Still, it's the same for everyone, I suppose. No sense in grumbling."

Dougal braked sharply and the car skidded on the gravel. He got out, leaving the keys in the ignition. The house loomed, a dream turned sour, against the blank winter sky: the windows were dirty; the rendering, once painted a brilliant white, was smudged with green; the flowerbeds on either side of the front door were thick with weeds. It was a cold day, and Dougal wished he had brought his coat.

"You have to take the consequences," Alan had said on Friday evening. "No point in whingeing about it. I'll pay your bill before you go, all right?"

"There's no hurry. The company will send you an invoice. That's what they usually do."

"It's up to you." Alan had swallowed another mouthful of brandy. "'Permanent Peace of Mind,'" he said, quoting the motto of Custodemus, the company Dougal worked for. "That's a laugh."

Dougal hadn't laughed then and he wasn't laughing now. He pressed the doorbell which chimed somewhere in the house. He tried the door, which was locked. He rang the bell again, stepped back from the door and looked up at the windows of the house. No sign of movement. The curtains were drawn back. There was a burglar alarm, not a Custodemus model, under the eaves.

He walked quickly along the side of the house, peering into the two windows he passed. The first gave him a view of the little room where he had sat with Alan on Friday. Alan called it his den. The bottle of brandy still stood on the filing cabinet. Above the desk were framed photographs of the two shops he had once owned, one in Staines, the other in Shepperton High Street.

"Hardware – DIY: that's what they call them nowadays," Alan had said. "But I was an ironmonger – that's the real word. That's what my old dad was. The Staines shop was his." The eyes behind the glasses were bright and moist.

Dougal pushed aside the memory. The next window belonged to the kitchen: a long thin room, expensively gloomy with fumed

oak, wrought iron and panels of leaded glass. The sinks and the
draining boards were piled with dirty crockery. Open tins and
frozen-food wrappings littered the work surfaces.

He reached the garage. The wide up-and-over door was closed.
Without much hope, he twisted the handle. It turned. The door
slid back into the roof space with a metallic rumble.

"Shit," said Dougal.

Alan's Rover was still there. The space beside it was empty.
Dougal felt the bonnet of the car as he passed: it was cold.

There were two doors at the back of the garage. Dougal tried
the one which led to the house. It was locked. But the other door
was slightly ajar.

The workshop, Dougal guessed. He gave the door a sharp
push. It swung back, but stopped abruptly halfway through its
arc. Dougal stepped into the doorway.

Oh Christ. No.

Alan Rushwick was hanging by a thin blue nylon rope from
one of the tie beams that held the roof together. Except that
it wasn't Alan any more. It was no more him than an empty
house is a home.

Unwelcome details flooded into Dougal's mind and lodged in
his memory. Alan was wearing the same clothes as on Friday:
brown corduroy trousers, a baggy cardigan and a checked
shirt; and his scuffed maroon-leather slippers lay untidily on
the concrete floor, one on its side. The body bulged against
the clothes as potatoes bulge against the sack containing them.
Alan's lank grey hair had fallen forward over his face. The lips
and the tips of the ears were a bluish purple. There were streaks
of dried blood at the base of the nostrils. The tongue had been
forced out, poking in the direction of Dougal, and the hands
were clenched. It looked as if the noose had been made not
with a knot but with an old-fashioned brass ring which had
lodged under the angle of the left jaw.

Primitive, Dougal thought, and very efficient. And at that
precise instant he noticed something else, something which did
not belong in Alan's workshop: the strong, fresh smell of a
woman's perfume.

Dougal pushed the door as hard as he could. There was a

gasp, high and sharp, on the edge of a scream. He grabbed the handle, stepped into the room and pulled the door back.

"Good morning, Mrs Rushwick."

"Who the hell are you?" Susie Rushwick was breathing fast, one hand raised to fend him off, the other touching her white throat as if showing on her own neck the precise spot where the brass ring was pressing into her husband's. "What are you doing here?"

"I'm doing a job for Mr Rushwick."

She lowered her hands. Susie Rushwick was a tall woman, much the same size as Dougal, with dark hair and very long legs. She was dressed for business in jeans and an open cashmere coat. "I've only just got here. God, what a thing to come home to."

"Where's your car?"

"None of your business." She glanced sideways through long lashes at him. "A friend dropped me off. Do you think it – he – do you think it was an accident?"

"Do you?"

"You read these stories about middle-aged men." She moistened her lips. "You know, they say it increases the pleasure if a man half strangles himself when . . ."

"Does he look as if he was on the verge of having an orgasm when he died?" Dougal asked.

"*I* don't know, do I?"

Dougal moved into the workshop and looked around. The woman watched. She seemed not to have recognised him. She hadn't asked about the nature of the job he was doing for her husband; perhaps she already knew.

The body did not move. Now Dougal was nearer to it, he noticed a smell of excrement mingling with Susie Rushwick's perfume.

"I – I need to make a phone call," she said.

"The police?"

She shrugged. "I suppose so. It seems so pointless."

"They usually like to be notified in cases of suspected murder."

"What? Are you out of your tiny mind? If it wasn't an accident, he topped himself. It's obvious."

"It would only be obvious if he'd left a note. Have you found one?"

Susie Rushwick hugged the overcoat around her body. "As it happens, no." She stared vaguely around the room. "But lots of suicides don't leave notes."

"But I don't think many suicides practise levitation."

"What are you on about now?"

Dougal nodded towards the body. Alan had been a small man. His feet dangled nearly three feet above the ground. There was a hole in one of his socks.

"How did he get up there, fix the rope, put the noose round his neck and hang himself at that height? If it was suicide, there'd be something he'd kicked aside, something he'd stood on. But there isn't." Dougal nerved himself and touched the right hand balled into a tight little fist: it felt very cold. "So if it was suicide, it must have been levitation." He swung round to look at her. "Don't you agree?"

The aggression seeped away from Susie's face. She wore bright red lipstick, applied in a way to make the lips look more generous than they really were. The colour served to emphasise the underlying pallor of the skin.

"Listen, I've been away for ten days." Her voice had become soft and low, almost seductive. "I only got here a few minutes before you did. He wasn't in the house so I thought he must be in here." She hesitated, choosing her words with care. "The door to the workshop was shut. When I opened it, it hit something – that stool, see?" She pointed at a tall, paint-stained wooden stool that stood beside the workbench several yards from the body. "I picked it up, I had to, didn't I, or I couldn't have got into the room. And it wasn't until I'd moved it that I realised—"

She broke off with a little sob. Her eyes flickered towards Dougal. Then she turned away, her shoulders heaving, and extracted a wad of tissues from a duffel bag made of soft black leather which was standing on the workbench.

Dougal stared at her. "Was Paul Newland with you?"

Susie Rushwick whirled round. "Have you been sticking your nose into my affairs? Who the fuck are you?"

Dougal dug a card out of the top pocket of his jacket. He

handed it to her and watched her lips moving very slightly as she read: *Custodemus – Permanent Peace of Mind – William Dougal – Private Investigation Division.*

"Are you telling me Alan hired you to *spy* on me?"

Dougal nodded.

"What did you tell him?"

"I'm sorry," Dougal said untruthfully. "I can't tell you that. Client confidentiality."

Susie Rushwick moved slowly towards him. For a moment he wondered whether she might intend to attack him. He tensed himself, ready for fight or preferably flight.

"So he knew. The bastard knew."

"Only since Friday. He didn't know for sure until then."

"I know what you're thinking but you're quite wrong. It's—"

"It doesn't matter what I think," interrupted Dougal. "But I have to warn you that it's company policy to cooperate fully with the police."

"And what's that supposed to mean?"

"I'll have to tell them exactly how I discovered the body. I'll have to tell them that you were here. I'll have to tell them that I couldn't understand how Mr Rushwick could have hanged himself. Not until you explained about the stool, that is." He glanced from the congested face of his former client to the cosmetically disguised face of his former client's wife. "They'll ask me why I'm here. And of course I'll have to tell them Mr Rushwick hired me, and why. The simplest thing would be to give them a copy of my report."

"What's in it?"

"The usual stuff. Photographs of you and Paul Newland. A detailed breakdown of your movements in the seven days up to last Friday."

"It meant nothing – it was just a fling. Alan must have known it wasn't serious."

"It wasn't just a fling. The weekend before last you were at an antiques fair. Paul Newland and you stayed there as man and wife. The chambermaid remembered the pair of you staying twice before over the last twelve months. I've got photocopies of the hotel register to prove it."

Her face twisted in disgust. "I hope it gave you a thrill."

"You spent three extra nights at the hotel and did a bit of business at a country house sale while you were there. On the Wednesday of last week you both came back to London. During the day you went to your shop in Staines, and at night you drove back to Newland's flat in Ealing. On Thursday evening you went out to dinner at an Italian restaurant called La Ventura. The waiter said you had three bottles of wine between you. By the end of the evening, you were talking rather loudly about how you wanted to get a divorce as quickly as possible so you could marry Mr Newland. The only problems seemed to be financial, didn't they? Mr Rushwick owned everything including the lease of your shop."

"You'll tell the police all that? You bastard."

"Company policy, I'm afraid."

There was a moment's silence. Unspoken words hung in the cold air between them. Susie was probably in her late thirties, and she was still very good-looking. Her good looks had won her a doting husband, a comfortable home, her own subsidised business and a handsome boyfriend who looked younger than she did.

"Do you know," Alan had said just before Dougal left him on Friday evening. "Me and Susie, we haven't made love for nearly two years." He had been in his fifties but looked an old man. "I don't think she ever really enjoyed it, not with me at any rate. Now she's always too tired, or it's her time of the month, or she's got a headache. You know. So I've stopped asking." He'd looked at Dougal, his face stern. "You don't want to hear all this, do you? And what's the point in talking about it? I've made my bed and I must lie on it."

Susie stirred. The smell of her perfume grew stronger. She moved slowly nearer to Dougal and touched his arm in a gesture that was almost a caress.

"Listen – he killed himself. It's as plain as the nose on your face. You didn't know Alan like I did. He'd cut off his nose to spite his face. If he hasn't left a note it's just so he could cause more problems when he's gone. Problems for me." She glanced at the corpse and quickly looked away. "Couldn't we talk somewhere else?"

Andrew Taylor

"Maybe I should phone the police now."

"No – wait a moment. Can we come to an arrangement? There's no need to say you've seen me here. It'd be much simpler, wouldn't it?" She looked at her watch. "Paul will be outside in a few minutes."

She was taller than Alan had been, younger and fitter. According to Alan, she took care to keep herself fit. She even went to karate classes. Physically she would have been perfectly capable of stringing up her husband and trying to make it look like suicide.

And morally?

"I bet Alan didn't remember to pay you," Susie said brightly. "Still, no harm done." She stretched out her arm and dug a red-tipped hand into the leather duffel bag, which was still standing open on the workbench. She produced a roll of notes and fanned them out like playing cards: tens and twenties and fifties. "There's fifteen hundred pounds there. Would that do for starters? Cash is easier than cheques, I often think. I do a lot of my business in cash. Of course if it's not enough your company can always invoice for whatever's owed." She tried the effect of a smile. "Take it – no need for a receipt."

Dougal wasn't looking at the smile or the money but at Alan's face.

The talons dipped back into the handbag. "Actually, I've got another thousand here. Twenty-five hundred: can't say fairer than that, can I?"

Dougal held out his hand. "I don't know. I just don't know."

With indecent haste she put the money into the palm of his hand and folded his fingers over it. Her hands were warm and sticky with sweat. "There'll be more, I promise. Look – the important thing is the stool. I'll put it back where – where I found it. OK?"

Dougal shrugged. "I'd better ring the police." He went out into the garage, saying over his shoulder, "I'll use my mobile: it's in the car."

"Just a minute." Though still low, the voice now held an unmistakable note of command. It was surprising what a little

220

bit of money could buy. Dougal heard the scrape of the stool's legs as Susie moved it across the room and the clatter of wood on concrete as she pushed it over. A moment later she joined him in the garage.

"There's one or two things I need to get from the house," she told Dougal. "It won't matter if you don't phone right away, will it? I shan't be a moment."

Dougal felt the rolls of notes in his trouser pocket and nodded.

Susie let herself into the house by the door from the garage. On the threshold she turned and bestowed another smile on Dougal. When the door closed behind her he walked through the garage and on to the gravel. It was even colder outside than in the workshop.

She needed to repair her make-up, he thought; the crocodile tears had caused several small blemishes to its perfection. More importantly, she would want to lay her hands on Dougal's report, assuming Alan had left it somewhere easily accessible. Forewarned was forearmed. And almost certainly there would be other things – passbooks to joint accounts, perhaps; portable valuables which she would prefer not to be included in the valuation of Alan's estate; or items which might interest the police if they searched the house. With luck she would be at least five or ten minutes.

Dougal opened the door of the Honda. He slipped the phone into his pocket and took the Polaroid camera from the bag on the back seat. Shielding it from the windows of the house, he returned to the workshop, where he photographed the body and its sur-roundings. He pushed the Polaroid into the pocket of his trousers, the same pocket which held the notes, to finish developing.

He was lucky in his timing. As he was putting the camera in the Honda, he heard a car pulling up in the road. Fragments of red glowed through the green of the privet. Dougal strolled down the drive.

Paul Newland was sitting in his Mazda, a red soft top, drumming his fingers on the steering wheel. Dougal tapped on the passenger-side window. The window slid down. Newland switched off Bruce Springsteen and stared at Dougal.

"I wonder if I could have a word." Dougal passed one of his business cards into the car.

"What about?"

"Your relationship with Mrs Rushwick. And the sudden death of her late husband."

Newland blinked. Then he opened his door, extracted himself from the car and marched round to Dougal. He was a big man with sleek fair hair, a small skull and very blue eyes. Dougal knew that he worked as a salesman for a garage in Shepherd's Bush which did a brisk and possibly suspicious trade in second-hand cars. He was wearing the suede jacket which Susie had bought him last week.

"Now what is this? And where's Susie?"

"You'd better see Mr Rushwick."

"See him *dead*?"

Dougal took out the Polaroid and showed it to him.

"Oh my God." Newland studied the photograph for a moment. "How – how did it happen?"

"That's the question. See that stool on the floor? When I got here a few minutes ago, it wasn't there. I actually saw Mrs Rushwick putting it underneath the body."

"But why would she do that?"

"Otherwise there would be nothing Mr Rushwick could have climbed on to reach the noose."

"He must have had something."

Dougal ignored him. "So the police will want to speak to Mrs Rushwick."

At last Newland understood. "They won't think she killed him, surely?"

'Why not? She had the opportunity, she certainly had the means, and as for the motive, well, I imagine she's Mr Rushwick's sole beneficiary: and of course, now he's dead, she can marry you. I think that's her general idea."

"Now look—"

"I'll have to tell the police about her moving the stool. They'll draw their own conclusions."

"This is nothing to do with me." Newland backed away as if Dougal had suddenly become infectious. "Nothing at all."

"I don't blame you." Dougal stared thoughtfully at the Polaroid. "Still, it's up to you, really. I'm going to phone the police."

He nodded pleasantly to Newland and walked up the drive. Before he reached the Honda, he heard the virile roar of the Mazda's starter motor. He glanced over his shoulder in time to see the red car streaking across the mouth of the drive. At that moment the front door opened.

"Was that Paul?" demanded Susie. "What's he think he's playing at?"

"I don't know."

"But I need him to drive me. I can't take Alan's car. I can't exactly phone for a taxi. Perhaps you—"

"I need to phone the police. Anyway, we shouldn't be seen together."

Susie frowned at him. "I suppose you're right." She came outside, her body lopsided because of the large black bag slung over her right shoulder.

"I think I saw a bus stop near the church."

"Oh for heaven's sake." She flounced down the drive.

"Susie," Dougal said.

She stopped and turned round. "What?"

"Do be careful."

She twitched her shoulders and scurried towards the road. Dougal walked back to the garage and through to the workshop. Alan's cardigan had deep pockets. Holding his nose, Dougal gingerly investigated the pocket on the right and found a small brown envelope. It was addressed to the coroner. He left it in the pocket.

Dead bodies made Dougal uncomfortable for all sorts of reasons so he went back outside. He patted his trouser pocket and felt the comfortable shape of £2500. In the other trouser pocket was a letter he had received that morning. He took it out and read it once more.

Dear William Dougal,

It was nice of you to listen to me. You didn't say much,

either, which I appreciated, because there was nothing much to say. I've thought it through and I think the best thing for all concerned is if I take the easy way out. I never much fancied growing old, anyway.

You should get this on Monday morning. If no one's found me before then, you can tell the police there's a letter for the coroner in the pocket of my cardigan. The cardigan I'll be wearing. Sorry to be such a nuisance.

Susie can have the money and live happily ever after with her fancy man. Except that she won't and he won't. But that's their affair. Nothing's for free in this world, is it?

All the best,
Alan Rushwick.

Dougal folded the letter and put it carefully away. Time to call the police: delay wouldn't make Alan any less dead. Dougal took out his phone. It was a cold day, so cold it brought tears to his eyes.

CHOOSE YOUR POISON

Tony Wilmot

*Tony Wilmot was a regular contributor to the long
series of CWA anthologies edited by the late Herbert
Harris and his presence among the contributors to
this book provides a welcome link with previous
collections of members' work.* Choose Your Poison
*is a new story which is a good example of his style
and technique. Wilmot is a craftman who specialises
in the well-made crime short story with a pleasing
twist at the end. Small wonder that the television series*
Tales Of The Unexpected *made much use of his work.
His best stories display an ingenuity to match that of
Roald Dahl.*

Her hand shook ever so slightly as she held the bulbous end of
the glass tube in the gas flame; thirty seconds was needed. She
checked the second-hand of her wristwatch.

On the workbench beside her were two other glass tubes,
slotted into a holder, and a beaker of colourless liquid.

Celia was alone in the laboratory; the staff had long since
left. Only the security man remained, but he wouldn't think
it odd for her to be working late even though she was the
company's MD.

Satisfied that the liquid was at the correct consistency, she
poured a dozen or so drops into the beaker; then gave the beaker

a few swirls. Next, she dipped the needle of a hypodermic syringe into it and drew up 3cc.

Her pulse quickened. The final stage had arrived. There's still time to stop, she told herself; still time to try to patch up her marriage to Jim . . . but did Jim want to try?

From the pocket of her white overalls she took a tissue; wrapped inside it were three gelatinous capsules, the kind the company used for its dietary vitamin products.

She was still hesitating. Do it, she told herself, *do it*.

Into each capsule she injected 1cc, then gave them a fresh coating of gelatine and placed them in the refrigerator to harden.

Now, everything she had used must be washed thoroughly; there had to be no trace of anything. Finally, she put the capsules in the paper-tissue again, looked round the lab. Had she forgotten anything? No, she hadn't.

The next morning she telephoned Jim at his pied-à-terre.

"Jim? Oh, it's me—" God, she thought, I'm doing it again, humbling myself. She had to be more assertive. "Can you and Ja – your actress friend – come over this morning? Yes, it *is* important; no, I can't tell you what it's about, not over the 'phone, but I think I have a solution to our mutual problem. Right, twelve noon then."

After she put the receiver down she realised she was trembling. Get a grip, she chided herself. *You* are the MD of a health foods firm and an enterprise awards winner; *he* is a philandering cheapskate; and *she* is nothing more than a trophy bimbo.

She checked that the drinks cabinet was well stocked, tidied the room, emptied the ashtrays, combed her hair and fixed her make-up. Then she began to clockwatch.

At last the doorbell went.

Be casual, Celia commanded herself; don't give that tarty homebreaker the satisfaction of thinking you are jealous.

But the hurt began the moment Jim walked into the apartment with the unlikely-named Jacie Starr in tow. Jim had never been very discriminating about his dalliances . . . a Page Three girl, a waitress, a film publicist, and now this ambitious trollop who had a bit part in the TV serial he was directing.

Until now Celia had done what was expected of wives who

Choose Your Poison

moved in Jim's "sophisticated" circle – by pretending that whatever he did was fine by her.

Jim flung himself in a chair. Now, what was so important that it couldn't be discussed over the 'phone?

"First, let's all have a drink." Celia was aware she was playing for time. "I've got Scotch, Scotch, or Scotch."

Her husband sighed. Was this going to take long? He and Jacie had a dubbing session at the studio before lunch.

"Not long," Celia said, handing round the glasses. She drank quickly from hers, hoping it would calm her nerves. "I thought we could reach an amicable settlement, Jim."

"I've told you my terms for a divorce. A fifty-fifty split."

Celia's heart raced; she took another drink. "You really expect me to hand over all I've worked for – just like that?"

"Just like that. Half of all our joint property and assets."

Cold fury seeped through her as she stared at her husband sprawled in the chair with that infuriating grin of his. She said: "By 'joint' you mean, of course, my property, my assets . . . I built up my business, single-handed. I bought the villa in Italy; and I paid for this apartment. What have you bought, Jim, apart from your golf clubs and sports car?"

Jacie Starr's eyes narrowed, vindictively. "You sound bitter, Celia dear. Jim's entitled to half and you know it."

"That's the attraction my husband has for you, isn't it – what he'll get from a divorce settlement."

"Being bitchy doesn't suit you, Celia," her husband said.

"Oh sorry," said Celia. "Mustn't upset poor Jacie, must we." A pulse throbbed in her temple. Avoid stressful situations, her doctor had warned her during the last consultation – and here she was, in the middle of a verbal minefield.

"Jacie loves me in a way you've never done, Celia. Makes me feel . . . alive; something I haven't felt in years."

Celia forced a laugh. "What soap did you get that little speech from? You're deluding yourself, Jim. She's like all your other bimbos – on the make." Could he be right, she asked herself; had she neglected him, their marriage, for her work? If she had, it hadn't been deliberate; she had done it for both of them; surely he had understood that?

227

Jim rose. "Look, we haven't got all day; get to the point."

Celia took the paper tissue from her bag and opened it out on the coffee table. She said:

"Three standard-type capsules, the kind used for vitamins, sleeping draughts—"

Jacie Starr, her tone waspish, said: "Aren't you sleeping well, dear? Jim and I don't have any problem – except that Jim doesn't let me spend much time asleep, the demon."

Ignoring the barb, Celia went on:

"Three capsules, all identical . . . except that one of them contains a poison which is fatal in fifteen minutes. I know, because I made it up in the lab myself. And only we three know about it."

"Your wife has hidden depths, Jim." Jacie Starr's tone was light, but her eyes had darkened.

Celia breathed in deeply. "What I propose is . . . we all meet in Jim's editing-room, at the studios, at eleven tonight. Then we each pick a capsule – and swallow it.

"If it's me who gets the poison, then Jim will be a wealthy widower . . . free to marry you, Jacie. If *you* get it, then Jim and I can try to make a go of our marriage." She had their undivided attention now.

"And if it's Jim . . . then Jacie and I will have to make new lives for ourselves."

There was a silence. Jim laughed hollowly. "Is this some kind of macabre joke, Celia?"

"No joke."

He stared into his glass. "So you're suggesting that we should risk killing ourselves in your lovers' lottery?"

"Nicely put, Jim. Yes, I am." She waited. "Well?"

"I think it's insane," her husband said. "Me, too," said Jacie Starr.

"But is it?" Celia asked. "We're mature adults, in charge of our own destinies, responsible to nobody but ourselves. And, let's face it, none of us will be a great loss to the world. What's more, there'll be no need for a messy divorce."

"It's ingenious, Celia, I'll give you that . . . but it's flawed."

Reading his eyes, Celia added: "Ah, you're thinking that the police would think it was murder . . ."

"Too right they would."

"Well, I've got an answer to that," Celia said. "Before we take the capsules, we each write a suicide note. Then, after it's all over, the two who survive destroy their suicide notes and leave. The victim – whichever one of us it is – will be found later, along with his or her suicide note."

Her husband gave her a keen glance. "You appear to have thought of everything."

"I think so, yes. Well, are you game?"

Jacie Starr was on her feet now; a sudden pallor emphasised her black eyeliner. She said:

"Jim, can't you see what her cunning little mind is cooking up. *She's* dispensed these capsules – so *she* knows which one has the poison."

"Well?" Jim said. "She has a point. How do we know you haven't marked them in some subtle way?"

"I haven't marked them; I give you my word."

"Your word isn't good enough, Celia," Jim said. "This isn't a game – we'd be gambling with our lives." He checked his watch. "Sorry, but we must be on our way. See you in the divorce cou—"

"Wait," Celia cut in. "Suppose I said you two could select your capsules first – and I'd have the one that's left . . ."

Her husband stared at her. "You'd be willing to do that?"

"I would, yes."

She watched his face; she could tell he was giving it serious thought. He would be weighing up the odds . . . a three-to-one chance of dying or inheriting everything. And if Jacie Starr were the unlucky one, he'd be thinking, he would still have his wife and her money.

He strode over to the window and looked at the city's skyline across the river. Finally, he turned to face her.

"For the first time in our marriage, Celia, you've surprised me."

She smiled fleetingly. "I think I've surprised myself."

He said: "We'll do it. No arguments, Jacie. I've thought it through and I've decided it's a risk worth taking."

"You – you can't be serious, Jim," said Jacie Starr.

Ignoring her, he said: "Eleven o'clock then, Celia. Use the rear door; that way you won't be seen entering."

The girl had gone pale. "But Jim . . . it's madness . . . why not just settle for half? The courts will be on your side."

"I've already given Celia my answer," he said. "I'm going through with it; so are you."

After the two had gone, Celia sat staring at the capsules in the medicine bottle. She was assailed by doubts. Shouldn't she agree to Jim's divorce terms? It would be risk-free, certainly; but giving in to him would mean giving in to the Starr girl, too. No, that was unthinkable!

The two were already there when she arrived at the studios. "You look worried, dear," the girl said. "Not having second thoughts are you?" To Celia's chagrin, the girl seemed totally in control of the situation.

"I just need a drink," Celia replied. The pulse in her temple was pounding. "I expect we all could, so I've brought a bottle of Scotch. Would you get some glasses, Jim?"

She took one of the glasses he produced, but her hand shook too much to pour.

Jim smiled at her. "You are in a state. Here, let me."

She watched him pour three drinks. He's showing no sign of nerves, either, she thought; what was their game?

He handed the glass to her. She drank it in one huge gulp. "Nerves, I guess," she said with a weak smile.

Her husband said: "Well, let's get on with it. Here's some notepaper; now, what do we write?"

"How about . . . we can't go on any longer, the situation's become too unbearable, et cetera, et cetera, so we've decided it's the only way out . . . or words to that effect." Celia looked at them both. "Agreed?"

Her husband shrugged. "It's a bit corny . . . but I suppose it'll do."

He scribbled his note, then handed the pen to her. Despite

the whisky, she was still a bundle of nerves. The scratching of the nib seemed excruciatingly loud as she wrote.

"Now me," said Jacie Starr, taking the pen with a theatrical flourish. "Oh don't be so po-faced, dear . . . it has its black humour, don't you think?"

"No," Celia snapped, "I don't; there's nothing funny about the prospect of dying."

Her husband said quickly: "I think we all need another drink." He refilled their glasses.

Celia took the tissue paper from a coat pocket and unfolded it on a worktop.

The three stared at the yellow capsules for what seemed an age. Then Jim picked one up, and gestured to Jacie Starr to do the same.

Celia took the remaining one. Nobody moved. Then Jim said: "After you, Celia."

"I thought we would all . . ." She tailed off. Were they attempting to out-manoeuvre her? "I was expecting we'd all do it together . . . at the same time."

"But it's your idea, Celia dear." Jacie Starr's eyes had a look of vicious triumph. "So you go first."

Celia placed the capsule on her tongue, took a sip of Scotch – and swallowed. "Now you two. Come on! You agreed—"

Neither of them made a move. The Starr girl laughed, a strange hollow sound. "Did you really think Jim and I would be fool enough to do it?"

"Yes, I . . ." Celia felt her heart give a lurch. "Oh, God, I've been such a . . . I've got to phone for an ambulance." She made for the door. He husband blocked her way. "Let me pass, Jim."

He said: "It takes effect in fifteen minutes, you said. Well, we can wait."

"Don't be stupid, Jim. If you don't let me get to a hospital, you'll have as good as murdered me."

"Technically, yes. But nobody's going to know that, are they. When they find your suicide note, they'll conclude that you were depressed . . . about my affair with Jacie . . . isn't that how it will look?"

*　　*　　*

231

Celia poured herself a glass of chilled white wine and turned on the midday news. It was the third item.

". . . a lovers' suicide pact. Their bodies were discovered this morning at City TV Studios. Police, who took away two handwritten notes and a half-empty bottle of whisky, said they were not treating the deaths as suspicious . . ."

Topping up her glass, she said to herself: The beauty of it is, Jim, we *all* took poison last night. Yes, that's right – I put it in the whisky before I arrived; the whisky masked the taste. I didn't die . . . because I took a capsule. It didn't matter which one: all three contained a substance which neutralised the type of poison I used.

Ironic, isn't it . . . you'd both be alive as well, if only you'd kept your side of the bargain. But you reneged, didn't you. . . . as I was sure you would when I first devised my plan.

And I was right, wasn't I.

THE MISSING LINK

Keith Wright

The British police story has come a long way since the days of Henry Wade, Maurice Procter and the founder of the CWA, John Creasey, who created Gideon of the Yard. Keith Wright has followed in the footsteps of Procter, John Wainwright, Peter N. Walker and others in making use of experience gained through serving as a police officer to embark upon a career as a crime writer. Wright is still a young man and his work reflects in style as well as content a world far-removed from Dock Green. It is a harsh world, but not one that is devoid of humanity. As Wright's skills continue to develop, we can expect him to become established as one of the standard-bearers of the contemporary police procedural.

"It was all a long time ago, Bob."

I caressed the stem of my glass, feeling somewhat self-conscious at having to raise my voice over the general hub-bub of noise in the smoky bar, particularly over such a sensitive subject.

I hadn't seen Bob for a number of years and it was good of him to show his face on this special occasion. We had done the "how's life" bit; that automatic conversation piece available for use in stemming the lull that is otherwise acceptable with closer

233

friends. Neither of us had been overly interested in the replies, but we were polite enough to appear attentive. We suffered each other with a respect dimmed over the years by sparse contact. Our common bond being a shared failure; that one thorn in my side; the case that had haunted my entire police career and that had now returned to infiltrate our previously cosy chat.

Bob's swarthy complexion, accentuated by his receding forehead, was glistening under the harsh lighting in the crowded room. He always smelled of garlic, or halitosis; I've never been quite certain which. He appeared keen to respond to what I had half hoped was a dismissive counter to his recollection of a different era of crime investigation. "I know the date off by heart; 25th July 1979. I was . . ."

I cut him off hoping to draw the conversation to a close. "I know you were a young Detective Sergeant, bright and eager to make your name. I've heard it all before, Bob. Let's not dwell on the past, mate, it's too bloody messy. Too many ghosts."

He kept my gaze as he sipped at his glass of whisky. He wouldn't let it lie. "By Christ I was keen, too keen I suppose, too impulsive, but you calmed me down, boss, playing your ruminative Detective Inspector game. However did you manage to appear so calm all the time?"

I smiled. Bob had been a good detective; cost him a marriage though. I had taken him under my wing a little, became good friends for a while. Our families shared a holiday one year I remember. "'*Appear*' being the operative word, Bob. Believe me I did not feel so bloody calm when the press accused me of not giving a shit about the Randall case. That was totally unjustified, after everything I . . ."

"Oh come off it, boss, they were right weren't they?"

Here we go again. "No, I . . ."

He raised a hand to cut me off. "Never mind 'No, I'. 'No I' nothing. Francisco Randall was a fucking perverted sad, sorry, child molesting bastard, so don't tell me his murder bothered you one iota. You forget I worked on the case 'til they pulled the plug on it."

I was shaking my head as I spoke.

"I haven't forgotten a thing, Bob, I am talking from a

professional standpoint. It was one murder case . . . one case out of, Christ . . . however many . . . a lot! And I couldn't solve it. Of course I gave a shit about it."

Bob placed his hand on my shoulder and whispered into my ear, his speech just hingeing on being slurred. He was, shall we say, relaxed rather than pissed. "WE couldn't solve it, boss, 'WE' not just you, mate, we were a team, maybe there was one thing that was overlooked, something one of us could have done. I don't know." There was an unnerving glint in his eye as he spoke.

Our reminiscing brought back ugly memories. Bob no doubt shared the images that I had. He had been first at the scene of the murder and had followed the inquiry through for many months until it was eventually wound down. The investigation into the life and death of Francisco Antonio Randall had uncovered many of his own victims, most of whom had never reported their defilement to the police. Young girls, not yet having reached puberty, violated by a man with a penchant for bondage, fellatio and amateur photography. The photos recovered from his seedy flat were the embodiment of evil itself. Occasionally he would smear his filth across the sexual spectrum and concentrate on little boys. Boys or girls, they all had one common bond, a look of fear, entwined with guilt. I found myself thinking aloud.

"Deserved a bloody medal, I suppose."

"Who?"

"The bloke who caved Randall's head in. How many more kids would he have got to before we caught him? I'd have liked to have nicked him, if nothing else just to shake the guy's hand."

Bob restrained a wry smile. "And then give him a life sentence, eh?"

I felt a cold hand grab mine from behind. The young woman was beautiful. Her teeth flashed white, as she spoke, her blonde hair filtering the disco lights flashing behind her.

"Come on, boring, don't spend all night stood at the bar, these people have all come to see you . . ."

She diverted her attention to my drinking partner.

"Stop hogging his attention, Bob." He was smiling. Her long fingers were tipped with scarlet nail varnish. She was so confident for a twenty five year old, but I was playing hard to get.

"I'll be over in a moment, Emma . . ." She squeezed my hand again. "Oh come on . . ." I wrestled free. "I'm talking to Bob, swinging the lantern a bit, shan't be long, only be a couple of mins."

I leaned over and kissed her cheek. A roar of jeers emanated from the crowd of younger officers standing in a circle by the cigarette machine. She walked away, her face slightly reddened by our contact, although her hand lingered in mine as we parted company. The prospect of an enforced termination of my chat with Bob had triggered a question in my mind. It was something that I had noticed as I had cleared my desk out only the previous week. The discovery had disturbed me, worried me even, as I drifted back through the mists of time. The case as dead and buried as Randall himself.

"You know Bob, I was looking at the scenes of crime photographs of the Randall murder. They were tab-eared and dusty, but they were still numbered at the index; 1 to 47, but when I counted, and don't ask me why I did, the actual photographs there were only 46. I'd never noticed that before, had you?"

My colleague, for the first time, would not meet my gaze, downing the remnants of his whisky, head tilting back somewhat exaggeratedly. The burn seemingly wincing his features. His eventual response was not a reply to the question.

"I won't be staying for the speeches, boss." He offered his hand. "Have a long and happy retirement." My mouth was agape as I received his gnarled, sweaty hand, my confusion frozen in exasperation on my face. Before I could recover Bob turned and made off towards the door. I wanted to call out, shout him back, but I had been stunned into a cocktail of curiosity and suspicion.

The decision was made for me as I watched him falter, turn, and walk back towards me. He pressed a package into my hand. A hesitant smile flickered across his now tense lips.

I mumbled "What's going . . ."

"You'll be getting some sort of present with your speech.

The Missing Link

A whip around by the lads. I wasn't going to give you my gift, but it will, maybe, set your mind at ease. It's your unofficial medal, boss. The scenes of crime photo and the negative have long since been burned." He slapped my shoulder, a little too hard. "Take care," he said, before leaving hurriedly, pushing aggressively through the crowd, attracting attention, heads turning towards him and then towards me. I turned self-consciously towards the bar and used my empty hand to fiddle around with the peanuts.

When it was safe I unfurled my clenched fist, revealing the piece of paper folded neatly in a square. As I unwrapped it, I saw the contents glisten. In shock I dropped it to the floor, but quickly picked it up, afraid of losing it once more. It had been lost in 1979. On the day Francisco Randall drew his last, wheezing breath. I wasn't clear in my mind if it had been the second or third powerful blow that had jarred the cuff-link clear from my sleeve as Randall attempted to parry.

I too had burned a photograph. It had been a photograph of a little girl, no more than ten years old. A girl who I had nurtured and held in my arms. A girl who needed her Daddy to be there when the foul deeds captured on film were being played out. But I hadn't been there. Despite her appearance of confidence, I still hear her sometimes at night, crying. Crying out for me to be there, but of course I never can be. I have been since. I've been there a thousand times since, in my dreams, in the cruel nightmares, and each time I awake with sweat stinging my eyes I pray it was real. Yet the dull ache in the pit of my belly heralds the realisation that it is not, nor will it ever be so. Part of me died the day that she disclosed her painful secret to me. She had said she was sorry, bless her. I had seen it all before, but not her, not my baby. I knew that she would carry the foul stench of that bastard's loins to her grave, and that any future happy times would be marred by a memory of hell.

I was in a haze. I could again sense my heart racing and perspiration fusing my grey hair to my collar. She knows. I'm sure she does, yet we have never spoken a word about it. Of anyone, she knows, by God does she ever know.

237

I felt the manicured hand of the belle of the ball take hold of mine.

"Come on, Dad, they want to make a speech. You retire today, you know, or had you forgotten?"

I took hold of her, hugging her tightly.

"Dad, stop it, what's the matter with you, everybody's looking."

"Let them look."

I released my hold reluctantly, whilst restraining the tears welling up in my eyes. A crowd had gathered around me. Emma craned her neck.

"Where's Bob gone?"

I was recovering again, I didn't want her to sense anything was . . . you know . . . not tonight.

"He, er, couldn't stay, he's jagged off, would you believe."

"Huh. Some friend he is."

I sighed. "Yeah. Some friend."

The crowd had rallied. One voice quickly became a dozen and then fifty; "For he's a jolly good fellow, for he's a jolly good fellow . . ."

And so say all of us.

BIOGRAPHIES OF CONTRIBUTORS

Catherine Aird is the author of seventeen crime novels and a collection of short stories, *Injury Time*. She has also been awarded an honorary MA from the University of Kent and was made an MBE for her services to the Girl Guide Association. She is a former Chairman of the CWA and in 1992 she was the first recipient of the CWA/Hertfordshire Libraries Golden Handcuffs Award for her outstanding contribution to detective fiction.

Kate Charles is an American who lives in England and sets her mysteries here. Since her first book, *A Drink Of Deadly Wine*, was published in 1991, she has enjoyed a rapid rise to prominence in the genre and is currently the Chairman of the CWA.

Mat Coward is a freelance journalist and crime fiction reviewer who has published a number of short stories. He contributes columns to the crime fanzines *A Shot In The Dark* and *Deadly Pleasures*. Formerly London based, he now lives in Somerset.

Lindsey Davis was born in Birmingham. After an English degree at Oxford, she joined the Civil Service, but now writes full time. The first of her novels about the Roman private eye Marcus Didius Falco, *The Silver Pigs*, won the Authors' Club Prize for best first novel. In 1995, she was awarded the CWA Dagger In The Library, a new award for the crime author whose work is judged to give most pleasure to library readers.

Eileen Dewhurst was born in Liverpool, read English at Oxford, and has earned her living in a variety of ways, including journalism. When

239

she is not writing, she enjoys solving cryptic crossword puzzles and drawing and painting cats. Her seventeenth and latest novel is *The Verdict On Winter*. Her other works include *A Private Prosecution*, *The House That Jack Built*, and *Death In Candie Gardens*. She wrote five novels featuring the policeman Neil Carter; currently, her principal series detective is the actress Phyllida Moon.

Martin Edwards has written five novels about the lawyer and amateur detective Harry Devlin; the first, *All The Lonely People*, was short-listed for the CWA John Creasey Memorial Award for the best first crime novel of 1991. The series has been optioned for television. He is also the author of five non-fiction books on legal topics and has edited three anthologies of regional crime writing on behalf of CWA chapters in the North and East Anglia.

Gösta Gillberg started writing crime and ghost stories in his early teens, under the influence of Edgar Wallace and M. R. James and sold his first story at the age of 15. He worked with Scandinavian Airlines for over 40 years; for part of that time he was based in Baghdad and Istanbul and his experiences provided the material for several short crime stories. He has also written articles about authors of detective fiction as well as translating about 300 crime and western novels from English and Norwegian into Swedish.

Lesley Grant-Adamson was born in North London and spent much of her childhood in the Rhondda in South Wales. She worked on provincial newspapers before joining the staff of *The Guardian* in London as a feature writer, then became a freelance journalist and television writer before becoming a novelist. Her first crime novel, *Patterns In The Dust*, was published in 1985; her most recent is *Evil Acts*.

Reginald Hill was brought up in Cumbria where he has returned after many years in Yorkshire, the setting for his award-winning crime novels featuring Andy Dalziel and Peter Pascoe; their investigations have recently been brought to the small screen by BBC Television. His latest series detective is the redundant lathe operator turned private eye, Joe Sixsmith, who has so far appeared in *Blood Sympathy*, *Born*

Biographies of Contributors

Guilty and a couple of short stories. In 1995, he was awarded the CWA Diamond Dagger.

H.R.F. Keating has written many novels and works of non-fiction, but is perhaps most famous for the Inspector Ghote series set in India, the first of which, *The Perfect Murder*, won the CWA Gold Dagger and was subsequently made into a film by Merchant Ivory. He has been President of the Detection Club since 1987 and in 1996 received the CWA Diamond Dagger.

Peter Lewis has lived in the North-East for more than 30 years. He is an academic and teaches courses in crime at one of the institutions for which Durham is famous. Among his books are "bio-critiques" of Eric Ambler and John le Carré; the latter received an Edgar Allan Poe award from the Mystery Writers of America. He and his wife run Flambard Press, which has published *Northern Blood 2*, an anthology of regional crime stories and collections of the work of Chaz Brenchley and H.R.F. Keating.

Peter Lovesey began his writing career with *Wobble To Death* in 1970, introducing Sergeant Cribb, the Victorian detective who went on to feature in seven more books and two television series. His recent novels have alternated between two contrasting detectives: the policeman Peter Diamond and the Victorian sleuth, Bertie. He is a past winner of the CWA Gold Dagger and in 1995 won a Silver Dagger for *The Summons*.

John Malcolm is the author of the Tim Simpson novels, the first of which, *A Back Room In Somers Town*, appeared in 1984. He is a successful businessman with an abiding interest in antiques. Under his real name, John Andrews, his publications include *The Price Guide To Antique Furniture*. He is a former Chairman of the CWA.

Val McDermid grew up in a Scottish mining community, then read English at Oxford. Her career as a journalist ended with a three-year stint as Northern Bureau Chief of a national Sunday tabloid. She is now

Biographies of Contributors

a full-time writer and the latest of her four novels about the Mancunian private eye Kate Brannigan is *Blue Genes*. Her non-series novel *The Mermaids Singing* won the CWA Gold Dagger in 1995.

Susan Moody, a former Chairman of the CWA, is the author of the Penny Wanawake detective series as well as suspense novels which include *House Of Moons*. Her most recent series began with *Takeout Double* and features Cassie Swann.

Ian Rankin was born in Fife in 1960 and graduated from the University of Edinburgh. Since then he has been employed as a grape-picker, swineherd, tax man, alcohol researcher, hi-fi journalist and punk musician. He is best known for his novels and short stories about Inspector John Rebus, but he also writes thrillers as Jack Harvey. His awards include The Hawthornden Fellowship, the Fulbright Raymond Chandler Award and the CWA/The Macallan Short Story Dagger Award.

Andrew Taylor grew up in East Anglia and went to the universities of Cambridge and London. He now lives in Gloucestershire with his wife and two children and writes full time. His first novel about William Dougal, *Caroline Minuscule*, won the CWA John Creasey Memorial Award and the third, *Our Father's Lies*, was short listed for the Gold Dagger. He has also written an espionage trilogy, books for younger readers, non-series novels such as *The Barred Window* and a couple of mysteries set in the post-war era and located in the border town of Lydmouth.

Tony Wilmot has been a newspaper reporter, book publisher's editor and feature writer on *Weekend* magazine (interviewing everyone from public hangman Pierrepoint to Salvador Dali). He has published a novel about Modigliani and won a CWA prize for a murder story set in a flea circus. Several of his short stories were televised in *Tales Of The Unexpected* and broadcast on Radio 4. He has been a full-time writer since the late 1980s.

Keith Wright is the one contributor to this anthology who works s a detective in real life. He published his first crime novel, *One Oblique One*, at the tender age of 27, while serving as a Detective Constable at Bulwell CID, Nottinghamshire Constabulary. Since then he has continued to combine careers in the real and fictional worlds of crime.